Ballistics at the Ballet

Ballistics at the Ballet

A MUSICAL MURDER MYSTERY

B.J. BOWEN

CAVEL
PRESS

Kenmore, WA

CAMEL PRESS

A Camel Press book published by Epicenter Press

Epicenter Press
6524 NE 181st St.
Suite 2
Kenmore, WA 98028

For more information go to:
www.Camelpress.com
www.Coffeetownpress.com
www.Epicenterpress.com
www.barbarabowenauthor.com

Cover design by Scott Book
Design by Melissa Vail Coffman

ISBN: 978-1-68492-032-7 (Trade Paper)
ISBN: 978-1-68492-033-4 (eBook)

Printed in the United States of America

To my daughter, Amy, who always provides encouragement and support, and serves as my emergency editor.

ACKNOWLEDGMENTS

MANY PEOPLE HELPED COMPLETE THIS MANUSCRIPT and turn it into a book. I would like to acknowledge a few here. In no particular order they are:

Jennifer McCord, my editor and publisher, who worked closely with me to fine tune my manuscript, and expressed and shared her love of music with me.

The La Dolce Vita Writers Group, which started me on the first book of this series.

Leisel Hufford, for her encouragement, extra interest, and editing.

Sarah E. Burr, who encouraged me, put together beautiful artwork for advertising the book, and helped this old fogie with social media, always making me feel like I "CAN DO."

Nancy Andrew, my flute expert. Both her father and my mother loved the Chaminade Concertino, and my character KC learns it as a tribute (though she doesn't know it). Any errors are mine.

Joshua Long, who patiently advised me on guns, which I know nothing about. Any mistakes are a result of my ignorance, not his tutelage.

Sergeant Jason Newton of the Colorado Springs Police Department, who graciously helped me reason through timing, explained "pinging" to me, and estimated whether my fictional police department had enough to arrest Charlie. Any blunders are wholly my responsibility.

Deputy Jesse Lance, El Paso County Sheriff's Office, who explained Colorado gun laws to me. Her explanation seemed very clear. Any inaccuracies are the result of my misunderstanding.

Lena Gregory and Debra Goldstein who gave unstintingly of their time and knowledge to help me find my way through the unfamiliar world of electronic promotion.

The Writers of the Roundtable—Marylin Warner, Anne Kohl, Leisel Hufford, Mary Zalmanek, Molly Lord, and Eve Guy—who gave me excellent advice, provided encouragement, read the fledgling versions, found the incongruities, and, most of all, were my friends throughout.

ONE

FOR MOST PEOPLE CHRISTMAS MEANS MANGER SCENES, lights, cookies, and decorations. For me it means the *Nutcracker* Ballet. It's my routine as an orchestra flutist. Happily unaware that routine is fragile and changeable and typically, as in my case, not missed until it's gone, I crossed the street and walked through the crisp Colorado evening toward this year's first *Nutcracker* rehearsal.

As second flutist in the Monroe Symphony, I've played the *Nutcracker* for 20 years, 10 performances a year. By the end of the run I get tired of it, but I always look forward to it each year. It's an indicator. I can tell if I've improved—or not—by playing the same music year after year. It's popular with audiences, it makes money for the symphony, and it helps pay the musicians.

The cycle starts when a traveling ballet company, not always the same one, joins the symphony, the children's chorus, and the children's ballet group to put on the production. The symphony has one rehearsal by itself; one run-through with all the collaborators, who have been rehearsing individually; and a dress rehearsal with costumes and all participants, which is attended by friends and families of the performers. Then it's on to the show.

And tonight, the complete cycle would start again.

I avoided the glitz and glamour of the front entrance of Fleisher Hall, walking past pawnshops and auto body garages to reach the rear door. A concrete canyon formed where the blank concrete face of Fleisher surrounded the stage entrance and met the similar façade of a multilevel car park across the street.

Although the orchestra would be rehearsing alone, apparently the ballet company had already rolled into town, because I saw a semi labeled "Emerald Valley Ballet" parked at the loading dock bay. Their stagehands were busy unloading sets and costumes.

The security guard greeted me as I entered the building with his usual, "Hey, Emily. Fancy meeting you here."

I knew the drill. For *Nutcracker* you signed in. "Hey, Bernie." I initialed the sign-in sheet, then moved downstairs to the green room. Not named for its color, it shared the term universally given to the backstage area reserved for performers. I ditched my coat and headed for the orchestra pit, lit only by musician's stand lights. Although the players had to squeeze to fit the too small space, it crouched below audience level (hence the term "pit"), so heads didn't block the audience's view of the stage.

One of the first orchestra players to arrive, I liked to take my time warming up. Even though I'd been teaching all afternoon and didn't need to accustom myself to playing, I wanted to get used to the acoustics and leave whatever problems and distractions I'd brought with me at the door. Generally, I started with long tones, then moved to scales, and finally difficult passages from the coming evening's music.

I nodded to my colleagues as they entered. Each musician had his or her own warm-up pattern, and as they began to play, each in his own world, the noise level built to cacophony, and didn't stop until the concertmaster, as leader of the string section and first violins, stood, and gave the signal to tune.

Our conductor, Felix Underhayes, entered then and announced, "There'll be a reception for the audience after Thursday's dress rehearsal. Come if you want." With that somewhat half-hearted invitation, the rehearsal began.

Things went smoothly until mid-first act. Chimes rang to create the striking of the onstage clock as it sounds midnight, but Felix cued only eleven chimes, then went on. That Felix made the error didn't stop him from attacking Charlie McRae, my nephew and the percussionist responsible for the chimes.

"Percussion! You need to count to twelve there. You *can* count to twelve, can't you? Or do you need a tutor? If you require classes, we can provide them."

I winced at Felix's disparaging comments. When I turned to see Charlie, his face reddened and his jaw clenched, but he knew not to speak. Better to take it quietly than to attract more attention by arguing or, worst case, lose his job.

Other than that, we ran the first half with just a few stops, mainly to adjust volume and balance the sound, then broke for intermission.

Behind me, Janet Archer, our second clarinet, greeted me. "Emily. How's it going?" A tall, beautiful black woman, Janet was one of my closest friends. She'd been a ballerina until her last growth spurt, and still walked with a dancer's toe out. She had divorced last year, and needed time to adjust to being a single mom. To give her a break, I occasionally stayed with her kids, but we hadn't seen each other for a while.

"I'm okay. How are you doing?" We walked together to the rest room, catching up on our lives since we'd last seen each other.

"Things are looking up. I'm getting the hang of this single mothering gig. I took your suggestion and told the kids I need more practice time. After all, my symphony job is our main source of income now. After some judicious nagging, Jimmie and Sherrie have been helping out more, and Mom has been great about baby-sitting whenever I need her. It'll only be a couple years 'til I can leave them alone with Jimmie in charge, and I can look forward to that. In other news, the kids want to get a dog, and I think now they may be responsible enough to take care of one, so I might say yes. Maybe as a Christmas present. I don't know. I'm thinking about it. What about you?"

We entered the rest room and talked through the stalls.

"Nothing new here. Teaching, dog walking, practicing, and orchestra. All the routine stuff. Mom and my sister, Kathleen, will be coming later in the month for Christmas."

"How's KC?"

"She's still my housemate, but I don't see her as often as I used to. She works as sous chef at the Articulate Artichoke, and they keep her busy six days a week. She loves the job, and she still has time for flute lessons, dog walks, and house cleaning. I do most of my own cooking now, though, which is to say I eat a lot of salads and frozen dinners."

"Same old Emily."

"Hey, pigs haven't flown yet, so I'm still not cooking."

We washed our hands together and headed to the drinking fountain.

Companionably, we moved in the direction of the pit and our seats. "See you later. Gotta get ready for the second half," I said.

"Later."

Act two flowed effortlessly, and though I worked on a couple spots with my section leader and the third flute after the rehearsal, the three of us were done quickly. I went home, toward bed and my retriever, Golden.

She waited for me, rolling over for the usual tail-wagging "welcome home" belly scratch. I made myself a cup of tea and sipped it, then let Golden out. She did her business while I brushed my teeth. When I let her in, we snuggled happily until I fell asleep. My life was oh, so satisfying. Little did I know it would soon be turned topsy-turvy.

TWO

WEDNESDAY, 7:30 P.M., NOVEMBER 30

Run-through with all personnel

THE FIRST, AND ONLY, RUN-THROUGH with all parties before dress rehearsal was business as usual for the musicians. Some of the ballet dancers were dressed in rehearsal clothes, while others wore full costume. I assumed the ones in costume wanted to practice costume changes.

For my part, I relaxed and enjoyed the music. I had played the *Nutcracker* so many times, it was like an old friend.

Besides Felix's small but nasty asides, things were going swimmingly when he stopped the orchestra, his face red. "First violins! If I see another bow out of synch, I'll break it over my knee! You!" He pointed. "Last stand! I'll see you two in my dressing room. Tomorrow. Six o'clock."

The suddenness and violence of outbursts like this intimidated, even frightened, the rest of us. No telling what the violins suffered. I couldn't help feeling squelched, my joyful mood spoiled.

At the end of the first act, while I, along with the rest of the orchestra, broke for intermission, the child dancers took the opportunity to run through their scene one more time. Their happy enthusiasm helped reconstruct my cheer, and I smiled.

When we returned, the ballet flowed easily until shortly before the end of the second act. Felix cued the harp for its big cadenza, introducing the Waltz of the Flowers. In the cold pit, not having been used for most of the second act. the instrument was slightly flat. Not much. But, to a trained ear, enough.

Felix stopped rehearsal. "Harp! Did you forget to tune, or are you just deaf?"

The harpist, a quiet brunette in her mid-thirties, new to the orchestra this year and not yet tenured, said, "Sorry, Felix. I'll try and do better."

"You *will* do better. We'll wait for you to tune."

Flushing scarlet, the harpist adjusted the pitch of individual strings as the eighty-five members of the orchestra and heaven knows how many ballet dancers waited, listening.

Finally, her voice breaking, she said, "I think I'm ready now."

"You *think* you're ready, or you *are* ready?" Unusual cruelty, even for Felix.

"I . . . I'm ready."

Felix gave the cue for the harp solo, but the cadenza sounded tentative and soft. "Louder please, and with confidence." Felix gave a downbeat and waited, the orchestra silent.

The harpist played louder, tears running down her face.

He twisted his mouth in a scowl. "I guess that's the best we'll do. We have to move on."

I cringed. Why had he been so unnecessarily spiteful? His fits of temper upset me, and probably my colleagues, too. I'd bet the union rep would be taking this to the Board. On the way out, passing by the harpist, who was covering her instrument for the night, I said, "Don't worry about it. He's a jerk who doesn't appreciate his players. You're doing a fine job."

Charlie, nearby in the percussion section, put in his two cents. "Guys like that end up getting theirs one way or the other."

She sobbed once before she caught herself and said, "Thanks, Charlie, Emily. I just hope I do well enough to be here next year."

Gladly, I left, but I felt sorry for the *prima* ballerina and *premier danseur*, who stayed late to work through tempos with Felix.

At home I took comfort from Golden's welcome and unconditional acceptance. Thank goodness I hadn't been the target of Felix's tantrums!

THREE

Afternoon and Evening of Dress Rehearsal

THE NEXT DAY, I TAUGHT PRIVATE instrumental students at home, as most musicians do. Outside, a snowstorm gathered, but my studio, in a back bedroom which doubles as a guest room, was warm and cozy. Furnished with a fold-away bed, a couple filing cabinets full of music, a desk, two music stands, and two chairs, everything I needed was at my fingertips. I loved my students and giving flute lessons, and the extra money didn't hurt, either. For me, private teaching offered continuing pleasure and excitement, right up there with skiing and hiking and standing ovations. Seeing understanding light a student's eyes, helping them achieve goals, or hearing an instant difference in their playing when they tried something new never failed to excite me. Furthermore, students adored me for helping and encouraging them, and they told me all about their lives.

In my book, students didn't come any better than Megan Green. Fifteen, a classic English beauty, with long curly brown hair, blue eyes, and rosy, pink cheeks, in another life she would have been fielding marriage proposals. Bubbly and full of enthusiasm, she caught on quickly and didn't mind working hard for a specific goal. She had been chosen for All-State Honor Orchestra last year. I couldn't have been prouder. Her parents were busy, her dad some sort of computer guru, her mom an insurance adjuster who used lesson time for errands. I always put Megan last in my teaching queue so that I'd end on a—excuse the expression—positive note.

But tonight something was bothering her. She didn't have her usual smile for me on arriving, and seemed tired and discouraged.

Megan ignored Golden's wiggling, enthusiastic greeting. Sensing the girl's distress, my dog stilled and cocked her head.

All I said was, "Anything the matter?"

Before we even sat down, Megan burst into tears and threw her arms around me.

Her angst took me by surprise. I'm not much of a touchy-feely sort, but I wanted to comfort her.

She sobbed long and hard and without pause while I awkwardly patted her back. When the sobs finally subsided into hiccupy, irregular breathing, Megan said, "My mom hates me!" She followed this pronouncement with more tears.

They don't teach you how to handle a situation like this at music school and, since my instincts didn't run in this direction, I was flummoxed. "I'm sure she doesn't hate you," I said, which only gave rise to hiccups and gasps.

I thought in silence, then tried a new tack. "Why do you think that?"

She calmed enough to sink into the students' chair and answer, "Mom says I'm just like my dad." She teared up again and cried softly, leaving me to assume the comment wasn't a compliment.

Despite feverish thinking on my part and muted crying on hers, a trite reassurance was all I could think of. "It'll be okay. I'm sure your mom didn't mean anything by it. She'll come around." Silently, I thought that for Megan to take her mom's remark as a grievous insult, her parents must be nursing long-standing problems.

I decided a lesson wasn't possible until we'd had tea, my family's cure for all problems, large and small. I got her a tissue and led the way to the kitchen, a pleasant yellow room at the back of the house, with large windows and skylights.

Golden followed, her nails clicking on the tile.

The kitchen still smelled of the oatmeal cookies KC had baked. I had pigged out and eaten most of them, but I served the last few to Megan for their moral support.

I didn't want to push her, and didn't know what to ask, so I didn't ask much, just concentrated on getting hot water ready. I gave her a task. "Can you get tea for us both? It's in the cabinet to the right of the stove."

Megan opened the cupboard and peered at the choices. I had twelve different kinds, most of them herbal. She hesitated. "What should I get for you?"

"Oh, I don't know. I like them all. Surprise me."

She got down two boxes, took them to the table, and put a bag in each of the two cups I'd set out. When I poured the boiling water, I saw she'd picked chamomile for herself, peppermint for me.

We sat at the round oak table together. She began to revive a little, sipping her tea, sniffling, and wiping her eyes, so I ventured a question.

"Don't your mom and dad get along?"

"I don't know. They don't talk things out, they just yell. Over the littlest things. One time Dad got mad because Mom served his hamburger with a pickle on it. Another time they got into it because she wore a dress he didn't like. Stuff like that."

"What does that have to do with you?"

"They criticize each other for big stuff, too. Mom says Dad doesn't take time for fun. When I told her I couldn't go shopping because I had to finish my report for history, she said I was just like my dad and slammed the door so hard, the pictures rattled."

I held my breath.

Megan's chin wobbled, but she giggled when Golden nosed under her arm.

Relieved, I let my breath out. "Well, it sounds like your mom and dad were mad at each other. But it wasn't your fault. It'll be okay." I tried to stay positive. "They'll work it out."

"Both of them will be mad if I get an F on that report."

"And it won't make you happy, either." The proverbial rock and hard place.

She nodded.

"Well, you can always talk to me. And really, I think this has more to do with them than you."

I wasn't sure I'd convinced her, but her eyes were dry, and she calmly stroked Golden's ears.

I'd done the best I could in unfamiliar territory, giving well-intentioned advice to an emotional teenager. Now I returned to routine. "I know from experience that music is a safe place to express yourself. It can make you feel better. Why don't we go back to the studio? I'll bet you can channel your mood into the Elegy. Did you practice it?"

She smiled. "Of course. It's a beautiful work."

We had a short lesson. Under the circumstances, that represented a major victory, and I naively hoped her natural sparkle would complete the healing.

FOUR

THURSDAY, 4:45 P.M., DECEMBER 1, 2011

Before dress rehearsal

Megan's problems troubled me, and I wanted to clear my mood with a nice, relaxing dinner before dress rehearsal. I chose the Articulate Artichoke, a vegetarian restaurant near Fleisher Hall, not so elegant that dinner would take forever. My friend KC worked there, but she would be in the kitchen, and I wouldn't bother her.

My vegetarian biryani went a long way to reviving me, and being waited on went the rest of the way. By the time I finished the vegan chocolate raspberry cake I felt completely myself again.

Even though rehearsal wouldn't begin for another hour and a half, the snow had started falling and I didn't want to drive home only to turn around and drive back again. I left for Fleisher, eagerly telling myself I would have privacy this early, and could practice some Bach in the Hall's large acoustic. It's always a special treat to singlehandedly fill the Hall with sound.

That never happened.

As I opened the stage door, I heard Felix shout, "No!" followed quickly by a shot. My ears rang with the sound. It had to have been close. The nearest hallway held Felix's dressing room and those of the *premier danseur* and *prima* ballerina.

Instinct took over and I ducked behind the security desk. Footsteps fled away from me, down the short dressing room hall, toward the "T" of the intersecting corridor. The assailant would have the choice of going downstairs, or exiting via an automatically locking exit door. A few fraught seconds later the exit door slammed, the ensuing silence broken only by Felix's moaning. I decided the threat had gone and moved across the entry and down the hallway, toward Felix's dressing room.

The *prima* ballerina's door was closed.

Next to it, the *premier danseur* emerged from his dressing room. "What's happening?"

"I don't know." I crept cautiously forward, the dancer following.

The next door, Felix's, stood open. He lay on the floor, groaning. And bleeding.

The *danseur* turned ashen and his chin trembled. "What . . . what . . ."

I spotted a cummerbund hung over a chair. "Take that cummerbund and press it over the wound on Felix's chest. I'll call 911."

I pulled the phone from my pocket. "Send an ambulance and police to Fleisher Hall. A man's been shot."

The *danseur* knelt on one side of Felix, pressing the cummerbund to the conductor's chest. I knelt on the other, holding Felix's outstretched arm, his hand in mine. "It's okay." I tried to reassure him. "Help will be here soon."

Felix whispered, "Tell her she's the only one . . ."

"Tell who, what?"

Felix's lips were moving, his voice too quiet for me to understand his words.

I sat beside him, continuing to hold his hand and stroking his arm, murmuring comforting nothings. I'm not even sure they made sense, but I couldn't think of anything else to do.

Felix's wife, Lorna, ran in a few minutes later and asked, "What's going on? I heard something that sounded like a shot . . ." She turned, saw Felix , and immediately fainted, slumping to the floor. The *danseur* and I couldn't help her, too. We chose to stay at Felix's side.

He died before the ambulance came.

The *prima* ballerina arrived a few minutes after the police and ambulance. "What is all the commotion?" At that point she saw Felix's body being loaded onto the gurney and slid down the wall, next to the conductor's door. "Oh. Oh, no."

After Felix's body had been removed, the EMTs revived Lorna and led her away, presumably to be checked over at the hospital.

Without a function now, I pressed myself against the wall and tried to stay out of the way, feeling useless. I heard the *danseur* telling police, "In less than an hour, performers will start coming by the dozens expecting to participate in a dress rehearsal of the *Nutcracker*. Invited guests will arrive shortly after that. What should we do?"

He addressed Lt. Gordon, chief of Monroe's homicide squad. I recognized him from our encounter last year when he falsely accused me of murder, an accusation which he later, to my relief, found to be untrue. Normally, he would have been the last person I wanted to see, but I was glad to have someone around who knew what to do under the circumstances. In the entryway he circled his underlings, ballet VIPs, security personnel, and Fleisher Hall dignitaries. Among them I saw my friend, the manager of Fleisher, Cal Nelson.

They huddled, and when Lt. Gordon returned to the *danseur*, who had been joined by the *prima ballerina* and someone from the ballet staff, the lieutenant said, "There'll be no dress rehearsal. Fleisher Hall is a crime scene. You won't be able to use it. We'll cordon off the Hall, and I'll post officers at all entrances to turn people away. We're searching the rest of the building now, making sure everything's safe. I'll use every officer available. But we need to finish, and it's going to take a while."

The ballet staffer said, "I'll tell the stagehands."

"I'll get my things." The *prima* ballerina turned to the *premier danseur*. "You'd better get anything you need, too."

"Sorry." Lt. Gordon blocked the doorway to her dressing room. "You can't go in there. If you need something, find a uniformed officer and he'll get it for you."

He turned to me. "Ms. Wilson, you're a witness." Jerking his head in the direction of a policeman, he said, "Derek, take Ms. Wilson's statement."

My friend Cal, Fleisher's manager, put his office at our disposal, and I gave my statement there.

By the time I finished, I was weary, heartsick, and ready to go home. Snow fell heavily. But when I headed for my car, my friend Janet leaped out of her vehicle.

"Thank goodness! When I got here police cars were all over. I recognized your car and saw the yellow police tape. They cancelled rehearsal. I waited and waited and worried. What's going on? I've asked people but no one will give me the scoop."

I closed my eyes feeling like a wall of words assaulted me. But Janet was my friend, and she needed reassurance. I couldn't blow her off. "Let's sit down, and I'll tell you all about it."

Eagerly, Janet sat in my car as I explained everything.

"So, who did it?"

I breathed heavily. "I don't know. I just want to go home, hug Golden, take a hot shower, and go to bed."

Realizing I had nothing left, Janet said, "Of course. Sorry. Let's go."

She followed me to my car and made sure I got to the house safely, trailing along behind me in her sedan.

FINALLY AT HOME, THE NECESSITY OF BEING BRAVE and strong ended. I sat on the floor, my back supported by the front door, hugged Golden tight, and let all the tears out. They were tears for Felix, tears for Felix's family, and tears for me, too.

Golden licked my face.

I cried until the weeping gave way to a desperate desire to scrub away the events of the evening.

Stripping and stepping into the shower, I stood in the stream, letting it soothe and comfort me. When the hot water gave out, exhausted and barely able to stumble, I let Golden out, waited for her to finish her business, and fell into bed, her warm bulk consoling me as I fell asleep.

FIVE

FRIDAY, 5:30 P.M., DECEMBER 2, 2011

1st performance

IT WAS A GOOD DECISION TO DONATE my inheritance from Olive to the city's kindness campaign. Now, though, I would have liked nothing more than to cancel today's students. I couldn't for two reasons: first, my budget wouldn't allow me to be that self-indulgent despite a hard, emotionally exhausting day yesterday, and second, my students counted on me. I'd been teaching all morning with only half my brain. I kept hearing Felix's last words, "Tell her she was the only one . . ." and seeing our imposing and sometimes threatening conductor lying weak and helpless on the floor of his dressing room.

I also worried about Megan. How was she doing? I was afraid she might be embarrassed about confiding in me. That afternoon, after it was late enough for her to be home from school, I called her between students.

"Hi, Megan. I just wanted to be sure you were okay."

"Miz Wilson, I'm fine. Much better now. I'm so grateful that you listened to me yesterday. I can't talk to anyone else about it."

Feeling flattered that she trusted me, and relieved that I needn't have worried, I answered, "I'm here whenever you need me."

"Thanks, Miz Wilson."

"I called during a break in my teaching schedule, and I see the next student just arrived. I'm going to have to go, but I'm so glad you're okay."

"No worries. See you next week."

I taught three afternoon students, and by the end of the day, I was more than ready to be done. KC wasn't home, so I'd have to fend for myself for dinner. I made a quick salad with canned garbanzo beans and the leafy greens in the fridge, then took a nap. The catnap revived me. I changed into my performance black and left for the *Nutcracker* hoping for a normal activity, something with no surprises.

Yesterday, the evening of Felix's death, should have been the dress rehearsal for the *Nutcracker,* with friends and family of the performers invited to stand in for the audience. That didn't happen, but by tonight the police had finished collecting evidence and released the Hall. We would hold the first performance as scheduled.

I arrived right on time and parked close to the stage entrance. After a warm day, more snow fell and, despite a nagging feeling of anxiety in the back of my mind—what awful thing might happen without warning?—I opened my mouth like a little kid and stuck out my tongue, trying to catch snowflakes as they drifted down. The junkyards and repair shops close by were covered with a clean, untouched layer of white. My footprints were clearly visible as I looked back toward my car, but they would soon be covered.

"Hi, Bernie."

Bernie greeted me with his usual, "Hi, Emily. Fancy meeting you here." Just what the doctor ordered. Even the process of signing in comforted me. Thank goodness for routine.

It would have been a financial catastrophe for the symphony to refund ticket money for the *Nutcracker,* even for so serious an event as the conductor's murder. So, instead, management went to the second string.

Most orchestras have an Assistant Conductor for minor concerts like pops, country western, New Year's, Fourth of July, and emergencies. Felix's murder fit in the category of emergency, extreme. Enter our Assistant Conductor, Douglas Jones.

He'd step in and conduct the concerts cold. It must be incredibly nerve-wracking to perform such a complex program involving orchestra, dancers, and chorus with no opportunity to rehearse, as he would do, but that's part of his job. Better him than me. As I arrived, I spotted him conferring with the choreographer backstage.

I left my coat in the green room and made my way into the orchestra pit, stepping over wires and threading my way through stands to the second flute chair. The oboes and bassoons were already there, trying reeds, looking for the ones with the best response and sound on that particular evening. I sat down, took out my flute, and began warming up. A warm-up routine is the musician's way to focus, and after long tones I ran through some scales and difficult passages, increasing my chances for a flawless performance. They say nobody's perfect, but you can set perfection as a goal. The audience and your fellow musicians appreciate it.

One by one other musicians arrived and began their preparations, and soon the discordant sounds became a welcoming dissonance. My warm-up took me to another world, a world with no grumpy parents, no unprepared students, and no dead bodies—a safe, comforting world.

I knew we were about ready when the last chair second violin snuck in.

The house lights began flashing, signaling to the audience the show would start momentarily. We tuned, and Doug entered to applause. He turned to face the audience and took a moment to breathe. "I'm sure you have all heard about the tragedy that happened here yesterday. We in the orchestra are heartbroken, but Felix would want us to carry on. So we dedicate this series of performances to his memory, his talent, and his joy in music making. He will be sadly missed."

The spin doctor's work. Felix hadn't treated Doug better than anybody else—lots of criticism and never a word of thanks.

At intermission I sat in my chair wiping out the condensation in my flute when our timpanist, Simon Cromwell, came to talk to me. Shaped like his drum, round, about fifty, he had a bald head, except for a thin fringe of graying sandy hair. Seeking me out was unusual, since the percussion section, my nephew included, generally kept to themselves, with their inside jokes and bawdy senses of humor.

"I wanted to let you know, there's something I need to tell Lieutenant Gordon. Charlie told me you're his aunt, and I know you proved yourself innocent of Olive's murder last year. I wanted to give you a heads up."

What in the world?

Simon stopped and rubbed his bald pate. "I like Charlie. He makes me laugh. Shortens the run. But I heard him arguing with Felix the night before the murder, at the run-through, during intermission. I need to let Lieutenant Gordon know."

He seemed to be asking permission.

I nodded.

He continued. "I wanted some peace and quiet during intermission, so I walked down the hall to the audience side of the auditorium. It's usually dark and deserted during rehearsals. I'd come to the place where the hallway turns a corner when I heard Charlie say, 'Touch her again and I'll make you pay!'"

My stomach filled with dread.

Frowning, Simon continued. "I stayed around the corner where neither he nor Felix could see me, and heard Felix say, 'Better tell *her*. I always get the girl.' Well, Charlie stormed past me, so mad he didn't even see me. I shrank back against the wall and waited a while, but Felix must have gone the other way because he didn't pass me." Simon stopped and looked tortured. "I don't want to tell Lieutenant Gordon, but I feel I have to. I figured if I told you first, you'd get a jump on figuring the whole thing out."

The Charlie who Simon described was *not* the Charlie I knew. I don't think I'd ever even seen him angry. Even as a little boy he was a charmer, blonde and blue-eyed like his mother, my sister, Kathleen. At the age of eight he saw *The Wizard of Oz* and began calling me "Auntie Em," a play on our relationship and my name, Emily Wilson. Twenty years and two linear feet later, at age twenty-eight, he still called me Auntie Em, and Golden wagged her tail and rolled over for a belly rub every time he visited. I trusted her.

Losing his father at sixteen hadn't made Charlie unkind. Both he and his mother were devastated, but he told me it made him even more miserable to see her so crushed. I watched him mother his own mother, trying to make her smile, using humor. When that worked, he became a clown at school, too. Kathleen told me his teachers complained, his grades sank, but his popularity skyrocketed, and no one suspected his pain. Thus, Charlie McRae, court jester, was born. He didn't let the mood stay solemn long.

In short, Simon's story stretched my credulity.

I did know the subject of the conversation, though. Charlie's first serious girlfriend, or at least the first I knew about, Ana Kekoa, had come to dinner with him a few times. He showed interest in settling down, and she was beautiful and intelligent; petite, with long black hair, blue eyes, and light brown skin. She'd met Charlie at his day job, where they both worked in IT. Her lively sense of humor, interest in Charlie, me, and our family charmed me easily. Charlie had discussed introducing her to his mom, and he planned that for her next visit, at Christmas.

"Thanks for telling me, Simon. That's not going to sound good for Charlie."

"I know. That's why I wanted to make sure you knew. Can you help him? Get a head start on asking questions?"

"I'll try."

Only a conversation with Charlie would clarify this. Until then, no point in worrying.

I ran quickly to the drinking fountain trying to avoid people The usual light-hearted chatter was muted. It was the first time the orchestra had met since Felix's murder. Somehow it didn't seem right to be flippant with Felix's death so fresh. Thanks to the grapevine, everybody knew my role, and my friends wanted to comfort me.

"Emily, you okay? I'm sure Felix was grateful. You did your best."

"Thanks, Janet. I wish I could have done more. And thanks for seeing me home last night."

"It was the least I could do."

I gave a quick nod to my friend and hurried away. Ordinarily I would have stayed, but I didn't want to talk.

"Quick thinking, Emily. You did the right thing." Clara James, one of the first violinists and a good friend, reassured me. Again, I nodded and scurried away.

Whatever I had done or not done hadn't helped Felix. He died. I couldn't bring myself to be good company, so I made myself as invisible as possible. After visiting the rest room, I returned to the calm safety of my second flute chair.

As the second act began, I felt relieved to play my part in peace, concentrating on the music, not worrying about other people's thoughts, or having to be sociable. I allowed the music to minister to my mood, finished the performance and packed up, hoping the orchestra would feel like home again next time. After all, people's memories are short, and you can't mourn forever, especially if you didn't particularly like the deceased.

I caught Charlie before he left. "Why don't you come to brunch before the first performance tomorrow. And bring Ana."

Charlie gave me a big smile. "That sounds great, Auntie Em. What time?"

"Eleven is fine." He had no clue that this wouldn't be an enjoyable social gathering.

SIX

THE SNOW WAS MELTING IN THE sunny aftermath of the storm. KC had left early for the restaurant, and I fixed myself a light breakfast of fruit and tea, mindful of my brunch with Charlie and Ana. Curious, I scanned the paper for the review of last night's performance. On page three of the Living section, I saw, "Nutcracker Overcomes Adversity; Performance a Delight." It mentioned the *prima* ballerina, Lily Hawthorne, for her "graceful and delicate" performance in the *Pas de Deux* and the Dance of the Sugar Plum Fairy. The article went on to say that the orchestra, led by conductor Douglas Jones, had accompanied the dancers with "sensitivity and feeling," and even mentioned the flutes for a "competent and sprightly" performance in the Dance of the Reed Flutes. The reviewer said that all of us were to be commended for overcoming Felix's murder and performing with "professional poise." In other words—excuse the expression—we dodged a bullet.

Charlie and Ana showed up for brunch at exactly eleven o'clock. Ana had brought her contribution to the meal, a plateful of grapes. Together with KC's vegetable soup, nuts, a salad, and bakery bread, despite my lack of culinary skills we would have a fairly healthy brunch along with our discussion.

"Come in. Come in."

Golden was excited to see Charlie, rolling onto her back and waving all four paws, begging for a belly rub.

Charlie, wearing a dog nose he produced from his pocket, dropped to the floor, rolled on to his back and, imitating Golden, waved his arms and kicked his legs. He asked "Who's a good dog? Who's a good dog? I am. I am."

Ana laughed and rubbed his stomach. "I suppose you want a treat now, too."

Their antics made me laugh.

Golden, of course, was delighted, and licked Charlie's face as he chuckled. He had to pull a squeaky toy out of his pocket and toss it to distract Golden long enough to climb to his feet.

She ran off, toy squeaking, while Charlie mopped his face with a tissue, also produced from his pocket.

When we had all regained our composure, he hugged me.

Ana said, "Good to see you, Ms. Wilson."

"Please, call me Emily."

I took their coats and Ana's purse and put them in the bedroom.

"I think we're just about ready to eat. Ana, can you take the grapes to the dining room table?"

Charlie plucked one from the plate as she passed. "Where's KC?"

"She's working. The restaurant is busy Saturday mornings, so she goes in early."

I had set the table and put out the bread, butter, salad, and nuts. I dished up soup in the kitchen, and Charlie took each bowl to the dining room.

With everything ready, we settled around the table, said grace, and passed food.

I managed to wait until everyone had served themselves before bringing up the real reason for our visit, wanting to get it over with. "Charlie, apparently someone overheard your argument with Felix Wednesday night." I didn't want him to know

Simon had told me about it. Charlie and Simon had to work together. "Can you explain?"

"What's to explain? We argued." Charlie directed his gaze at his lap and didn't meet my eyes. Suddenly he seemed the surly teenager he'd never been.

"The man was murdered. An argument with him doesn't create a good impression, especially with the police."

Ana put down her spoon, looked at Charlie, and said, "Let me tell your aunt the whole story."

Charlie, who sat beside Ana, took hold of her hand and kissed it. Keeping hold of it between both of his, he gazed intensely at her.

Turning back to me, Ana said, "I waited for Charlie after rehearsal last Tuesday. He didn't leave on time, and I couldn't get warm in the car, so I came inside. The other orchestra members streamed out, but not Charlie." She glanced at him.

Charlie interrupted. "I'm sorry. If I had known—"

"Hush. You couldn't know." Ana looked long and lovingly at him. Then turning to face me she said, "Felix stood beside the stage door, and we started talking. He asked me what I did for a living, and when I told him I worked in IT he told me that was a waste, and I should be a model. By this time I didn't see anyone else around. Even the security guard had gone to lock the front and side entrances, now that almost everyone had left. Felix . . . well, Felix . . . he embarrassed me. First, he stood too close. Then he put his arm around me and talked about how he had his finger on the pulse of opportunities. I didn't know what to do because I knew he was Charlie's boss, but I also knew I didn't want him to touch me. It was creepy. Fortunately, Charlie came up the stairs with one of the stagehands just then. They were laughing, but Charlie read the signs right away and knew that I felt uncomfortable."

"He had no right—" Charlie's face turned red.

"Hush. Let me finish." Ana put her fingers gently to his lips. "Charlie hustled me out of there so fast we were gone in a blink. I told him what had happened, and he fumed. He said Felix shouldn't be allowed to take advantage of his position that way. Charlie went on a rant about how Felix's behavior embarrassed the symphony and the community, and the Board should know how he acted when they weren't around."

Charlie took over. "I didn't rant. I told the truth. The next day, Wednesday, at intermission, I warned Felix I'd go to the Board if he ever did it again. That's what we were arguing about. Basically, he laughed in my face."

I certainly understood. But I needed a full explanation. "You were heard saying, 'Touch her again and I'll make you pay!"

Charlie blushed. "Yeah. I probably did say that. But I didn't mean I'd kill him. I meant I'd go to the Board and the management and tell them he'd behaved like a sleaze."

That did little to ease my concern. "You can see that it sounds like a threat. It can be taken the wrong way."

Charlie dropped his head and rubbed Ana's hand, which he still held, with his thumb.

After a hefty silence I tried to make him feel better. "Well, don't worry about it too much. It's not illegal to have an argument with the man. But I needed to find the facts. Your comments raise suspicion, and I want to help if I can."

"Auntie Em—"

"Don't worry about it. Let's have a nice meal."

"There's more."

I didn't have a good feeling about this.

Charlie continued. "After rehearsal Felix ordered me to meet with him before dress rehearsal the next day. At that meeting he told me that he had put me on probation because of my 'insubordination.' He started talking about my sounding one too few chimes in rehearsal, and I had to yell over him to point out that was his mistake. He yelled back and . . ."

Ana looked sick.

". . . and one thing led to another . . . and . . . and I hit him."

"Charlie!" I was shocked.

He looked up quickly, still holding Ana's hand. "But I didn't kill him. Felix hollered at me. Ordered me to get out. Believe me, I couldn't leave fast enough. He was alive and still yelling when I banged the door behind me."

Charlie ate no more, but gazed at Ana, continuing to rub her hand with his thumb.

In fact, I don't think Ana or I ate any more, either. I could see how this would look to the police, and I was consumed with concern for Charlie—not a good prelude for either Charlie or me to the day's two shows, a matinee and an evening performance.

SEVEN

SUNDAY, 3:00 P.M., DECEMBER 4, 2011

Next day, the grapevine buzzed with excitement at intermission. Alice Smithson, cellist and chief grapevine communicator and instigator, told me all about it. ". . . and then Charlie said, 'if you ever do it again, I'll kill you!' and then Felix is murdered less than twenty-four hours later."

I rolled my eyes and hoped Alice didn't see. That *wasn't* what Charlie had said, but then nobody ever accused the grapevine of being a reliable source. I felt like defending him, but it would only make things worse. Besides, Alice had gone on.

"Well, I'm not surprised he came onto Charlie's girlfriend. Everybody knows Felix was a player. Thank goodness *I* wasn't his wife. I'd have killed him for sure!"

With a jolt, I remembered Lorna, Felix's wife, running into his dressing room and fainting at the sight of his fallen body. Why was she in Fleischer Hall at the time of Felix's death? Could she have shot him, run around the building, entered Felix's dressing room, and pretended to faint? A possibility I couldn't afford to dismiss. I put those musings aside for later and refocused on Alice's words.

"There were rumors about Felix and all sorts of different women."

I wanted out of this conversation. I'd learned last year that gossip could be dangerous, as well as inaccurate. "Well, nice talking to you Alice, but I have to get back and get ready for the second half."

Truly, I needed longer than usual to settle down and concentrate. Poor Charlie! It had to be difficult to work with everybody talking about him. I turned around and glanced at the percussion section. Charlie sat slumped and alone. Odd. Normally he socialized with the other members of the percussion section. I gave him a thumbs up and a smile.

He returned the thumbs up, but his smile seemed artificial, and quickly faded.

It was a relief to return to the second half and play the part I'd played a thousand times before. If only real life were as innocent and beautiful as the *Nutcracker!*

Speaking of innocent and beautiful, Golden was made of that same stuff. When she greeted me at the door that night with her Christmas tree squeaky toy and turned her tummy and heart toward me, I warmed all the way through.

EIGHT

MONDAY, 11:00 A.M., DECEMBER 5, 2011

IT WAS A TYPICAL DECEMBER DAY, COLD BUT DRY. KC and I were working on the Chaminade Concertino in her weekly flute lesson when I got a phone call from Charlie. He sounded tired and hopeless. "Auntie Em, they're taking me into custody. I need a lawyer and I don't know anyone. Can you help me?"

"Don't worry. I'll call Barry. He was my lawyer last year, and he's a friend."

"Ana and Mom need to know, too. And work—my day job. The symphony'll have to get a sub. And I only get one phone call."

"Okay, Charlie. I'll let your mom and Ana know. Ana will know who to call at work, and I'll call the symphony." I hung up. I was afraid of this.

"Em?" KC had heard only my end of the conversation. I hadn't told her my concerns about Charlie, hoping the police would see he was innocent, in spite of his arguments with Felix. Surely there were other leads. When I told her the part of the story I knew, she said, "That can't be good for Charlie. Can I help?" Her gentle concern and the earnest look in her eyes were touching.

"Any ideas you have are always welcome. Other than that, I don't think so."

"I'd better get out of your hair. You have a lot on your plate."

"Thanks for understanding, KC. I'll keep you up-to-date on any developments."

Who should I call first? Probably Barry. Maybe he could get Charlie out of jail sooner, rather than later.

Barry and I are good friends, and possibly becoming more. The romantic part of our relationship is developing slowly, though. Barry rings my chimes, but not too loudly. He's well-informed, relatively handsome, with a good sense of humor and lively intelligence. But he wants an agreeable mate, someone he can care for, who will care for him.

As a recent divorcee, I treasure my freedom. His protectiveness feels smothering. He has heard *that* before—from his ex-wife.

When Barry and I get together we enjoy each other's company. I would have liked spending more time with him if I hadn't worried about the obligations that might develop. I *did* worry, though. So our calls were few and dates even fewer, the relationship complicated by the fact that our schedules rarely coincided, since I worked during Barry's leisure hours, and vice versa.

Figuring he might be busy during the workday, I texted. *Call me when U can.*

Within five minutes he phoned.

"What's up? It's unusual for you to text while I'm working."

"It's my nephew, Charlie McRae. He's been arrested for the murder of our conductor, Felix Underhayes."

"I saw the coverage of the murder on the news. Why Charlie?"

I described the situation. "The only thing I know is that Simon Cromwell overheard their argument. The police found out about that a couple days ago. Charlie told me about another run-in he had with Felix just before the murder. The cops arrested Charlie today."

Barry grunted. I thought he must be writing things down because there were a couple of silent moments before he said, "Okay." Barry sketched out his next steps. "I'll visit Charlie, let him know what we discussed, and tell him not to talk without me present. When I know more, I'll get back to you."

"Thanks, Barry."

Now for the hard part; calling Kathleen.

My big sister and I are close. She protected me in grade school. A third-grade bully is afraid of a sixth grader, even if she's a girl. Kathleen helped me through high school, gave me advice on boys, and cushioned emotional bumps and bruises whenever possible.

Mom encouraged both of us. Kathleen had always been artistic and intuitive, if impulsive. Mom paid for private art lessons, and Kathleen's paintings, pottery, and jewelry were spectacular. But my sister didn't like marketing and, after a short try, decided she'd rather keep her office manager job and create crafts as a hobby.

I didn't have the intuition or imagination of Kathleen, but I loved music. Mom had never complained about providing private lessons, which I knew were a sacrifice. She somehow paid for new instruments whenever I needed them. I'd gotten into honor bands and orchestras and finally gone to Juilliard. I had a few extremely part-time, barely-paid orchestra jobs 'til I'd landed second flute in the Monroe Symphony. There I'd found friends and satisfaction. Some people might say any success I'd had was due to discipline, but to me music didn't require discipline. It was fun, challenging, and something I felt talented at. Even scales didn't seem like work.

When we grew up, Kathleen and I buoyed each other whenever necessary. I helped her after Charlie's birth. He had to stay in the NICU for a long time, so I kept house while she and her husband drove back and forth to the hospital, praying for Charlie's recovery.

I supported her, too, when her husband died. I planned her husband's funeral, comforted Charlie, and stayed with her until little by little, between me and her grief recovery support group, she began to embrace life again.

After my divorce Kathleen listened and listened and listened. She came to visit for a few weeks and did the cooking, staying 'til my wounds were a little less raw.

Charlie went to school at the Boston Conservatory. When he won the audition in Monroe, Kathleen was delighted he had kin in town (that would be me). He stayed with me while he found an extra job and his own apartment, but that lasted only a few weeks. He's super-busy, and I'm busy, so now we only see each other at orchestra and occasional family dinners. Kathleen often comes to town for holidays and special concerts. When she does, Mom comes, too, and we have a reunion of our small family. I love seeing Kathleen and Mom more often than I did before. We're family, even if there aren't many of us. Sure, I get annoyed with Kathleen sometimes, as I'm sure she does with me, and we both get exasperated with Mom occasionally, but I can count on them, and they can count on me.

I hated to give Kathleen bad news, but she needed to hear about Charlie's arrest from me. He was her only child, her miracle baby, so I reminded myself to be gentle. I pushed the button for her Indiana number.

"Hi, Emily. What's new?"

"Kathleen." Now that it came down to it, I couldn't think of any tactful way to break the news. "It's Charlie."

Instantly her voice changed, alert and rising in pitch. "What happened? Is he alright?"

I answered the last part first. "Yes, and no."

"Emily, tell me what's going on!"

"He's been arrested. For murder."

"Murder!"

I explained.

"Where is he now? Can I talk to him? What about bail?"

"I don't have any answers, Kathleen. Charlie called me from the police station. I wanted you to know as soon as possible and to hear it from me. I'll call as soon as I find out more."

"Oh, poor Charlie! I'll be there as soon as I can get a flight. I already have my ticket for later in the month, but I'll try to move my departure date earlier. In the meantime, please help him as much as you can."

"I've already gotten him a lawyer. Barry helped me out last year, and he's a talented criminal attorney."

"Thanks, Emily."

I heard the sound of sobs as I hung up.

I called Ana, too.

"Impossible! Charlie would never kill anyone. Even Felix. I know Charlie was pretty ticked off, but . . ."

"We have to do our best to encourage him. Do you want to come with my sister and me to visit him in prison?"

A moment's silence followed. "I can't afford to miss another shift at work. Especially with Charlie gone. It'll be easier for me to plan a solo visit. But both you and Charlie can count on my help, if you need it."

I sympathized. I could hardly imagine meeting my boyfriend's mom under these circumstances. And I guessed I wouldn't have wanted to be saddled with Charlie's mother and aunt, either. Ana wanted to have more important, intimate conversations than she could have in our presence. We'd cramp her style.

"I understand."

"If you see Charlie before I do, please tell him I love him."

"Of course."

"And I'll contact work. I know Charlie's got vacation time coming, so maybe I can convince them to use that."

"Thanks, Ana. You're the best."

Next I called the Symphony's personnel manager. He was dismayed. "But we've got a performance Thursday, and no rehearsal before then." He tsked, then calmed down. "Well, thanks for calling me, Emily. At least I have a couple days to find somebody."

We hung up, and I realized that, for now, I'd done all I could. What next?

NINE

MONDAY, 1:30 P.M., DECEMBER 5, 2011

Later, when the living room phone rang and the caller ID showed Barry's number, I answered quickly, eager to get some information I could give Kathleen. I hoped to get a report from him, but I didn't know if he would talk to me because of confidentiality issues.

We exchanged greetings, then I asked, "Did you see Charlie?"

"I did. Normally I wouldn't be able to tell you anything we talked about, but he signed a release enabling me to talk to you or his mom about his case. "

"Good." I knew Kathleen would voraciously devour information, and I wanted to know, too. "What's going on? First tell me how he's doing. Kathleen will want details."

"He seems pretty shell-shocked. He wanted to talk about getting out on bail—all the details of how that's arranged." Barry paused a moment, then continued. "I explained that the judge would set bail—or not—at the arraignment hearing later this afternoon. We'll have to wait for that. Charlie wasn't happy to hear there'd be no immediate release." Barry cleared his throat. "We spent most of the rest of our time talking about what happened."

I flopped down in a chair. "What did he have to say?"

"He absolutely denied that he killed Felix, and said he had never owned a gun and didn't know anything about them. But he admitted that at intermission Wednesday night they argued about Felix's advances to Ana, and that he shouted at Felix and stormed away."

Barry cleared his throat. "By then I'd talked to my source at the PD and learned that, beside the argument on Wednesday, which Simon overheard, the cops found Charlie's fingerprints in Felix's dressing room and rude conductor material on his Facebook page."

I'd seen that page. It wasn't full of "rude conductor material," it was full of jokes—the musician's way of venting—jokes so standard they were like knock-knock jokes. "Q: What's the difference between an orchestra and a bull? A: The bull has the horns in front and the ass in the back." They were harmless stress relievers, but apparently, open to misinterpretation.

Barry continued. "Then on Thursday just before the murder, Charlie and Felix had another argument which turned into a brawl. The *primeur danseur* overheard it."

"Yeah, Charlie told me about that."

"Charlie claims he left about five-fifty, and, although he admits to his anger, he swears Felix was alive then. But the cops think the dispute escalated to the gunshot. They confirmed the *danseur's* report when they discovered Felix's DNA on Charlie's ring. Several people also reported friction between Charlie and Felix. The cops felt they had sufficient cause to arrest Charlie for the murder and a judge agreed, even though they haven't found the murder weapon yet. They'll keep digging."

"Wait. Let me get this straight. Correct me if I'm wrong. Charlie's story is that Felix came on to Ana after rehearsal Tuesday night. Charlie and Felix had an argument about that Wednesday night at intermission. Then, after rehearsal Wednesday, Felix ordered Charlie to come early to Thursday's dress rehearsal to discuss his 'attitude'. During that meeting, Felix told Charlie he was on probation. Charlie lost his temper and hit Felix. The *danseur* heard the scuffle. Charlie left angry, but Felix was alive."

"That's right."

"And it's only Charlie's word that he left at five fifty, and that Felix was alive when he left?"

"Uh-huh."

"And on top of all of that, there were disrespectful conductor jokes on Charlie's Facebook page." I thought a moment. "But why would Charlie bother to have a fistfight with Felix if he could just shoot him?"

"Don't know, Em. It doesn't make much sense, does it? Murder never does. I'm just saying, those are the facts the police have."

"The timing does sounds damning. Even I'd be mad enough at Felix to kill him given that series of events."

"Heaven, forefend!"

We chuckled, though it wasn't very funny.

"Do you think Felix's advances to Ana set off the whole mess?"

Barry snorted. "What do you think?"

The silence that followed didn't need words to speak.

"What about Charlie's everyday attitude to Felix? Can you describe that?"

"The *Nutcracker* is fresh in my mind, so I'll tell you about that." I took a deep breath while I organized my thoughts. "Felix directed critical comments to Charlie in the first rehearsal, but Charlie didn't retaliate." I told him about Felix conducting the wrong number of chimes, then taking it out on Charlie.

I paused and thought a moment. "And in the run-through, he constantly accused Charlie of going too fast. Charlie followed Felix's beat. Nobody thought Charlie rushed except Felix. I think his tempo hurried the dancers and he criticized Charlie as an excuse. Charlie didn't make any secret about his dislike of Felix, but he didn't criticize him in public or to the powers that be, either. Charlie doesn't like making trouble."

Barry must have been taking notes, because I thought the call had been dropped before he spoke again. He hesitated. "Em, I think you have to consider that Charlie may be lying."

"That can't be. He's my nephew. He's grown up with me beside him. I don't believe he's a killer. Besides, he's my only sister's only child. He's her life."

"I figured." Barry sighed. "All my clients are innocent anyway, at least as far as I'm concerned." He continued, "So in that case, nothing will convince the police or a jury that Charlie is innocent except finding out who really killed Felix."

I nervously started pacing. "Give me your honest opinion, Barry. Do we have a chance?"

"Well, if Charlie's telling the truth, the cops won't be able to connect him with a gun. If there are no records to support gun ownership, that backs up his story. But that's pretty weak. He could have gotten the weapon from an illegal source. Or stolen it. If the cops can't find the gun and link it to both Charlie and the murder, they're gonna have difficulty proving their case. They may even drop the charges. But if they pursue charges, I'll call the prosecutor on it."

Barry paused and cleared his throat. "I pressed Charlie hard and asked him to convince me he wasn't the murderer. You said yourself that it sounds bleak." Barry spoke faster. "That rattled him. He couldn't come up with an argument. Stuttered and stammered and said he didn't do it."

My heart hurt for Charlie and all he must have been through in the last few hours. "Not good, then."

"Actually, I believe him. I wouldn't expect an innocent person to have a glib explanation." He paused. "I didn't soften his situation. I told him a jury would find his story difficult to believe in the face of all the evidence against him. I did my darndest playing devil's advocate, but he maintained his innocence."

"It's good that he stuck to his story, I guess, but it doesn't sound very convincing. Did Charlie have any ideas?"

"I asked him to think about it. Would anyone want to frame him for a murder? I was straight with him. Unless we can find the murder weapon and its owner, and that person had a motive and an opportunity to kill Felix, it's going to be tough. Charlie said a lot of people don't get his humor, but he didn't think anyone had anything serious against him."

"Not everybody likes Charlie. His jokes rub people the wrong way sometimes. I've heard several people who've described him as 'that crude clown,' or 'that bawdy buffoon,' or even 'that vulgar funnyman.'"

"That's a good place to start. I'll tell the cops to check out the negative feelings Charlie generated." Barry must have been writing again because he paused a long time before he said, "I'm wondering who else could have hated Felix." He paused, then continued, "You've gotta help me here, Em. Tell me more about the people Felix had contact with backstage."

"What do you want to know?"

"For starters, exactly who might have had business with him?"

"Hmm . . ." I thought out loud. "Felix had fingers in quite a few more pies than usual for *Nutcracker*. There were kids and dancers." I tried to paint him a picture. "Small children play the mice, and kids sing in the children's chorus. They're all backstage, dropped off by their families. The ballet dancers roam around in various stages of undress, there are people who sew, wrangle kids, and do makeup, and of course the regular orchestra members."

Barry started to say something, but I interrupted him with more details. "The kids playing the mice have a large room set aside for them, the children's chorus has another room, the *corps de ballet* has a large dressing room, Felix has a dressing room, and the two lead ballet dancers—the *prima* ballerina and the *primeur danseur*—each have individual dressing rooms. And then of course the orchestra has the green room and the orchestra pit." I hesitated. "Theoretically, Felix oversaw all that."

After another moment I concluded. "But of all those people, in reality only the *primeur* and *prima* ballet dancers, whose dressing rooms were in the same hall as Felix's, would have direct contact with him." I thought a moment longer and added, "He might talk to the kids' dance master and the chorus' conductor, the ballet choreographer, or he might need to talk to the stagehands, too. And of course, he normally interacted with the orchestra."

"Seems like lots of people had contact with Felix," Barry said slowly.

"The security guard supposedly keeps track of them all. But Felix was murdered early enough that the guard hadn't arrived yet."

Barry said, "Why did the *danseur* arrive so early?"

"I'm not sure. There could be a lot of reasons. The point is, he had a right to be there, even two to three hours before the performance."

"Seems like he should have gotten to Felix right away, before you, not after."

"I guess that's true."

"The *prima* ballerina wasn't there yet, so the *danseur* would have had the best opportunity to shoot Felix, since his dressing room is right next door. Would he have time to shoot Felix, return to his dressing room, and then come out again as you arrived after the shot?"

"I don't know. He would have to be awfully fast. And I heard the exit door slam, too. He couldn't have gotten back in through the same door because it locks automatically, and I would have seen him if he came in by the stage door. He could only have done it if he ran down the hall, slammed the door but stayed inside, and then ran back up the hall to his dressing room. I didn't hear any returning footsteps. Besides that, as I say, he would have had to be incredibly fast."

"He might know something, though, or have heard something."

He paused before changing the subject. "I always like hearing from you, Em. Even under the circumstances." He sounded shy.

Sincerely, I answered, "It's been too long." I enjoyed his company, and it had been a while since we'd talked.

"I wondered if you'd like to see a play Saturday. Theatre in the Round is—"

With genuine regret I interrupted. "I wish I could. It sounds like fun, but I've got another *Nutcracker* performance Saturday. After Christmas the symphony will have a break." I hoped it didn't sound like an excuse. I *did* want to see Barry. It had been too long.

"Sure. I should have known."

"I'm free before performances, though. How about lunch tomorrow? Charlie's mother should have arrived by then. We can all eat together."

"That sounds like a good idea."

"She's flying stand-by and will be here as soon as she can. I'll call you with exact times when I know what flight she's on." We made arrangements and hung up.

I'd tell Kathleen that Charlie had seen his lawyer and mention lunch arrangements. I wouldn't tell her that, so far, the news wasn't good.

TEN

TUESDAY, 9:00 A.M., DECEMBER 6, 2011

KNOWING KATHLEEN WOULD BE BESIDE HERSELF, I made my home as welcoming as I could. Remembering that cookies had eased Megan's trauma, I stretched my culinary talents to the max and baked chocolate chip cookies. Their sugary aroma scented the air. That's love. Hopefully I wouldn't burn them.

Unfortunately, my housemate and friend, KC, didn't often have time to cook anymore. When *she* cooked, the smells were truly mouthwatering. But her job as sous chef at the Articulate Artichoke, a local restaurant, kept her busy. In fact, she'd gone in early this morning to help with preparations for a business luncheon being held there. Usually, I'd gone to a rehearsal or a concert by the time she got home, so we hardly ever saw each other. I "cooked" for myself, getting by on foods that took little or no prep, and she cleaned and took flute lessons from me on Monday, her day off. Sometimes she joined me and Golden for dog walks.

In my three-bedroom home I used one bedroom and KC had the second. The third bedroom doubled as my studio and a guest room, with its hide-a-bed. During Kathleen's stay I planned to temporarily teach in the living room so she could sleep in the guest room and have her privacy. I had readied her room and made sure there were fresh towels in the bathroom.

When the doorbell rang unexpectedly, Golden barked and followed me to the entrance.

At the door a broad-shouldered man towered over me. He wore a grey parka and carried a notebook under his arm. I stifled a groan. The chief homicide detective.

"Lieutenant Gordon. Come in. How can I help you?" I tried to sound welcoming. From our exchanges last year, I knew he didn't like dogs, so I held Golden by the collar despite her efforts to greet him, and led the way down the hall. *Déjà vu.*

My mother could be a little odd, but she'd taught me manners. I asked, "Can I get you tea?"

"No thanks, Ms. Wilson. I'll stick to business."

We sat in the living room, where he dwarfed the surroundings. All efficiency, he avoided the sofa and seated himself in a straight-backed, armless chair, where he slipped off his parka and prepared to take notes.

"As you know, I've been investigating the murder of Felix Underhayes. You were first on the scene, and one of only two who tried to help him after the shot. Kind of you. Why were you at Fleisher Hall for rehearsal so early?"

What was he thinking? I did my best to put any suspicions he might have to rest. "I'd just taught a flute student having family problems. I wanted to think about the situation as well as pamper myself a little before the dress rehearsal, so I went to dinner. I finished early. With time on my hands, I thought I could get in some practice time in a big auditorium acoustic." I didn't tell him I hoped to play Bach in that surrounding and heal my soul a bit.

He noted my comments. "I understand Charles McRae, the alleged killer, is your nephew." Lt. Gordon met my eyes before he asked, "How do you get along with him?"

"We're family. I love him."

He scribbled in his notebook. "Can you tell me about him?"

"There's not much to tell. He's my sister's son, a gentle soul, and a clown. He does his best to make everybody laugh, and Golden loves him."

"Golden's the dog?"

"Mmhmm." He didn't sound very impressed, so I continued. "Charlie shovels my walks sometimes in the winter and helps me however he can." For the sake of clarity I added, "He's the last person who'd murder anyone."

"Hummph."

I didn't think anyone "humphed" except in the funny papers, but there you have it.

"I understand Mr. Reitman is Mr. McRae's lawyer. Isn't he the same attorney you used when we had our little misunderstanding last year?"

What did he mean, little misunderstanding? He'd tried to lock me in jail and throw away the key. To be fair, at the time I suppose he'd had good reason and strong evidence. "Yes, Charlie has the same lawyer. I recommended him. Is that a problem?" I knew the lieutenant suspected Barry had been involved in my evasion of police, but hadn't been able to prove anything.

"No. No problem." He stood. "Thanks for the background. Here's my card. Call me if you think of anything else."

That interview seemed innocuous, and had given me the chance to put any doubts he had about me to rest, as well as support Charlie. I felt my stomach relax.

I followed him out, relieved and grateful.

After he'd gone, I entered his office and cell phone numbers in my contact list.

I *would* think of something else. Something that would clear Charlie. I had to.

THE LITTLE TOWN IN INDIANA WHERE KATHLEEN lives wasn't a major airline hub and wasn't close to one. She'd hung out at the nearest airport and found space flying stand-by, then called and let me know she'd arrive on a flight at noon today, the day after Charlie's arrest and five days after Felix's murder.

I let Barry know the time of her arrival and arranged to meet at the Articulate Artichoke, then drove to the airport. I left the car in short-term parking and walked to the terminal. Kathleen and I had arranged to meet at baggage claim. I soon spotted her long hair bobbing above the crowd.

We had always been Mutt and Jeff—she the tall, stunning blonde who took after my father; me the dark, run-of-the-mill child who resembled my mother. Now we were both turning gray—she, gorgeous silver-gold; me, plebian salt-and-pepper.

Kathleen usually looked like she had stepped straight out of a fashion magazine. Even at her husband's funeral she had managed to look terrific, in a formfitting black dress that showed off her long, elegant legs.

How miserable she must be to arrive like this! She wore baggy gray sweats and no makeup, hair in strings, her eyes red and bleary, as if hadn't slept since hearing news of Charlie's arrest.

She was three years my senior, but now I felt as protective as I would of a little sister rattled by a nightmare. "You're a sight that makes my eyes sore." I smiled and opened my arms.

Recognizing one of Mom's contorted clichés, she smiled momentarily as I had hoped, then hugged me long and desperately, and we rocked together for a moment. She paced restlessly as we waited for her suitcase, seemingly unable to sit still, as if the unceasing movement could help Charlie.

When her luggage finally appeared, I started in the direction of the parking lot.

Kathleen stopped me. "I have to pick up my rental car. It's already reserved."

I felt a stab of disappointment. "You didn't have to spend money on a car. I planned to drive you around." I had hoped for some good sister time.

"I didn't want to be any trouble."

This would probably take a while. Steeling myself to be patient, I followed her to the rental car counter. To my surprise her car, a white, late-model Toyota Corolla, waited outside. We were ready to leave in short order.

Kathleen wanted to visit Charlie right away.

I had foreseen this might be an issue. "Non-professional visitors have to give twenty-four hours' notice, so I scheduled us for three o'clock today."

"You're kidding!" She took a deep breath, exhaled and closed her eyes. When she reopened them she said, "Well, I've waited this long. I suppose I can wait another two hours."

I realized how hard this was for her and put my arm around her. "Sorry, Kathleen."

She struggled to smile, and then said, "If you hadn't taken care of it, we'd have to wait longer. Thanks, Emily."

"Let's go to a restaurant and eat. We'll meet Barry, Charlie's lawyer, there. By the time we finish a nice meal it will be almost time to see Charlie."

As she headed for her rental car, I hoped good food and a talk with Barry would help settle her nerves.

I LED THE WAY IN MY NEW SUBARU. Kathleen followed in her rental car. We caravanned to the Articulate Artichoke.

KC, my housemate and friend, worked there. Toiling long hours as a sous chef, she had suggested numerous techniques and recipes to the head chef that were helping gradually turn the struggling restaurant into a gourmet's delight, with its own little niche in the city's gastronomic life. Her perceptions were sometimes strange and surprising, and often good for me. I knew I could depend on her friendship, and I counted on her to welcome the sister I'd talked so much about.

The lunch rush had ended. Barry hadn't arrived yet, so after the hostess seated us, Kathleen and I left our table and went to the kitchen window. We were in luck. KC looked up from her chopping task, and I waved.

She wiped her hands on a towel and met us at the doors.

"KC, this is my sister, Kathleen. She's in town to help Charlie McRae. He's been arrested for Felix's murder. You've heard about it?" Oh, Emily! Open mouth, insert foot. I couldn't believe I'd introduced them so tactlessly.

I heard Kathleen gasp.

KC paused, then said softly, "Well of course! It's been in the news, you know? But why are you two involved?"

Quickly, I explained, "Charlie is Kathleen's son, and my nephew."

Kathleen looked a little sick.

"Oh, I'm so sorry!" KC responded, turning to my sister. "I'm sure he'll be relieved to see you. It's great that he has such a supportive mom in his corner, you know?"

"I hope so." Kathleen tried to smile.

"I'm glad I got to meet you. I've heard a lot about you. I wish I had time to talk, but I have to get back to work. We can get acquainted later."

This time Kathleen smiled sincerely. "I understand. Until then."

We returned to our table and sat down. As we awaited the waitress, Kathleen asked, "How did you meet KC?"

I decided not to tell her KC and I had become acquainted in jail, during a time in my life I'd rather forget. "She plays the flute," I said. "She helped me find my friend Olive's murderer." There. I hadn't told a single lie. "I discovered her culinary talents and talked her into applying for a job as the Artichoke's sous chef. It doesn't pay very well, but she has a good chance for advancement."

Barry arrived just then, and I made introductions all around.

I sat down and felt Kathleen bouncing her leg next to me. I realized Charlie and his predicament preoccupied her.

The waitress took our drink orders and left, and our conversation went straight to Charlie's plight. Without giving anyone a chance to look at the menu, Kathleen asked, "How can the cops think Charlie would ever kill anyone?"

I let Barry handle it.

"There are some pretty damning particulars against Charlie." Barry enumerated the facts on his fingers as he talked. "Felix forced his attentions on Charlie's girlfriend; he and Charlie argued on two separate occasions, once violently; Felix put Charlie on disciplinary probation; the police found Charlie's fingerprints in Felix's dressing room and insolent conductor jokes on Charlie's Facebook page; and Charlie's ring held Felix's DNA. It all sounds bad, but it's all circumstantial."

Her leg still bounced. "Charlie would never kill anyone. He couldn't."

"I know. We'll prove it isn't true. Don't worry." Barry's voice was soothing.

That's easier said than done. I remembered Charlie's efforts to make his mother laugh. I saw him as a gentle jokester, more inclined to sophomoric puns than vicious bloodletting.

Kathleen continued, "This is all a bad dream—somebody's mistake."

I patted her arm. "We'll get through it somehow. Barry'll help us. He's very experienced and highly recommended. He helped me last year." I had hoped Barry's qualifications would make Kathleen feel better, but she made no comment, continuing to bounce her leg.

Barry picked up where he left off. "I know it's easy to say, 'Don't worry,' but it's very early in the investigation. The police haven't found the murder weapon yet, and when they do, I'm sure they won't be able to connect it to Charlie."

That seemed to lessen her stress. She stilled her leg for the moment. "What about bail?"

"I'm afraid the judge decided not to allow it."

"Oh, no!" Kathleen's eyes filled.

"The prosecutor presented the murder as a high-profile capital case and convinced the judge Charlie was a flight risk, since he hasn't been in Monroe long and has no close ties here. She reminded the judge that violence had been involved and recommended against bail. The judge agreed."

Kathleen's chin trembled. "So he can't get out until the police release him?"

"I'm afraid not."

Kathleen silently processed this information, then blinked her tears back, took a deep breath, and changed the subject.

"Emily, what do think of this girl, Ana, Charlie keeps mentioning?" Off the hook for a moment, Barry attended to the menu.

I answered, "I don't really know her very well, but she seems to care for Charlie a great deal and be very intelligent. He met her at work. They're assigned to the same unit."

"I want him to be happy, but I want it to be with the right girl." Kathleen leaned her head on her hand.

"I wouldn't worry. They're a long way from marriage, and Ana seems very nice."

Kathleen mumbled and finally studied the menu. When the waitress came, we ordered and continued the conversation with trivial subjects, Kathleen quiet, for the most part. At some point the leg began to bounce again, and as soon as everyone finished Kathleen said, "Where's the waitress with our checks? We need to go."

Barry urged, "You two go ahead. I'll take care of the bill."

I thanked him. While we were collecting our purses to leave, KC came out of the kitchen and stopped us. "Em, I haven't heard anything about how the symphony is handling Felix's death. Will they cancel the performances? I have tickets for Steve and me next week."

"Who's Steve?" She hadn't told me about him at yesterday's lesson.

She blushed. "He's just a guy. We've had a few dates. I met him the day after Thanksgiving."

Interesting, I thought. They'd had "a few" dates, and Thanksgiving had only been a week and a half ago. KC's past history of choosing men didn't exactly shine with success, and I felt my protective instincts kick in. But back to the matter at hand. "With or without Felix, the show must go on. As usual, the symphony is teetering on the edge of bankruptcy. Any cancellations and we'd lose our shirts. The Assistant Conductor, Doug Jones, took over, and he's doing a great job. We've already given four performances."

I glanced at my watch. I knew Kathleen anxiously anticipated our visit to Charlie.

Kathleen nudged me. "If we get to the jail early maybe we can see Charlie sooner."

I couldn't justify a lengthy discussion while Kathleen's son waited in a cell, so I finished my conversation with KC as quickly as I could.

"I expect full details on Steve later."

"Sure, Em. See you."

We said our goodbyes and conveyed our thanks to Barry once again before we left for the jail, where Charlie waited.

THE MONROE JAIL IS IN A BUILDING next to the courthouse, convenient I suppose. It's a four-story structure, completely gray concrete. The upper two floors are all cells, and the only windows are tiny slits.

Kathleen, who had followed me in her rental car, fidgeted through check-in. We surrendered our cell phones and metal objects, and I waited while Kathleen showed her Indiana ID. I produced my Colorado driver's license, then a female guard patted me down.

Kathleen came to my defense. "Do you have to treat my sister like a criminal?"

My cheeks warmed. "Kathleen!"

"It's procedure." The matron didn't suspend her search.

"You don't mean to say you intend to put me through that, too?" Kathleen sounded unbelieving.

"Sorry, ma'am. It you don't want to go through the process, you're welcome to remain in the waiting room."

"But . . . my son . . ."

"I don't make the rules." Her emotionless response said she'd heard it a million times before.

Kathleen let herself be searched without further protest.

We locked our purses in a locker and were both sent through a metal detector. Only then were we escorted to a small wire elevator that smelled of stale sweat, creaked, and moved *very* slowly. It took us to the fourth floor where Charlie was being held. We stepped off the elevator into the visitor's reception room and more gray, this time a gray-painted concrete floor, smelling faintly of urine and strongly of disinfectant. An officer directed us to sign in again, then escorted us to a room with a Plexiglas barrier and bright orange molded plastic chairs. He told us to wait while a guard got Charlie.

Kathleen sat on the edge of her seat, bouncing her leg. "Oh, this is awful!" She flinched and jumped when the metal door clanked, opening to let Charlie through.

In an orange jumpsuit—not his best color—his ordinarily pale face, framed in shaggy blond hair, looked ashen, like someone had whitewashed him. A prison guard accompanied him, then backed off a few feet—near enough to hear and respond if necessary, but far enough away to give the illusion of privacy.

Kathleen glanced at her hand, then the Plexiglas that separated her from Charlie. For good reason, I knew she wished she could pull a packet of sanitary wipes from her purse and scrub it. That wasn't an option, though. She apparently decided closeness was more important than cleanliness, and put her hand on the glass, fingers spread. Charlie trembled as he did the same. It was the closest they could get to a hug, I guess. We all sat and lifted our respective phones.

"Oh, sweetheart!" Kathleen moaned, scooting her chair forward and putting her hand on the Plexiglas again. "How could they do this to you?"

"It's a mistake, Mom. You know that, right?"

Both of them were so single-mindedly occupied with the other that my presence went unnoticed, which was okay by me. I had no idea what to say.

Kathleen gave Charlie a barely visible nod.

He continued. "It'll be okay. They'll straighten this out, and I'll be home in no time."

My eyes filled. Charlie comforted his mother as best he could, even though he was the prisoner behind bars.

"What can we do to make you comfortable?" Without waiting for an answer, she continued. "I'll make sure . . ." She sniffled. ". . . you have your therapeutic . . ." A sob. ". . . pillow and . . ." Kathleen began wailing, in a way that I thought only a five-year-old avoiding her nap could. I comforted her as best I could, put my arm around her, patted, and whispered encouraging words.

Charlie looked uncomfortable, to say the least, during this outburst. "Mom, I . . ." He never finished, just put his hand on the Plexiglas.

It seemed a long time before Kathleen hiccupped to a stop. She took a tissue from her pocket and honked into it noisily. Somewhat recovered now that she had given vent to her feelings, she said, "The prosecutor must think she has a strong case, based on what the police have told her. But don't worry. Emily and I will help you. Emily knows how these things are done."

I figured she must be referring to proving my innocence last year, an experience I didn't want to repeat.

Kathleen gave me a trusting, confident look. "The murderer must be one of the orchestra members."

That seemed like an unsupported leap of logic. "How do you figure?"

"Felix treated the orchestra members horribly, and they had to come into contact with him on a daily basis. One of them must be the killer. You're the expert, Emily. You know them. You can talk to them."

It seemed premature to convict one of my colleagues of the crime, but Kathleen was right. No one else would help Charlie. "I don't know about that. But we'll do everything we can. Ana will help, too."

Charlie gave us both a grateful look. "You guys are awesome! It's great to finally have somebody on my side."

For the first time since the beginning of our visit he sounded hopeful.

"Ana told me she'll be visiting later," I said.

"Thanks, Auntie Em."

The guard approached then and told us we were out of time.

We rose to go. Kathleen exchanged handprints on the Plexiglas with Charlie once again. "Bye, sweetheart. We'll solve this and get you out of here."

"Thanks, Mom." Charlie left only when the guard clutched his shoulder and led him away.

Kathleen followed me home in her rental car. When we arrived, nervous energy fueled her conversation. "It sounds positive. Barry seems confident the police won't be able to connect Charlie to the gun and we'll be able to prove Charlie's innocence. And your help will be invaluable. You know the orchestra. What shall we do first?"

"Kathleen, I'm really sorry, but I have students coming soon."

She only said, "Oh! I thought . . . Charlie needs . . ." She paused, cleared her throat, and wiped her eyes. "Well, I guess I need to settle in anyway. I'll take a shower. We'll get started later."

Seeing how she worried, I felt guilty. I'd do my best, but I couldn't spend all my time sleuthing. I had to earn a living. Kathleen would have to have a little patience.

ELEVEN

TUESDAY, 8:00 P.M., DECEMBER 6, 2011

THAT NIGHT KATHLEEN AND I HAD OUR FIRST good discussion of Charlie's situation. KC was still at the restaurant, and I missed her ideas. I went over what I'd heard and seen, and what Charlie supposedly did, and we discussed what our next move should be.

"Barry thinks we should talk to the *danseur*. He arrived first on the scene besides yours truly. And he had the dressing room next to Felix's. He might know or have heard something important. Maybe we should start there."

My sister demurred and insisted the murderer had to be one of the orchestra members. "Felix doesn't sound like a very nice man. They couldn't have liked him much, whereas the ballet dancer wouldn't have known Felix long enough to develop strong feelings."

"That's true. But for *Nutcracker*, the stagehands would have had to deal with Felix more than the orchestra."

Kathleen seized on the idea. "Okay. Then let's start there. Who's first?"

I thought a minute. "Jim Plank leads the stage crew. Ken Sands and Leon Brown are the other stagehands. Ken is such a sweetie.

I can't believe he'd do anything to Felix, no matter how much he disliked him. Let's start with Jim. We can ask him to give us contact information for the other two."

I got Jim's number from the orchestra directory and turned possible approaches over in my mind as I picked up the phone. It felt awkward to set up a meeting. What if he wouldn't talk to us? In the end, I gave up trying to be clever and just asked to meet with him.

"Meet with me? Why?"

Naturally, he was puzzled. I wouldn't ordinarily say more than a sentence or two to him at work unless I needed something, so I explained. "Charlie McRae is my nephew. I'm trying to help prove he's innocent."

"Your nephew! I didn't know that," Jim said. "I don't know how I can help, but sure. Why don't we meet before Thursday's performance."

We'd have to wait a day and I knew Kathleen wanted to get started, but I agreed, and we ended the call.

I wasn't wrong. Kathleen fretted over the delay. We discussed waiting until we could talk to Jim. Sounding frustrated, Kathleen told me, "I thought you wanted to help Charlie. We can't sit and do nothing."

She had a point. We needed to move as quickly as possible. "We have to be considerate of other people's schedules, though." I tried to mollify her. "What if we do as Barry suggested and talk to the *danseur*?"

Kathleen wrinkled her nose. "I doubt it'll be helpful, but it's better than doing nothing." She shrugged. "What can I do? You know. By myself. While you're teaching or performing?"

Her question gave me pause. She handled social situations extremely well. Naturally outgoing, people liked her. She also exuded mother-bear energy in defense of her cub. That sounded like a useful combination, but I couldn't think how to employ it at the moment. I worried, too, because my sister could be unpredictable, a character trait she got from Mom, so I gave a vague response. "I'm sure you can do something. Exactly what will be clearer later, as we find out more."

I brought up a more immediate, and difficult, concern. "Have you told Mom about Charlie?"

Kathleen avoided my gaze.

Mom lived in Denver and called Charlie every week. "She'll wonder what's going on when she can't get hold of him."

Kathleen didn't respond, instead looking down at her fingers.

"Better she hears it from us, than that she gets concerned and drops in unexpectedly." I wheedled. "You know she'd do it."

"She dotes on Charlie. He's her only grandchild. I can't bear to tell her." Kathleen behaved like a marshmallow. What had become of my big, strong, older sister?

"Do you want me to talk to her?"

"You shouldn't have to do that."

True—I shouldn't have to do any of this—nobody should. But we didn't have any choice.

"Could we talk to her . . . together?" Kathleen sounded timid.

"Okay. I'll get on the studio phone while you call from the land line in the living room." I picked up as Mom answered the phone.

"Hi!" Kathleen put on a chipper, happy voice.

"Kathleen! Sweetie!"

"Emily is here with me, too. We're at her house."

"You're together? A family reunion and nobody told me?"

"Of course not, Mom. There's a reason we're together."

"A reason?"

Kathleen hesitated. "Charlie's been arrested." There. She'd said it.

"Arrested! What for? I know he's not perfect, but he's so—"

"He's accused of murder." Kathleen blurted it out.

"Murder! Who made that blunder? Charlie doesn't have a vicious bone in his body."

Silence. I stepped in to fill the void. "Mom, someone shot our conductor, Felix Underhayes. Twice people heard Charlie arguing with Felix before his death, and then Felix put him on disciplinary probation. Besides which, there's DNA evidence and Charlie's Facebook page is open to misinterpretation. In the police view, Charlie had good reason to hate Felix. He had a fistfight with Felix and they've picked up on that."

"Ridiculous! Charlie couldn't hurt a mosquito."

I almost corrected "He couldn't hurt a fly" out of habit but decided to save that particular losing battle for later. Instead, I explained that we were going to try to find someone else who could have murdered Felix.

"Well, I'm glad you're helping him, because Charlie's a dear. I'll call that detective and give him a piece of my mind. Tell me his name!"

"Mom!" Kathleen and I said together. We'd been afraid of this. As unpredictable as sheet music in a windstorm, Mom didn't hesitate to attack loudly, without mercy, in defense of her young. Charlie didn't need anyone to make things worse for him. Besides, she couldn't afford to give away pieces of her mind.

"Emily, is this the same detective that put out an APB on you last year?"

"Yes. Lieutenant Gordon heads the homicide squad in Monroe."

"Gordon! That's the name!"

Uh-oh. Now I'd done it. She might really call him.

"He's brainless." Mom's voice trembled with anger. "As a policeman you'd think that he would have learned that if it looks like a duck, walks like a duck, and quacks like a duck, it's probably something else. I'll go straight to the mayor!"

"Now, Mom. We don't want to make Lieutenant Gordon mad too early. We'll save the big guns for later and bring you in if we need to." I prayed enough flattery would keep her under control.

"Well . . . if you think we should wait. Do you want me to come out there?"

"You're coming out for Christmas next week anyway. We'll let you know if we need help sooner."

I hurriedly changed the subject by asking about the boyfriend she'd met on her Alaskan cruise last year. He came out every two weeks to visit her. Telling me the details of his latest visit distracted her. She didn't mention Charlie again until we were about to hang up.

"Now don't forget. I can come out and help if you need me. And call with updates."

"Okay, Mom." I crossed my fingers, praying she'd stay put. "But there shouldn't be anything to worry about. The police'll find the truth."

I wished I could believe it.

TWELVE

WEDNESDAY, 9:00 A.M., DECEMBER 7, 2011

THE BALLET DANCERS WERE STAYING at the Regis Hotel. I didn't know the name of the *premier danseur*, so I looked it up under his picture in the program I'd kept, then asked the desk clerk, "What room is Manolo Simka in, please?"

The clerk picked up his phone and dialed a number, then handed the phone receiver to me.

"Manolo, this is Emily Wilson. I'm the one who helped Felix with you the day of his murder. Can I come up?"

"Sure. Room 222."

"Thanks."

I handed the receiver back to the desk clerk and Kathleen and I took the stairs in deference to my sister's desire to burn calories.

A gorgeous, well-muscled male specimen with wet hair, dressed in sweats, answered my knock. "Manolo?" I knew the face from our experience last week.

"Come in, come in." He stepped out of the doorway so we could enter, then hugged me. "My friends call me Manny."

Feelings I didn't know I had bubbled up, and tears filled my eyes. I blinked them back and said, "This is my sister, Kathleen McRae."

"Glad to meet you." His speech sounded precise, absolutely correct.

Manny had a large suite. He led us to a connecting sitting room. "Sit. Sit."

We settled ourselves on a leather-covered loveseat. "I just wanted to find out how you were doing. Thank goodness you were there to come to Felix's aid—to my aid. I keep seeing Felix . . . I thought you might understand."

He sat in an easy chair and blinked, and I wondered if he, too, held back tears. "I'm okay. I knew Felix hardly at all, but finding him . . . like that . . ." He swallowed. "It must have been much harder for you."

"I was okay while I did something. The shock set in later."

"You functioned very well."

"Thanks. And thank you for trying to help Felix."

"It's the most worthwhile thing I've done in a long time."

"I'm so lucky you were in your dressing room and could help." I hoped the question I planned to ask sounded natural. "When I looked around and saw you were right behind me, supporting me, it gave me confidence. Why were you there so early?"

Manny avoided my gaze and looked down at his fingers. "It is somewhat embarrassing to admit." He stopped.

How could it be embarrassing?

After a pause, he continued. "Men are not supposed to have feelings. They are supposed to be brave, drink beer, play pool, and have sex." He lifted his gaze. "But the dance company has been touring a long time. It has been over a month now. I miss my friends, my mother, my cat, my significant other, so many things. I am fortunate. I have my own dressing room. I planned to luxuriate in the silence, escape the need to be social, the need to be 'on.'"

Manny frowned. "But it had not been quiet next door in Felix's dressing room. There were shouts, arguing with another man, thumps."

"Did you recognize the man's voice?"

"Regrettably, no." He looked at me curiously.

"Did you hear any specific words or phrases?"

"Again, no. I just heard raised voices and wished for quiet."

When I asked no further questions, he continued. "There were a few moments of silence. With relief, I had just begun to settle myself for meditation when the shot came. I froze and waited for a few minutes to make sure the danger had passed before I stepped out to investigate the gunshot."

I calculated. I'd been at the stage door when the shot sounded and had stayed hidden until I heard the murderer's footsteps running away and the outside door slam. I didn't come out until I thought it was safe, then crossed the lobby to Felix's hallway and moved cautiously down to his dressing room, arriving just before Manny.

Meanwhile Manny, whose dressing room was next to Felix's, had also waited until he thought the murderer had gone. I certainly understood that. The outside door had slammed behind the murderer and locked automatically. If Manny had been the killer and had stayed inside, only slamming the exit door as a ruse, I would have heard his footsteps running back down the hall. He couldn't be the murderer.

"How did you and Felix get along?"

"I did not have much to do with him. Like many conductors, he cared only about the production. We said 'hello' a few times, but he was not friendly."

"Well, I just wanted to see how you were doing. I know Felix's death has been in my nightmares."

"Mine, too."

Kathleen spoke up. "You acted with wisdom and caution. You didn't see or hear anything that might hint at the identity of the killer?"

"I'm afraid not."

"Well, thank you for helping."

We thanked Manny and left. In the corridor, I said, "I guess you were right. He was no help at all."

"I'm not so sure about that. He heard the fistfight, but he also said there were a few minutes of quiet after the fight and before the shot. That supports Charlie's claim that when he left, Felix was alive."

We walked in the direction of the staircase.

I smiled and used my hip to bump hers. "You're right. Thanks for picking that out, Kathleen. It's a small fact, but an encouraging one."

MY STUDENTS WERE A WELCOME RETURN TO NORMALCY. I gave them my full attention. Megan Green had changed her lesson to Wednesday, and by the time she arrived I felt calm and happy.

Megan seemed distracted as she began the etude I had assigned. Uncharacteristically, she played wrong notes and missed time changes. Finally, I stopped her. "What's wrong, Megan?"

She wiped away a single tear with the back of her hand. "I'm sorry."

I guess I'd asked for this by inviting her to talk to me, but I didn't feel any more competent to handle the situation than last time. I gave her a tissue, patted her back and asked, "Do you want to talk about it?"

"Maybe." She didn't speak, though. She had put the flute in her lap and kept pressing the keys up and down. Finally, more to the flute than to me, she said, "Mom and Dad were shouting at each other all night. I couldn't sleep." She sniffled, then whispered, "Dad called Mom a thief. He says she steals money. How could he think that?" Not waiting for me, she answered her own question and, in a more normal voice said, "He said that he gives her an allowance and she shouldn't need more."

"Your mom has a good job. Why would she need an allowance?"

"I don't know. I guess it's their way of budgeting."

"*Steals* is a strong word. What did your mom say?"

"She didn't say much, just that she wasn't a thief. Then she cried. I wanted her to defend herself, but Dad's pretty scary when he's mad."

Golden had been laying in her place in the corner as the lesson began. Now she rose and lay on Megan's feet.

Doing my best therapist imitation, I asked, "And what do you think of the whole situation?"

Megan, whose eyes had been slowly spilling over, wiped her tears and sniffled, then bent down and patted Golden. After a moment she straightened and said, "I don't know what to think.

I love my dad, but my parents even fought about money after my youngest brother fell off the jungle gym at the playground and broke his arm. Mom had to take the day off to take him to the ER. She had to pay for parking and painkillers, plus the snacks my sister and brother and I got from the hospital vending machine while Mom talked to the doctors . . . I don't know. It seems like Dad should understand. And I don't think she should have to account for every penny, anyway. She's a grown-up. She has a job and makes good money."

I thought Megan was absolutely right.

She continued, "And when he's drinking it's worse."

I led the way to the kitchen and tea, Golden trailing behind. Should I ask more questions, I wondered, or just be there?

Megan decided the matter. She continued, "What he says then doesn't make any sense at all. He accuses Mom of not keeping the house clean enough, and never being on time . . . oh, I don't know what all . . . but he's so mad . . . he's really scary."

"Megan," I asked carefully. "Does he ever . . . hurt you or your brothers and sister?"

She shook her head as she sat down at the kitchen table.

"Well, alcohol usually doesn't bring out the best in people." I filled the tea kettle and put it on to boil. While it heated, I found the Lemon Zinger. "I can see why the whole thing's upsetting and confusing, but I guess they'll have to work it out. The important thing is to realize that it's not your fault, and there's nothing you can do." I listened to my own words and realized how lucky Kathleen and I had been to have sober, loving parents, even though Mom could be a little, or a lot, odd. I felt a quiet glow of gratitude.

Golden put her front paws on the chair between Megan's knees, and nose to nose with her, licked her cheek.

Megan laughed and wiped dog kisses from her face.

I watched, realizing my dog knew skills I hadn't taught her.

Pulling another tissue from the box on the table, I handed it to Megan.

She dried her face and eyes, then rubbed Golden's ears, and put the dog's paws down on the floor. Even though she had calmed down, Megan still seemed troubled. "There must be something I can do."

"The best two things you can do are to stay out of it, and take care of yourself." Self-doubts left behind, I spoke confidently. My ex and I had plenty of fights before we split up. None of them were rational, and none of them included outsiders. But Megan was only fifteen. I'd give her all the concrete help I could. "Do you feel safe at home?"

She didn't hesitate. "Yes. Of course."

"What about your mom? Is she safe, too?"

Silence. Then, "I guess." After another moment of silence she said, "We're all safe."

I wasn't convinced. She didn't seem sure, but I didn't want to lose her trust by pushing too hard. Could someone else do a better job? Ask better questions? "Is there a school counselor you could talk to?" My own school counselor had been straining herself when she made recommendations on classes, but hopefully school counselors were better now.

"No way. I don't want anyone else to know about this. Especially at school."

It looked like I could only give her reassurance and hope and be interested. I was no psychologist. "That's the best advice I can give you, then. Stay out of it and let them work it out. You can talk to me anytime, and I'm willing to support you however I can."

Megan smiled at that. "Thanks, Miz Wilson. That helps."

I glanced at my watch. Time to end the lesson. I suggested that we go back into the studio and play a quick duet before she put away her flute. At least we'd get in a little playing. The music lifted both our spirits, but even so, her farewell smile was small and strained.

THIRTEEN

THURSDAY, 6:00 P.M., DECEMBER 8, 2011

T HE NEXT DAY I TAUGHT UNTIL SIX. KC, of course, was at the restaurant. I wasn't sure what my sister had been doing, so when my last student left, I went in search of her. I found both Kathleen and a Christmas tree in the kitchen. "What . . .?"

"I couldn't stand doing nothing. I know it doesn't help Charlie, but at least it kept me busy. They've set up a tree lot in the parking area of the MegaMart."

"That's fantastic, Kathleen. Let's transfer it to the living room so the students can see it."

We moved it, then found the tree stand and stood it upright.

That left us just enough time to wolf down dinner before we interviewed Jim.

My sister, who'd always watched the *Nutcracker* with Mom, wanted to wait for her to arrive so they could see it together, so she followed in her rental car and would leave after we talked to Jim.

It had been a warm day. The snow had melted, and the drive to the hall relaxed me. Although the junkyards adjoining Fleisher offended the eye and the concrete canyon around the musician's entrance felt cold and sterile, the unseasonably warm night air made for a pleasant walk to the stage door, and I waited outside for Kathleen to park her car.

As we entered backstage, dancers floated by. Dance masters wrangled the young children who played the mice, nudging them toward their dressing room in preparation for applying makeup and donning costumes for the performance.

Jim moved among the dancers, making sure they had everything they needed. He greeted us, then said, "Be right with you, Emily. Shouldn't take long. Don't have much to say."

That discouraged me. He'd already decided he couldn't be of much help. "Thanks for making time, Jim."

He had on his "performance" clothes, a black suit. "Why don't we sit on the steps outside. It's a warm night." In the open air, he parked himself on the stairs, leaned back, then lit his cigar. As a flutist, I can tell you that there's nothing more disgusting to a wind player than secondhand smoke. It could have been worse, though. At least he puffed on a cigar, and not a cigarette. Reluctantly, we sat upwind from the smoke, and I introduced Kathleen.

"Nice to have an excuse to sit and smoke out here, but I really don't see why you want to talk to me."

"We're trying to help Charlie, and we wanted to find out about Felix, what kind of relationships he had around the symphony. We were hoping you could fill us in."

"What do you want to know?"

"It would help if we knew who would have been around when Felix died, before the show. Besides you, who's backstage?"

"We got off to an earlier start than usual the day Felix died. Typically, no one's around that early. Even me. I usually don't come 'til about an hour and a half before we start unless there's set-up to do. The crew is the next to come, usually about an hour and a quarter before the show, after I put out the task schedule." As I took a breath to ask, he continued. "The conductor arrives before anyone in the orchestra. Felix gives—I mean gave—pre-concert talks to the audience about forty-five minutes before the show. He came early enough to dress and review his notes; I'd guess an hour before the curtain." Jim took a draw on his cigar.

He blew the smoke into the air and then continued. "But he warned me the day before he died that he'd have three people to meet with before the dress rehearsal, so he'd be here about two hours early. Charlie'd be coming by himself. The other two would be arriving later, together, and he told me to make sure all three could get in. So that meant I had to come early, too. I let Charlie and Felix in, and then, about half an hour later, all hell broke loose."

"When was that?"

"Just before six."

"Who were the other two he expected?"

"Josh Regan and Mark Thurmond."

They were both violin players. In fact, they were the last stand first violinists Felix had demanded meet with him. The meeting must have been intended to discuss the bowings that upset him during the run-through.

I searched my memory, but I didn't remember seeing any of them. Of course, I'd been in shock mode. In my concern for helping Felix, I hadn't seen much of anything else.

Kathleen asked, "Where were the three of you when Felix was shot?"?"

"What business is it of yours?" Jim looked her up and down.

Kathleen and I exchanged glances.

There must be a different way to find out where he'd been, and what he'd seen. "Did you hear the shot?"

"'Course. You'd've had to be deaf not to."

"Where—"

"Look. I don't have to answer your questions. You're not the police. Is there anything else?"

On the brink of leaving, he leaned forward and straightened his jacket.

I changed the subject, hoping he'd stay. "What interactions did you guys have with Felix?"

"As few as possible."

Short and definite. And angry. "Meaning . . .?"

"Felix was a real bastard. The other guys didn't talk to him at all. If he had a complaint, he talked to me as leader of the stage crew.

The first time I tried to have a conversation he obviously wasn't interested in what I had to say. After that, as long as I assured him we'd get it taken care of, we got along well. I didn't tell him about any glitches or voice any thoughts of my own."

Sounded like Felix had been his usual charming self with Jim. "So, you didn't have much to do with him?"

Jim tsked. "Isn't that what I just said?" He stomped out his cigar.

The air crackled with hostility. I could see we wouldn't get any more information from him. "Well, thanks for talking to us."

"Whatever. You're welcome, I guess." He gave Kathleen one last dirty look, then went into the building.

Kathleen's eyes grew big. "Eeyow! He has a chip on his shoulder, doesn't he? He's hiding something."

"You're right. He just rose to the top of the suspect list for me."

"Me, too." She hugged me "I'd better let you get ready for the show." She left and walked toward her car.

I stood and glanced at my watch.

I didn't want to start warming up this early, so I left the Hall, went for a walk, and reviewed what we had learned from Jim. Clearly, he had the opportunity to kill Felix. Why was he so reluctant to help us? Exactly where was he when the shot was fired? Or did he fire it? We needed to find out if he had the motive and the weapon to kill Felix.

I continued to mull over the possibilities until the performance began. Then, I put my questions to the back of my mind and focused on my playing.

FOURTEEN

FRIDAY, 8:00 A.M., DECEMBER 9, 2011

K ATHLEEN AND I HAD BREAKFAST WITH KC before she left for work.

Our interview with Jim Plank had kept me tossing and turning, so I brought up the subject with Kathleen. "What would you think of having lunch with Ana? That way you could meet her, and we could run the problem of Jim Plank past her. She can work magic with a computer. Hopefully she can get more information."

"Oh, Emily, that's a great idea! Jim's hiding something. And I want to meet Ana. I'm sure Charlie knows what he's doing, but this'll be the perfect excuse to get to know her."

I called and we made arrangements to meet for an early lunch. It would be a hurried affair at a fast-food place near her office.

When we met I introduced Kathleen. "I've heard a lot about you, Ana."

"And I you. It's great to get to meet you. Charlie says you were a wonderful mom."

Kathleen blushed. "He was a delight to raise." They had a short conversation about how wonderful Charlie was—surely his ears were burning—and I could see Kathleen approved of Ana. We ordered and took our food to a table in the corner.

I explained our problem. ". . . so Jim put an end to any discussion of where he was when the shot was fired. You're so good at research, I wondered if you could learn anything more. I'm particularly interested in his motives—whether he might have reason to bitterly resent Felix—and whether he owns a gun."

"I'll do what I can, but I make no promises." Did I fail to mention, in addition to all her other attributes, she's modest?

"Thanks so much."

In a hesitant voice she asked, "I don't mean to worry you, but when I visited, Charlie seemed awfully depressed to me. What do you think?"

Kathleen buried her gaze in her lap, and then answered, "I'm not sure that what we see is accurate because he always tries to be positive. But he seems to be doing pretty well for someone in his situation. He wants it to be over and be free, but that seems natural."

"I guess." She sounded beyond unhappy. "Thanks for finding something I can do to help. Let me know if I can do anything else. I think I'm more anxious than Charlie for all this to be done."

I assured her. "Not to worry. We'll discover the truth. And what you're doing is incredibly helpful."

Kathleen looked up and nodded, squeezing Ana's hand.

She smiled and said, "I'm sorry to rush off, but we have a big project. I'm covering for Charlie as well as doing my own work and . . . well . . . I'd better get back."

We assured her we understood and planned our next moves after she'd gone. I suggested talking to the rest of the stage crew, Ken Sands and Leon Brown.

Since the rest of the crew weren't listed on the orchestra roster and Jim had been too hostile to give us their contact information, I had to get it another way. I pulled out my phone and called the symphony office.

"Monroe Symphony. This is Belinda."

"Hi, Belinda. This is Emily Wilson, the flutist." We'd spoken often. As the intern, Belinda performed "duties as assigned" *ad infinitum.* "I'm painting my house, and I wondered if one of the stagehands would be available to help. I've already spoken to Jim Plank, and he can't do it."

"I can't answer for any individual's availability, but I can take a message and ask Ken and Leon to call you."

"That'd be great."

"Have a nice day, now."

"You too, and thanks again, Belinda." We hung up.

Ken Sands called back almost immediately. I explained that we needed to see him, and he told us to come any time before four.

Glad of Kathleen's company, I asked her, "When do you want to go?"

Eagerly she answered, "How's right away?"

KEN LIVED IN A SMALL, SINGLE-STORY HOUSE, square with faded yellow paint, set in a big lot south of downtown. Winter-bare bushes and a chain link fence surrounded his home. An orange jeep with a rag roof occupied the parking space in front. We opened the gate and walked up a long sidewalk.

I almost rang the doorbell before I noticed a sign which requested that visitors knock. I knocked, and multiple dogs barked.

Ken came to the door in chinos and a blue button-down shirt, open at the neck. Tall, about 35, with shaggy brown hair, he sported a thin goatee. "I didn't realize you'd come so soon."

"We can come back later, if that would be better." I didn't want to antagonize him before we even started.

"No, no. I don't want you to have to come back. I'm just surprised is all."

On entering we were engulfed by large dogs—a black lab, a golden retriever, a brown and black mutt who looked like he had some Rottweiler in him, and a rust-colored dog with curly hair and a square muzzle.

Kathleen raised her arms and her purse and stood on tiptoe while the lab sniffed her crotch.

Ken pulled the dog away and said, "Sorry."

I reached for the golden and scratched it behind the ears, addressing it directly. "What's your name?"

"That's Mo," Ken answered for him.

"Short for Mozart?" I looked up from Mo's ears to Ken and smiled.

He looked confused. "No. Just Mo. The lab is Larry, the poodle mix is Curly, and that's Lucy." He pointed at the black and brown dog.

So, the wrong world of entertainment: these dogs were all comedians.

Ken corralled them and we moved from the entry into a dim room. A dark green sofa embroidered with maroon anchors and a matching easy chair furnished the place. Kathleen and I sat on the sofa. Ken took the chair. The room smelled like, what? Damp wool? Then I noticed a pair of beige socks drying on the radiator.

"Sorry about the bell. Curly goes crazy, beyond just barking, if you ring it."

Larry had approached Kathleen again as soon as she sat down, and she ran her hand along his back.

"I understand." I continued to scratch Mo's ears. "I have a dog, too."

Ken looked interested. "Really? What kind?"

"She's a golden, like Mo, here." That created instant camaraderie, and we traded stories about puppyhood. Mo had been a klutzy goofball, not unlike Golden. We exchanged tips on the best places to take dogs. I could have swapped stories and information with him for a lot longer, but Kathleen, who sat on the edge of the sofa, tapped her wristwatch.

I shifted on the sofa, stopped petting Mo, and got down to business. "I don't want to take up your whole day, Ken. We really came about Felix's death. As you know, Charlie McRae's been arrested. Kathleen," I nodded in her direction, "is Charlie's mother. I'm his aunt, and we really can't see him as a killer. We're hoping you can help us come up with another explanation."

"Wow. Big task. Charlie sure didn't like Felix."

"That's true. But nobody really did."

Ken seemed genuinely puzzled.

"For now, we're just flailing around. The police seem to have accepted that Charlie's guilty. We figure it won't hurt if we ask a few questions. If you'll tell us what you remember, maybe there'll be something we can sink our teeth into."

"I don't see that I can help." Ken stroked Lucy as he spoke. Curly sat beside his chair. Kathleen captured Larry's head and scratched his ears. Mo rested his head on my feet.

"It's okay. Just tell us what you remember about Felix and his relationships, backstage and otherwise. I don't know much about Felix and the way he interacted with the crew. Can you tell me about that?"

"Well, let's see." He hesitated a moment while he absently stroked Lucy's ears, rolling his eyes upward.

The poodle mix moved away from Ken and started to pace.

Ken paused. "Excuse me. I think Curly needs to go out."

He disappeared for a minute, then reentered the room and sat down. "To answer your question, lucky for us, Jim was Felix's contact. He would only deal with the head of the stage crew and then only to give orders. He didn't approach the rest of us lowly hired hands. Or know we were alive."

Jim had been at Fleisher at the right time to kill Felix. I didn't know exactly where, thanks to his attitude. What about his motive? I asked Ken, "Did Jim have problems with Felix?"

"Jim vented in private, alone with us guys. I can tell you for sure that he didn't like Felix but he knew how Felix wanted things done, and knew how to take orders, so they didn't have any blowups. Not since I've been here, anyway."

"What about before then?"

"There are stories." Ken squirmed in his chair.

I pushed. "Who'd you hear them from?"

"The guys. I don't remember who. It's been a long time." He crossed his arms.

I persisted. "But Jim didn't like Felix?"

He tugged at his shirt and shifted in his chair again. "Don't make too much of that. Not many people did."

"Yeah, I know. I don't have to go further than my own feelings to understand."

That loosened his tongue. Lucy had flipped onto her back, and he bent to rub her tummy while he said, "It's bad enough when you're a musician. I've seen it. But when you're manual labor, well . . . Felix didn't even think we were human. Jim blew off steam with us all the time."

"Do you think Jim held a grudge?" I glanced at Kathleen, who gazed intently at Ken.

"Depends on what you mean by 'held a grudge.' Jim sure didn't like Felix, and didn't have any more to do with the man than he could help, but whether Jim was pissed about any particular thing? That I'm not sure of."

"You don't know if his attitude was work-related or something more?"

"Nah. I'm sure Felix being Felix annoyed him. But beyond that? I'm not sure. Like I say, Jim blows off steam with us, but never mentions anything but that day's frustrations."

After a moment's silence, Ken said, "There's something else. Something I just thought of."

I looked at Kathleen, who had picked up her purse in preparation to leaving. "Yes?"

"You said you were interested in Felix's relationships backstage and otherwise?"

"Uh-huh."

"Well, there used to be a guy who worked with us."

"Another stage hand?"

"Yeah. His name was Myles. Myles Lewis."

"I remember him." I gave Kathleen the sisterly "This is important" look. I hadn't brought a note pad because I didn't want to intimidate anyone, but between the two of us we should be able to remember the name.

"Myles had a pretty little wife. She'd come visit him occasionally between shows."

"Why? Isn't that frowned upon?"

Ken didn't answer. "Just a sec. I better let Curly back in. It's cold out there."

While he was gone Kathleen and I exchanged glances, our curiosity—and hopes—aroused.

Ken returned and sat down. Curly lay on his feet. "Sorry. Where was I?"

"The reason Myles's wife visited?"

"Oh, right. Sometimes she brought him meals. Sometimes she brought him things he'd forgotten. Anyway, one time she wore Daisy Dukes. Boy, were they short." Ken smiled at the memory.

"Well, you can be sure Felix took note. Pretty soon they were flirting, and not long after that Myles and his wife divorced."

"Oh, no." Kathleen sounded distressed.

Ken looked her way, then continued. "Myles blamed the divorce on Felix. Said Felix had an affair with his wife. That probably wasn't the whole story—it's never that simple—but Myles quit the crew. Said he couldn't stand to kowtow to Felix another second."

"How long ago did he resign?"

"I'd guess two months ago."

"That's really helpful. I hadn't heard a whisper, even on the grapevine."

"Myles kept it pretty quiet. I hate to throw him under the bus, but you said you were interested in Felix's relationships."

I tend to believe anybody who loves dogs is sensitive, and what Ken said next confirmed that, in my mind. Addressing Kathleen he said, "I'm really sorry you're going through this. It must be hard."

Kathleen looked at him, her eyes filling.

"It is," she whispered. "Thanks for your help."

KATHLEEN WAITED ONLY UNTIL KEN closed his front door before she said, "Well, that was heartening, wasn't it?" She wiped her eyes and, in a confident voice, said, "It's pretty clear that both Jim and Myles hated Felix. They're both really good suspects."

"How do you figure?"

"They both had a motive. "

"Myles has a good motive, I'll admit." I paused for a moment, considering. "But what about method and opportunity? We don't know if Myles even has a gun. And nobody's placed him at Fleisher Hall at the right time. All we have is a new possibility to investigate."

Kathleen just looked at me.

I thought out loud. "But Jim had opportunity. He hung out at Fleisher at Felix's request and refused to tell us what, exactly, he did after he let Charlie in. We don't know for sure if he had motive or a weapon, though."

"According to Ken, Jim had a motive."

I tried to temper Kathleen's enthusiasm. "I heard 'maybe.' Ken didn't know for sure."

Ignoring my comment, Kathleen said, "So, Jim had opportunity and a probable motive. That just leaves method. We have to find out if he had a gun."

I thought Kathleen's enthusiasm was premature. But I hoped Jim or Myles had committed the murder, too. It would be a simple answer, one that wouldn't involve my colleagues or anyone I loved. I couldn't take either man seriously as a suspect, though, unless, or until, real evidence turned up. Ana might be able to come up with more information. I'd call her before tonight's performance.

We got into the car and silently digested the interview with Ken, each in our own way.

Opening the garage, we went through to the kitchen via the connecting door. Kathleen made tea and I set out the cookies I had baked. We sat at the round oak table and nibbled companionably on them while we sipped our tea.

Kathleen asked, "So, what's next, boss?"

"I don't have a student 'til later this afternoon. It's a good opportunity to interview Leon, the other stagehand."

I checked my phone. Leon had left a message which said he was free 'til two-thirty, but he had an appointment later that day. I consulted my watch and called. Leon okayed a visit, as long as I understood that he wouldn't have long.

"Then we're off." Kathleen stood, filled with eagerness.

FIFTEEN

FRIDAY, 1:30 P.M., DECEMBER 9, 2011

L EON LIVED IN A HUGE BROWNSTONE apartment building, the ultimate in luxury in, say, 1910. Now, however, it screamed shabby, with rusty ironwork gates, unshoveled sidewalks, and residents' names taped helter-skelter across mailboxes in various handwritings and at various angles. The building was within walking distance of Fleisher Hall. Leon had told me his two roommates, neither of whom I knew, would be at work during the day. I figured that with three guys splitting the rent, the apartment would be a mess. I rang Leon's place, and he buzzed us up without question.

Inside the halls, the lights were out, and the scent of garlic and curry welcomed us. The elevator wasn't working, so we began the climb to Leon's apartment. A couple on the second floor bellowed a loud and vicious disagreement, and I gladly rounded the staircase and continued up to the third floor.

Leon opened the door wearing a navy-blue turtleneck and beige Dockers. A short man with light brown skin and a tummy that overhung his belt slightly, he said, "I have to leave in forty-five minutes, but I want to be as much help as I can in the meantime."

As we went inside, I introduced Kathleen.

"Charlie's mom. He always speaks so well of you. Says you live in that little town in Indiana with a funny name. How was your trip?"

Kathleen responded politely, but I could feel her impatience, and I hurried to move the conversation forward. "We're shaken by Felix's murder, and by the idea that Charlie could have been the killer."

"Yeah. I wouldn't pick him as a murderer."

Leon made room for us by sweeping some papers from a threadbare purple sofa to the floor. "Sit down, sit down."

We sat. "You sound like you know Charlie pretty well."

"Well as I do anybody. I only got the job a couple months ago."

He must have been Myles' replacement.

"How did you strike up a friendship?"

Leon sat on the floor in front of us. "The percussion section is at the back of the orchestra. That's where the stagehands hang out, in case Felix or somebody else needs something. The percussionists talk to us when they have long rests, which is often. They're nice guys. Not like Felix."

"Do you know who might have hated Felix enough to kill him?"

"Felix wasn't anybody's favorite person. But I don't know who would have wanted to kill him. He was just a jerk. And he got away with it because of his position."

"I know what you mean, but can you explain to Kathleen?"

Leon turned toward Kathleen. "Felix communicated with demands and insults. It had gotten so only Jim talked to him because, as the leader of the stage crew, he had to, not because he wanted to. Felix seemed happy with that arrangement. Ken and I were, too. Jim—not so much."

I asked, "What do you mean by demands and insults?"

"For starters, he never said 'please.' I know that's a small thing, but it would have gone a long way to making things more pleasant for everyone. And he'd say things like, 'You should have known I'd need it,' or 'Is it too much to expect you to anticipate this or that . . .'" He imitated Felix's voice flawlessly.

Leon's complaints described an unpleasant work environment, and I could hear Felix saying those things, but that wasn't a reason to kill.

Kathleen declared, "I know my son wouldn't have murdered Felix. We need to find someone else that could have done it."

Leon paused. "I'm sure you're right. Charlie isn't the murdering type, but I can't think of anyone who had it in for Felix, at least not more than anybody else."

Jim looked more and more interesting to me as a suspect. "You said Jim dealt with Felix for the most part. Did the two of them get along?"

"Jim took Felix's orders without complaint, but sometimes, to me Jim seemed like a volcano about to erupt. Everyday he'd have some new complaint and he'd vent to us about it. He hadn't blown yet, but he was not a happy man."

"Hmmn. Do you know if he had a gun?"

"I think he might have mentioned going to the shooting range once."

"Do you know what kind of gun he had?"

"Not even sure about the comment. Maybe he borrowed a gun? Don't know. It's a fuzzy memory."

I changed the subject. "How about Myles?"

"Myles?"

"We heard he was a stagehand who didn't like Felix very much." I glanced at Kathleen.

"Oh. You must mean the Myles who worked the crew before me. I didn't know him at all, but I've heard stories."

"Stories?"

"Yeah. Just that he really hated Felix and quit because Felix was such a prick."

"The day Felix was murdered when did you get to the Hall?"

"I didn't get there 'til around 6:20. We'd set everything up before we left the night before, at the run-through. We just had to make sure the dancers had all they needed and check the orchestra pit and the sets. But I never got in Fleisher. There was chaos by the stage door—police cars and an ambulance—and yellow police tape was up. A cop said to go home. That there'd be no rehearsal."

"Did you see anyone you knew?"

"Nope. I figured I had a night off and went to play pool at Barney's."

"Well, thanks for talking to us."

"No problem. Hope you find what you're looking for."

He walked with us to the door.

Slowly moving down the three flights of stairs and out into the street, Kathleen and I discussed what we had learned.

Thoughtfully I said, "That's a different slant on Felix and Jim's relationship."

"Different people see things differently."

Thinking about my mental list of suspects I said, "Until we get some confirmation one way or the other, we can't excuse Jim for lack of a motive."

"And he might have a gun."

"Don't forget that he wouldn't tell us where he was during the shooting." I suspected we were on to something. "I'll put Ana to work finding out about the weapon. For now, he's looking pretty good as a suspect."

On the way home both of us were quiet. Thinking in my case. I assumed Kathleen had her own thoughts. I knew she worried about Charlie, and rightfully so. I wanted to reassure her. "We're making good progress. We have some confirmation of Charlie's story and a couple of good possibilities as suspects. We'll get this."

"I know, Emily. Thanks for helping."

BERNIE, THE SECURITY GUARD, GREETED ME for the evening's performance with his usual "Fancy meetin' you here!"

I left my coat in the green room and settled into my chair in the pit, trying to put the day's students and the interviews with Ken and Leon behind me. Cacophony took over as other musicians arrived and everyone warmed up and prepared to play. The familiar routine soothed my nerves and focused my thoughts on the performance. As usual, when showtime came the lights flicked on and off, and the oboe sounded an "A." The orchestra tuned, Doug came out to applause, recited the speech in memory of Felix and gave the downbeat. The performance had begun.

During intermission Ken, the stagehand, busied himself sweeping the "snowflakes" off the stage. The *prima* ballerina joined him and pointed towards the set. He dropped his broom and went backstage with her. When they returned, Jim accompanied them. Ken returned to his sweeping duties, while Jim and the ballerina were deep in discussion, involving frequent pointing to the set and emphatic hand gestures. Wonder what that was about? Unobserved, I watched Jim's movements, trying to picture him as a murderer.

I made the usual rounds of restroom, drinking fountain, and fresh air, listening to gossip from several people about how well Doug was doing and how nice it was to feel the orchestra pulling together with the conductor, instead of against him. The atmosphere seemed different than before, though. I sensed that several people went out of their way to avoid me. It could have been my imagination. Or maybe the heroic glow of helping Felix had faded as word spread that I was Charlie's aunt. Somehow, my home away from home, the symphony, didn't feel safe anymore.

With relief, I finished the second half, packed up my flute, and headed home.

Golden's welcome enfolded me, undiminished in its enthusiasm. KC and Kathleen had both gone to bed, so I reflected on the loyalty of dogs and the fickleness of people.

SIXTEEN

SATURDAY, 9:00 A.M., DECEMBER 10, 2011

KC HAD LEFT EARLY FOR THE RESTAURANT, and Kathleen and I were having breakfast and planning our day.

"According to Jim, those violinists, Josh and Mark, were at the Hall at the time of Felix's murder. My visit with Charlie isn't scheduled 'til this afternoon. Do you think we can talk to them before then?" Kathleen sounded eager to get going.

"The symphony has a matinee today, too, but I think we'll have time to talk to them first. I'll get the orchestra roster."

Mark Thurmond didn't answer my text, but Josh Regan gave the okay to visit, as long as we gave him about half an hour.

Josh lived in a luxury townhouse complex in the suburbs with a pool and a clubhouse. I wondered how he could afford it on a musician's salary. Possibly his wife made big bucks. I didn't know anything about her.

He came to the door in beige dockers and a long-sleeved white knit shirt, looking fresh and scrubbed. "Right this way." He led us across the entry hall into a living room with no clutter; not a single item out of place, or dusty, or conflicting with the color scheme. The room looked like a *Simple Living* set. It had to have been decorated by a professional.

Kathleen and I perched on opposite ends of a leather love seat, while Josh sat across from us on the matching sofa, behind a coffee table.

I scarcely knew Josh, so, hoping for the best, I said, "Everybody has heard by now that Charlie McRae has been arrested for Felix's murder. Kathleen is his mother, and I'm his aunt. We're trying to help him."

"So that's why you wanted to see me. I wondered. How does that involve me?"

"We're trying to figure out exactly what happened the day of Felix's death." Kathleen and I exchanged glances.

"So?"

"We know you and Mark had been ordered to meet with Felix. How did it go?"

"Like everything else about that situation."

That meant nothing to me. "You'll need to explain."

Josh tsked. "Mark drove me crazy." Josh sounded well and truly annoyed. "He insisted on changing the concertmaster's bowings. I kept telling him that the concertmaster is the section leader and we need to follow her, right or wrong. But Mark claimed the concertmaster's bowings weren't as good as the ones he, Mark, came up with. He'd edit the bowings at home, then bring the changed part and demand we use it. When I followed Mark's part, my bow went every which way, totally unsynchronized with the rest of the section. The phrasings sounded different, too. When I'd talked to the concertmaster before, she didn't feel like she could take sides in a 'squabble' between members of her section. Then Felix stepped in and yelled at both of us during the run-through. It was humiliating."

"You were counting on Felix to help?"

"Nah. Felix just wanted to embarrass us some more, but what could I do? He demanded that we come see him. I had to go."

"I see."

Josh paused and looked at me, but when I didn't question him, he continued. "I got there about ten minutes early. You know—I mean knew—Felix. Being alone with him would have been a special kind of hell. So, I stayed outside, figuring Mark would show soon.

"I waited across the street kitty corner from the stage entrance and paced. It seemed like forever 'til I saw you arrive and heard the shot. I sure didn't want to hang around, so I scrammed."

Excited, I asked, "Did you see anyone leave the building?"

"Sorry. I wanted to get out of there as fast as I could. I didn't stay to watch."

"Did Mark ever show up?"

"I don't know. I just bolted. I didn't want to get involved in whatever went on in there."

Kathleen cleared her throat. "You weren't curious?"

Josh snorted. "No ma'am. Curiosity killed the cat. Anybody would have reacted the same way."

"A good decision under the circumstances." Kathleen soothed any hackles she might have raised.

Josh nodded.

"Well, thanks for talking to us, Josh. I appreciate you taking the time."

"No problem."

AS WE WALKED TO THE CAR Kathleen said, "If he'd stayed to watch even for just a few minutes, he would have seen the murderer." She sounded disappointed.

"Well, he didn't. And it's possible he's alive because of it."

My sister sighed. "I suppose. But you should have pushed him a little. He might be lying. Maybe he's the killer."

"In that case we'll find it out some other way." But, I reflected, what we *had* found out was tantalizing. He'd been on the scene. He'd heard the shot. He *said* it was fired by someone else. But could I believe that? We needed to find corroboration.

SEVENTEEN

SATURDAY, 3:00, DECEMBER 10, 2011

I ASKED MARK AT INTERMISSION if he'd like to go to dinner at the Bangkok after the show. Average height and fiftyish, he had thick glasses, wore suspenders, and had never moved out of his boyhood home. He responded with an enthusiastic "yes", maybe thinking I wanted to flirt. Whether I'd get more or less information out of him that way I didn't know, but I figured I could handle one dinner, and I needed to know where he'd been and what he'd done the evening of Felix's death.

The Bangkok, a small Thai fusion restaurant, was on my way home. Mark and I took separate cars and met outside. He tried to put his hand on my back on the way in, but I hurried ahead. Doubtless due to an erroneous assumption by the hostess, we were seated at a small table in a dark corner in the mostly empty restaurant. I'd eaten here before, but Mark took his time studying the menu. When he'd finally made up his mind, we ordered from a small man with a thick Thai accent.

When the waiter left, I said, "You're probably wondering why I asked you here tonight." I'd decided to use a business-like approach.

"I assumed you're as hungry as I am, and that you wanted a pleasant dinner companion." He gave me a suggestive smile.

Eew. "Well, that's true enough." I scooched further away from him. "I'm also Charlie McRae's aunt, and I'm trying to help him. I thought you might have some information I could use."

"Oh." He sat up straighter and wiped the silly smile off his face.

We were interrupted by the waiter, who brought egg rolls, sweet and sour sauce, and hot mustard.

I took an egg roll, and put it on my plate. While I helped myself to hot mustard sauce, I continued. "The whole orchestra heard Felix command you to meet with him the day of his death."

"Unfortunately."

"Can you tell me more about it?"

"Do you know Josh Regan?"

"A little."

"Well, he's a prig. Totally attached to doing things by the book. I've been with this symphony for twenty-five years, and I know how music, especially the *Nutcracker*, should be played. When I changed some of the bowings, he complained to the concertmaster, even though the bowings I marked were infinitely superior to the ones she chose. Then, as you heard, Felix got involved. He embarrassed us. In front of the entire ballet and orchestra he ordered us to meet with him in his dressing room before dress rehearsal. And on top of that, he didn't even know our names. I've played with this orchestra for twenty-five years, and he didn't know my name!" Mark's voice rose, and his face flushed.

"How did the meeting go?"

"It never happened. I'd run overtime with a student, and I didn't get to Fleisher Hall until well after six. By that time there were police and an ambulance and all kinds of activity. Yellow police tape blocked the stage door and the cops said there wouldn't be a rehearsal. I left. I thought if Felix was pissed, I'd explain and hope he understood, not that he ever understood anything. As it turned out, I didn't have to worry."

The waiter brought our dinners then, Pad Thai for Mark and

Panang for me. He asked for chopsticks, and the conversation didn't continue until after the waiter had brought the utensils.

"So you never even went inside the building?"

"Nope."

"How did you get on with Felix?"

He chuckled. "He was a bastard, but what conductor isn't? Like I said, I've played with this symphony for twenty-five years. I've seen conductors come and go, and I know I can outlast them. The next bastard is waiting in the wings, and I'll outlast him, too."

Cheery outlook. Wonder if he ever enjoys playing?

We made small talk then, about the symphony, the *Nutcracker*, possibilities for a new conductor, and the union. I had nearly run out of conversation when we finally finished the meal.

ONLY GOLDEN ACCEPTED MY RETURN HOME with undiluted joy.

"Where were you?" Kathleen had been worried.

KC knew better, but she said, "I figured you must be having dinner somewhere else."

"Yeah. Sorry. I should have called."

I explained to them where I'd been and what I'd discovered. "So," I summed up, "both Josh and Mark claim they never entered the building, one because he arrived early, the other because he arrived late. Mark didn't like either Felix or Josh, but would he murder over bowings? He *is* a little nuts, but that nutty? It's hard to believe. They both claim they didn't see anything. And either one could be lying. Jim might be a better lead, but we can't dismiss Josh and Mark. I wonder how we can find out more."

To me, it sounded like a job for Ana. I called and asked her to add Josh Regan and Mark Thurmond to her list of computer investigations. "I'm particularly curious about Josh Regan. He spends money like he has a printing press at home, but he's on a musician's salary, just like I am. And it's only his word he didn't fire the shot that killed Felix."

"Okay. I'll check into it." She paused, as if writing it down. "While you're on the phone—I've been researching Jim Plank. So far all I've found are a couple of overdue parking tickets. I'll keep looking, though."

"Thanks, Ana. You're the best!"

I'd done all I knew how to do, so I set about cheering us all up. The Christmas tree Kathleen had bought sat in the living room, unadorned. I retrieved ornaments from the storage closet and brought them into the living room. "We can't let our tree go undecorated."

KC clapped her hands like a child. "A real Christmas! With a real tree!"

I wondered why she was so excited.

Kathleen said nothing, but she smiled and helped KC get the lights working, twinkling in the best places.

Soon all three of us were smiling as we placed the ornaments. Kathleen and I boosted KC, the smallest among us, to place the star atop the tree. Golden barked, and we all laughed.

We needed the Christmas cheer, but whirling thoughts returned as I readied myself for bed, and kept me from sleep for a long time.

EIGHTEEN

SUNDAY, 10:30 A.M., DECEMBER 11, 2011

I T HAD BEEN A LAZY MORNING. Golden quietly slumbered along
with me until 9:00, when I woke slowly. KC would be at the restaurant helping with Sunday brunch, but where was Kathleen?
Not too worried about it—maybe she'd taken a walk or gone to
church—I fed Golden, fixed myself a boiled egg and spent a couple
hours practicing with no specific goal, other than to enjoy myself.
I had just put my flute away when the phone rang.

"Hello?"

Momentary silence. "Emily, I . . . that is . . ."

"Kathleen?"

"It's embarrassing." She paused again. "I'm at the police station."

"Why? What happened?"

She sounded uncomfortable. "I followed Myles Lewis. You
know, the ex-stagehand? I looked him up on the internet. My GPS
got me to his place and I waited 'til he came out, then tailed him. I
don't know . . . he headed for a patrol station. I waited in the parking lot, but the police came out and made me come inside the station and wait while Myles left . . ."

"I'll call Barry and be right there."

I filled in the blanks for myself. Once Ken had told us about Myles Lewis, Kathleen figured he had an excellent motive to commit the murder. To her, following him had seemed the best approach to finding more facts.

Barry didn't hesitate. "Let's meet at the police station."

I am all too familiar with the station where Kathleen waited. It held mixed emotions for me, because I had been questioned by Lt. Gordon there, some of my worst memories, but I had also made KC's acquaintance. She had added life to my quiet existence.

Barry waited in front of the building, and together we climbed the steps to a marble columned façade.

He opened the door for me. "Let me handle this, Em."

No problem there. "She's all yours, Barry."

I stood inside the door while Barry had a short conversation with the policeman at the main desk.

He returned to report. "It's okay. She's free to go. Apparently when Myles noticed her following him, he came straight here, went inside, and told the cops. Kathleen waited in her car in the parking lot. That didn't seem like very threatening behavior, either to the cops or Myles, but they held Kathleen while he left, just in case. She's not even in a jail cell. The cops didn't want the paperwork. She doesn't need a lawyer and you can take her home. It wasn't really necessary for her to call you, but I guess she couldn't remember the way to your house. When she tried to put your address into her phone's GPS, she dropped the phone in the toilet." He shrugged. "Your sister is kind of unpredictable, isn't she?"

I rolled my eyes. "I'm sorry to call you out here for no rea-son. And on a Sunday." But at least my sister hadn't been arrested. "Thanks for being here for Kathleen—for us—on short notice, Barry. I'm sorry."

"Oh, it's more than fine. I'll put it on Charlie's bill." He grinned at me. "Besides, I got to see you."

My stomach flipped.

"But seriously, you need to warn her. If she follows Myles again, she's opening herself to stalking charges. It only takes twice to make a case. That could get messy." He held my gaze. "Remind her as often as necessary. This is serious. Let me and Lieutenant Gordon handle things." He paused. "I know she's worried about Charlie, but do your best to restrain her."

"Okay. I'll try. And really. Thanks." I appreciated Barry's good-natured help.

"One more thing." He hesitated. "I have some bad news."

Just what I needed.

"I talked to my friend Tom, at the PD, last night. The cops still haven't found the gun that killed Felix, but when they retrieved the bullet, they learned it was from a nine-millimeter Glock 27. "

"That should let Charlie off the hook, right? How can that be bad news? He doesn't have a gun, let alone a Glock."

"He *says* he doesn't have a gun. The cops think he must have, and with all the other incriminating evidence against him, they're convinced they have probable cause to continue to hold him."

Great. "Well, thanks for telling me."

"No problem. I'm sorry to rush off, but I'm having lunch with my brother and his wife."

"Okay, Barry. Thanks again."

"I'll be free after that, though. Are you grateful enough to have dinner with me?"

"Sorry. I have a performance this afternoon, and with all the excitement I'll be lucky to get there in time. After that, I'd better make sure Kathleen's okay."

Barry sighed. "Figures. Our schedules don't match, do they?"

With real regret I agreed.

"Well, good luck." He gave me a quick hug, then disappeared out the front door.

I started down the hall to the room where I'd been told Kathleen waited, but heard her laughing. I followed the sound, turned a corner, and entered the cafeteria.

Kathleen and Lieutenant Gordon were kneeling close together, a napkin between them. When they saw me, they both rose quickly.

Strange to see these two together. "What's going on?"

Kathleen giggled and glanced at the lieutenant, who smiled back at her. She lowered her chin, then raised her eyes in a big-eyed, seductive gaze. The sparks between them could have lit the building afire.

"We're just cleaning up." Kathleen looked into the lieutenant's eyes.

Turning toward her I said, "Kathleen, we'd better go."

"You two know each other?" Lt. Gordon sounded interested.

"You haven't met?" Could things get any stranger?

He shook his head.

"Kathleen, this is Lieutenant Gordon, *the arresting officer* in Charlie's case." I paused. "Lieutenant Gordon, this is my sister, Kathleen McRae. *Charlie's mom.*"

They shook hands, both with dawning dismay written on their faces.

Meanwhile, a uniformed officer entered the lounge. "Hi, Paul." He glanced around quickly, felt the chemistry between my sister and Lt. Gordon, noticed the awkward silence, and said, "I need to, uh, get something. If you'll excuse me." He used the vending machine and left without another word.

Lt. Gordon recovered first. "Nice to meet you, Miz McRae. I'm sorry we're not meeting under happier circumstances."

Emphatically, Kathleen removed her hand from his and said, "Charlie is *not* a murderer. I trust you to find the truth."

"Finding the truth is my job, so I hope you're right."

Kathleen looked up into his eyes. "When you find Charlie is innocent maybe I can spill hot coffee on you again."

"Good idea. I'll wear a helmet next time."

I interrupted, and urged again, "We'd better go, Kathleen."

Looking my way, she said, "Okay, okay." Turning back toward Lt. Gordon she smiled, and said with conviction, "'til we meet again."

As we left the cafeteria and walked down the hall Kathleen said, *sotto voce,* "I'm shocked that man is the officer in charge of Charlie's case."

I nodded.

Her look met my eyes. "You described him as humorless and a bit slow."

"He is, as far as I know."

"I didn't expect him to be so handsome and charming."

I looked at her sideways.

Kathleen continued. "It's just . . . I wasn't looking where I was going. I ran into him and his coffee spilled. I bent to help him mop it up. We bumped heads and . . . I didn't know . . . Did you see the way he looked at me?" She smiled as she remembered.

"Yeah. The heat nearly burned me. Now let's just get home, huh?"

"I don't know the way to your house. That's why I called. Without my phone and its GPS, you'll have to lead me or give me directions."

We walked silently for a few moments.

"I guess I'm a horrible mother, huh?" Kathleen's voice sounded soft and squelched.

"You just responded to a handsome man."

"When you said he was in charge of Charlie's case I nearly died. If I'd known . . ."

I didn't say anything.

Kathleen continued. "But he'll find the truth. I know he will. Then maybe we can start fresh."

As we reached the exit I asked, "Why were you following Myles Lewis, anyway?"

She stopped and her eyes widened. "Don't be stupid, Emily! He hated Felix. He had a motive. A strong motive. You were asleep. I didn't have anything to do . . ."

I thought of Mom's saying. *The devil finds tasks for idle hands.*

". . . So I got his address. The GPS gave me directions and I waited 'til he left and then followed him. I thought he would lead me to information. I'm not sure what. Maybe a gun shop or a shooting range. I took a gamble. Charlie's been in jail too long and I wanted to do something."

Exasperated, I held my breath, then let it out in a noisy gust. "Kathleen, I know you're worried about Charlie, but there are some things you can't do. You and I are helping as much as we can. So are Barry and KC and Ana. But there are limits. The police need to handle the rest."

Kathleen bristled and started walking again. "Well, the police haven't done such a good job so far. I suppose they're trying, but they need help."

I couldn't have been more annoyed, not least of all because I couldn't argue the point. I changed the subject by sounding Barry's warning, repeated to groans from Kathleen. "Think orange, Kathleen. You won't be any help at all to Charlie if you're wearing orange, jailed for hounding the suspects."

"I know. But I want to help so badly." She rubbed her forehead and said, "I'll follow you." After a slight pause she added, "But first we need to get me a new cell phone."

KATHLEEN AND I DIDN'T TALK AGAIN 'til she served lunch—stir-fried veggies in some kind of sauce, over leftover tofu and brown rice—a good meal under the circumstances.

"Are you mad at me?" Kathleen pushed the food around on her plate.

"Not mad. I know you're trying to help Charlie. I know he's your son, but he's my nephew. I want to help him, too, but I don't think shadowing the suspects is the way to go about it. It won't help Charlie."

I churned. This degree of turbulence in my life wasn't usual. Besides Kathleen's near arrest and her flirting with Lt. Gordon, I'd been turning Megan's situation over in my mind. How could I best help? "I don't have time to talk." I ate as fast as I could. "I have a show."

Speeding, I screeched up to the hall in record time.

Fortunately, Bernie's "Fancy meeting you here," greeted me. I realized I needed to calm down and turn my thoughts to the *Nutcracker*, so I compartmentalized, shoved the day's events to the back of my mind, and left my coat in the green room.

In the orchestra pit I focused on my flute playing. Because I'd gotten here in such a hurry, I had time for a warm-up, though not as much as I'd like. With every long tone I concentrated on the sound and the speed of vibrato, and slowly Kathleen's rashness and Megan's distress were replaced by peace.

I felt much calmer when KC leaned over the rail separating the audience from the orchestra pit below, and said, "Hey, Em! I wanted you to meet Steve."

Her new boyfriend.

"We're here for our annual *Nutcracker* fix. I had to give the restaurant a week's notice to get the day off, so I'm thankful the performances weren't cancelled."

The tall, dark-haired man beside her lifted his hand in greeting, and said, "Glad to meet you. I've heard a lot about you." KC leaned against him.

"Oh, no! Did she tell you what a bad cook I am?"

Steve chuckled. "Just that you were there when she needed someone. Are you a bad cook?"

I laughed. "The kitchen police are watchful whenever I boil water." Apparently KC had been honest with Steve, and he didn't hold her past against her. So far, so good. Maybe things *would* work out between them.

At that moment the lights began flashing, warning that the show would begin soon. KC smiled up at Steve and said, "Later, Em," then winked at me.

Her happiness cheered me and I was glad to be playing a concert. It allowed me to get my mind on ordinary things. It would all be okay.

NINETEEN

MONDAY IS THE SYMPHONY'S DAY OFF, and I planned a busy day. Felix's funeral, visiting Charlie, and KC's lesson were all on my calendar. Kathleen, who had cooked breakfast, would keep me company at the funeral, we would see Charlie together, and she would keep herself busy during KC's lesson.

Felix's funeral was his final performance. I couldn't believe it had been only eleven days since he died. It felt like another lifetime. I attended to see if I could get any ideas that would help Charlie. Kathleen accompanied me for the same reason, quiet and discreet.

Sunshine filled the crowded chapel. Who were all the mourners? The cluster seated in front near Felix's wife, Lorna, seemed to be family. Scores of orchestra members attended, along with the stagehands. I saw Manny and the *prima* ballerina, Lily Hawthorne, talking with several people who must have been dancers too, judging by their slender bodies and pronounced toe outs. I identified city royalty from past newspaper pictures: the police chief in full dress uniform, most of city council and the mayor, and of course Lt. Gordon, who watched Kathleen with interest when she wasn't looking. There were also a lot of strangers. The public respectfully honoring Felix's position in the community, I guess. After all, he'd given them joy through music over many years.

As the service began, Felix's wife, Lorna, sat in the front row. On her right sat her three young children. On her left sat her best friend, Celee O'Connor. Lorna and Celee were both of a type: perfectly groomed and wearing expensive jewelry. Though Lorna was blonde and Celee copper-headed, neither of them had a hair out of place. Lorna seemed numb, staring straight ahead and occasionally crying or speaking softly to the kids. Celee murmured to both Lorna and the boys.

A string quartet made up of symphony members played Barber's *Adagio for Strings* as people came in. I kept watching Lorna. What a blow for her. One minute she had been a rich, adored wife and mother of three, an hour later a widow and a single mom. If it were me, I would be devastated by the shock of my husband's death, the manner of it, and the new responsibility of raising my children alone. For Lorna's sake, I hoped Felix had organized his affairs well.

Someone had carefully thought out the service, with the string quartet providing musical interludes throughout, and several people giving witty and moving tributes to Felix detailing his kindness, his playfulness, his generosity, and his devotion to music. None of the speakers, I might note, were orchestra members. The Felix we knew blamed his mistakes on the musicians, picked on specific players, including Charlie, and barked orders with no patience or tact. But I guess death is good for the character, and bad for people's memories.

Throughout the service I continued to watch Lorna and Celee. The way they fussed over the children pulled at my heart strings. The two older kids looked a little dazed and sat silently, but I don't think Tom, the youngest at age six, understood the occasion or what it meant. He busied himself playing with a toy robot man and, loudly enough for me and everyone else in the chapel to hear, poignantly asked his mother why she cried.

Kathleen and I attended the reception afterward in Fellowship Hall. Diane Gelbart, president of Friends of the Symphony, acted as hostess, and supervised the volunteers. We had become good buddies when I played flute at a fundraising luncheon Friends held last year. A grandmotherly sort, round and soft, and a hugger, she enfolded me. "Emily! So glad to see you. I wish the circumstances were different."

"Hi, Diane." I stepped back to allow Kathleen room in our circle. "This is my sister, Kathleen." Diane didn't need to know about Kathleen's relationship to Charlie. It wasn't important, and it might stop her from talking to us. Or she might already know. "The reception is lovely, going so smoothly. Thank you for helping Lorna out with it."

"I couldn't do less. I was with Lorna when Felix was shot, you know."

"Were you?" I glanced at Kathleen.

"Friends of the Symphony had scheduled a meeting before the dress rehearsal to go backstage and meet the dancers. It's one of the reasons people join the group. Lorna and Celee and I—we're the Membership Committee—we figured it would be a good time to meet and clean up a couple things, so we got together even earlier, in one of the conference rooms."

Fleisher Hall was an immense facility, a block square. The conference rooms were upstairs on the northwest side of the building, upstairs from Felix's dressing room and the stage door downstairs, on the southwest.

"We had just wrapped up the meeting and agreed to a quick meal at Sandwich Smorgasbord before the Friends meeting. Celee had to go the rest room and Lorna and I talked a bit longer. But we needed to hurry, so I said I'd go ahead and find us a table. I had just gotten to the front doors when I heard the shot. I should have run back and made sure Lorna and Celee were okay, but I was afraid. My family and friends are important to me, and I want to meet my new grandbaby later this month. So instead of running back to Celee and Lorna, I ran to the car and took off. I've been feeling guilty ever since."

I said, "There's no reason to beat yourself up, Diane. There was nothing any of us could do for Felix, or for Lorna, either."

"I guess that's true. But still . . ." She was silent a moment. "I hear you comforted Felix in his last moments."

"I was there, but I couldn't do much."

"At least he didn't die alone. That's something." Diane patted my arm.

"I guess." I shifted uncomfortably.

"Diane! We're running out of cookies." A white-haired volunteer sounded harassed and in a hurry.

"There's lots more in the kitchen. I'll get them." Diane turned to us. "Gotta run." She hugged me, then turned to Kathleen. "Nice meeting you." She left before my sister could reply.

Kathleen's reaction was immediate. "So, Celee and Lorna were both at Fleisher early. They had split from Diane and each other, so any one of the three could have committed the murder."

"Diane? Celee? Lorna?" The idea seemed so outrageous to me that I didn't even consider it.

"We can add them to our list of people who were at Fleisher. They would have had opportunity."

"True." I couldn't argue. Looking around, I noticed many of the orchestra members had stayed for the reception, including Alice Smithson, my connection to the grapevine. Josh Regan and Mark Thurmond stood on opposite sides of the reception room, Mark alone. Josh held the elbow of a woman who must have been his wife. Beautifully turned out in a knee-length wrapped black dress, she looked as if she might have been wearing a designer creation, though I would be the last person to act as a fashion expert. I wondered again what she did for a living, because orchestra members like her husband couldn't afford designer dresses. Had Felix threatened to fire Josh over the bowing issue? If he had, he might have endangered Josh's lifestyle. Josh admitted he had arrived early at Fleisher Hall the evening of Felix's death. His finances could be a motive and his early arrival an opportunity for the murder. *Food for thought.*

I saw Lorna across the room, and Kathleen and I wove our way through the crowd to join the line waiting to speak to her.

Kathleen hung back until I introduced her as my sister, keeping her relationship to Charlie hush-hush. She expressed her sympathies and moved on, leaving me to convey my condolences.

What can you say on these occasions? "I'm so very sorry about Felix's death."

Lorna's floral perfume overpowered me, and her pupils were enormous. Was she medicated? It was a reasonable guess. I might need medication to get through the shock of my husband's death and the stress of the funeral, too.

"Thank you, Emily."

The line of mourners wound out the door, and I had nothing to say once I had expressed my sorrow and regret and given her a hug, so I moved on quickly.

The prevailing mood seemed to be "What-a-great-guy. Sorry-he's-gone." An act for the grieving widow I presumed, or a tribute to sides of Felix's character that orchestra members didn't see. I'm sure no one celebrated his murder, but I had to doubt the sincerity of people who called him a great guy.

I noticed several odd looks directed at me. The orchestra grapevine voraciously devoured any tidbit of gossip, and my efforts to save Felix the evening of the shooting wouldn't have occupied it for long. Did it already know that I was Charlie's aunt? What type of tale could be made from that? Something shocking, I'm sure. The stories people make up! Alice would notice my presence at the funeral and make the most of it. Suddenly I felt out of place and awkward, in hostile territory. I wanted to go home to Golden and her unconditional acceptance.

I have to say that the orchestra's spin-doctor had done a great job with the funeral. A flawless performance. Like all performances, though, everything was not as it seemed.

AFTER WE LEFT THE RECEPTION, I figured I just had time to stop at the bank before our visit with Charlie. My students' lesson fees for the month needed to be deposited. Many were checks, a few were cash. The deposit was too cumbersome to make in the drive-through or by smart phone. I preferred to go to one of the teller's windows in the lobby. Kathleen waited in the car.

I entered the bank at almost the same time as the woman who had been with Josh Regan. The senior employees had offices with glass walls and their name and position stenciled on the door. The woman in the black designer dress opened the one marked "Margo Regan, Branch Manager."

So. She *was* Josh's wife, or sister. I remembered their affectionate intimacy. I'd say wife. And her dress was way more expensive than even a bank branch manager could afford. True, she must have made more than a teller, but . . . a designer dress?

As I made my deposit I considered. I remembered the Regans' perfectly decorated townhouse and wondered if they were in debt. If they weren't, surely they had some other source of income or were barely scraping by. I speculated again. If Felix had threatened to fire Josh, it would be a blow to the family budget. He might have committed the murder to save his job. But I shouldn't jump to conclusions. Possibly the dress was a one-time splurge and Margo had a flair for decorating, or the family lived off inherited money. Maybe. But Josh had just moved up my mental suspect list.

TWENTY

MONDAY, 2:00 P.M., DECEMBER 12, 2011

AFTER DRIVE-THROUGH BURGERS AT DONNELLY'S, Kathleen and I visited Charlie. We went through the jail check-in procedures, rode the elevator to the fourth floor, signed in again, and waited for him.

"I don't think I'm ever going to get used to seeing Charlie this way." Kathleen dabbed at her eyes with a tissue she took from her skirt pocket. "It must be so hard on him."

I felt awkward about being included in the visit. Even though Kathleen's angst tore at my heart, and I loved Charlie, I couldn't match the depths of my sister's sorrow.

At that moment the iron door clanged, admitting Charlie and the guard.

Kathleen jumped up, ran to the Plexiglas, and gave Charlie a tender handprint. "Sweetie!"

"Mom!" Charlie returned Kathleen's greeting, matching his handprint against hers, then sank into a chair. His eyes were red and outlined by dark circles, giving him a haunted look, and his smile seemed stiff and mechanical.

He lifted the phone on his side of the glass to his ear, while

Kathleen and I raised the handsets on our side.

"How are you holding up?" How like Charlie! Concerned for his mom.

Kathleen sniffled into her tissue. "As well as can be expected, I guess."

Charlie turned to me. "And you, Auntie Em?"

I answered, "Missing you."

Kathleen continued. "We're trying to help, looking for someone with a motive. We're working on it." She paused, then explained further. "We went to Felix's funeral earlier today. We found three more people who were at Fleisher during the murder."

"Really? Who?" Charlie sat up straighter and focused on his mom.

"Celee, Lorna, and Diane."

Charlie slumped again. "Not very likely killers."

"Anybody's a possibility," Kathleen said.

Charlie wanted more details about the funeral. "Who showed?"

I took over. "The people you'd expect. Family, audience members, dancers, city VIPs, and the police."

"Any orchestra members there?"

I nodded. "Oh, sure. We couldn't ignore a death in the 'family.' And the musician's union sent a representative, too."

Charlie glanced down in silence a moment. "How are Lorna and Felix's kids doing?"

"It's hard to tell. I don't think Tom, the youngest, understood what was happening. The other two kids seemed quiet, and Lorna cried off and on."

As I talked, Kathleen sank back in her chair, glum and distant.

Charlie could be counted on to clown when his mother seemed sad, but even he apparently couldn't think of anything to laugh at.

After a lengthy silence, I changed the subject, addressing Charlie. "Is there anything we can bring you? Soap? Shampoo?"

"Crossword puzzles and Sudoku would be nice."

"Consider it done." Relieved he asked for something simple, I made a mental note.

"There's not a whole lot to do here." Charlie looked down at his hands, then into Kathleen's eyes. "It's kind of lonely, too, and hard to sleep. There's no quiet, and no privacy."

I remembered the lengths I'd gone to avoiding jail when Lt. Gordon falsely accused me, and I grieved for Charlie and his plight.

"Oh, sweetheart!" Kathleen's eyes filled again.

"The police don't seem like they're working very hard to find another suspect. Isn't there something you can do?"

"Like your mom said, we're looking into it. We're doing everything we can."

I must have sounded defensive because Charlie said, "I wasn't criticizing. I know you're trying hard to find the truth. But I thought if you could hurry . . . hire someone . . .?"

He sounded afraid and desperate. It broke my heart.

Kathleen responded. "I wouldn't mind spending the money, even if I had to borrow, but I don't know anyone, and besides, no one I could hire would care. It has to be someone who knows you, and knows you couldn't kill anyone. That's what will make the difference."

"I guess." Charlie collapsed against his seatback.

The rest of the visit Charlie and Kathleen made small talk, mostly about people I didn't know. I guess it connected them.

I let my mind wander.

Charlie's life and freedom could be in real danger. I knew, without doubt, that he wasn't a killer. Just a human being who'd lost his temper at the wrong time. But believing in his innocence and proving it were two different things. Kathleen and I needed to get busy, before Charlie's bad luck got him life in prison—or worse.

TWENTY-ONE

MONDAY, 5:30 P.M., DECEMBER 12, 2011

Because of the busy day I'd scheduled, KC was the only student I taught. When I met her a year and a half ago, she had let her flute playing slide. Then she became my housemate and started lessons again, and we brushed the rust off her playing. After she got her new job, she kept taking lessons for fun and relaxation. We had sessions on her day off. KC loved the instrument. I think flute playing may have been her only pleasure besides cooking and reading cooking magazines and romances. Her keen mind and sense of humor made her one of my favorite students. But she's also a close friend, and sometimes lessons become gab fests—like today.

As she took her flute out of the case and assembled it, KC asked, "How's it looking for Charlie?"

My flute in my lap, I answered. "Not good." I paused to organize my thoughts. "I've started interviews, but so far no serious suspects." I took a breath.

"I've gotten some good information. Josh Regan and Mark Thurmond were set to meet with Felix at the time he died, and Jim Plank planned on opening the door for them, though he says he didn't see either of them. So all three were at Fleisher at the time of the murder. Both Josh and Mark claim they didn't see Felix, but admit to being at the Hall at the right time. Josh might have a financial motive for the murder. That'll take more investigation to determine. And Mark seems to have been hostile to Felix, but no more so than a lot of people. Jim was confrontational and evasive when I asked him to be specific about his whereabouts during the shooting. That's suggestive. And he had an opportunity to be in Felix's dressing room and possibly had a gun, so I'm interested in him. Diane Gelbart, Lorna, and Celee were at the Hall, too. Until I do more research I'm treading carefully. No one seems to have liked Felix, so either everybody has a motive or nobody has a motive, depending on how you look at it. Having said that, there's a former stagehand, Myles Lewis, who had a grudge against Felix. Apparently, Felix seduced his wife. Myles blames Felix for his ensuing divorce."

"It does sound like Myles has a good motive. How does Kathleen feel about it?"

"Beyond optimistic. But she hasn't considered means or opportunity. Certainly, I can't think of Myles as a likely possibility 'til we find out more."

KC understood. "How can I help?"

I lowered my head and pressed my fingers to my temples. "If you could listen, and give me your ideas. It might help me think it all out."

"Sure. Tell me."

"Even though it's your lesson time?"

She laughed. "I'll just leave your bathroom dirty next time." We traded lessons for housecleaning.

I chuckled. "Fair enough." I gathered my thoughts. "It's maddening not to know whether people are telling the truth. Any of them could be lying. Only Myles seems to have a compelling motive, but I have a lot more investigating to do there to find means and opportunity. No one liked Felix. He was rude, impatient, and insulting to everybody. If that's a motive, I'm as likely a suspect as Charlie or anyone else."

KC waited silently for me to continue.

"And I guess I'm afraid because I love Kathleen and Charlie and want to help them, but I'm not sure we can prove what she and I both believe—that Charlie didn't kill Felix. She loves him, so she's convinced he didn't do it. As for me, I love him, too. He's always been an endearing clown. Period. I can't see him committing cold-blooded murder."

KC frowned.

In the silence that followed, I picked up my flute, then put it down again and continued, "What's more, I'm no detective, but the police, who are supposed to be the professionals, aren't looking at any other suspects. They think they've solved the case, and that Charlie killed Felix. They're trying to pin down details so they can get a conviction, but not seriously considering anyone else."

This time KC's silence lasted long enough that I began to be embarrassed by my outburst. But eventually she said, slowly, "As far as motivation, sex is usually pretty important."

"You mean if Felix had sex with Myles's wife?"

"Yeah . . . and there might have been others. Guys in the public eye . . ."

"The grapevine describes in magnificent detail all sorts of rumors about Felix and his affairs. The pig! He had this perfect wife, Lorna. Why would he want other women?"

KC sighed. "I don't know. But a lot of men step out on their wives."

"I know. I'll check into it."

Feeling guilty that we'd done so little flute-playing, I changed the subject. "Weren't we working on the Chaminade when we were interrupted last week?

As usual, KC had practiced hard, and we both enjoyed her lesson, laughing with pleasure. She had prepared well enough that she could play with the accompaniment on YouTube, and her performance improved as she did. We ran through the piece, then worked on some spots. I glanced at my watch. "I'm sorry to talk so much of your lesson away."

"That's okay. You needed a friend."

As KC packed up I asked, "How's it going with Steve?"

I'd swear she blushed. "Oh, Emily, it's wonderful! He seems to like me. He's interested in my opinions, actually listens, and shares my values. He's really with me when he's with me, you know? And I respect him. He's smart and kind and generous."

So far, so good, I guessed, though based on my own experience with men, I'm inclined to be skeptical of relationships. This one sounded good, though, and KC smiled more than I'd ever seen. "How did you meet him, anyway?"

KC responded with the enthusiasm of a teenager recounting her date with a "hot" guy. "Remember a couple weeks ago? The day after Thanksgiving? I had the night off, so I went to the symphony performance. Steve's on the Board and was there, too. At intermission we both arrived at the drinking fountain at the same time and started talking. I wound up giving him my phone number."

"The Board?" I didn't know the members very well and didn't know them by sight.

"He's the Symphony's media expert."

The spin doctor? The one who made Felix sound like a saint at his funeral, responsible for the positive press it got? He had done a remarkable job. All the press articles were extremely complimentary to Felix and the symphony, and Felix's funeral eulogies were amazing. Not a negative word.

"Steve Palmer? Owner of Media Masters? Why didn't you tell me you were dating a Board member sooner?"

"I didn't want to say anything too early. I still don't. It seems like I'll jinx it, you know? It's only been a couple weeks."

"Don't worry, KC. I understand."

We headed for the kitchen, where Kathleen had already started lasagna, one of my favorites, for dinner. She confined herself to instructions for the culinarily challenged, that is, me. I helped her and KC prepare dinner, stretching my comfort zone by buttering garlic bread.

During dinner Kathleen told KC that Diane, Celee, and Lorna were all present at Fleisher when Felix was shot. Since this wasn't news to either of us, we didn't respond beyond an acknowledgement of new possibilities, and Kathleen grew quiet. KC tried to

keep the conversation going and introduced several different subjects, finally settling into a conversation with me about Cecile
Chaminade, and how unusual she must have been as a woman
composer in Paris in 1902, leaving Kathleen to listen or tune out,
as she chose.

After dinner KC said, "We all need something to take our minds
off our troubles."

Considering Kathleen's abstracted silence at dinner, I agreed.

"How about we finish decorating for Christmas?" KC grinned.

"That'd be fun. I'll get the decorations." From years of
Christmases I had mistletoe, wreaths, holly, centerpieces—just
about everything you could imagine.

KC and Kathleen worked together, winding the holly into the
bannister going upstairs while I hung a wreath on the front door
and draped mistletoe throughout. We consulted and arranged glittering angels flying through the air, and two manger scenes, one
of which Mom had created as a girl. Golden investigated every
opened box and barked with excitement when, standing under the
mistletoe, I kissed her on the nose.

It *was* fun. Just what I needed. Felix's funeral, the visit to Charlie,
and my frustration with the police investigation had been a strain.
Even KC's lesson, which had been the high point of my day, had
me worrying. My venting had shortened one of KC's most precious
forms of relaxation. The evening's activities, though, had freed me
from guilt. I let loose like an uncoiling spring as we all relaxed into
the Christmas spirit.

When I turned out the light, Golden jumped onto the bed and
graced me with her accepting company and healing energy as we
fell asleep.

TWENTY-TWO

I WANTED TO THINK.

KC had gone to the restaurant, but Kathleen, who ate breakfast with me, asked what my plans were for the day. When I responded that I intended to teach and then play a performance, she impatiently asked, "We're not working on Charlie's case?"

"I need to decide what to do next."

"What do you mean? It's perfectly obvious. We need to keep investigating the suspects—Myles, Jim, Josh, and Mark—and now Celee, Diane, and Lorna, too."

Privately thinking the three women were not even possibilities, I said, "How? Except for Diane, I don't know any of them very well. I have to think about how to get more information—about *whether* I can get more information. Maybe we should just let the police take over. I wonder what Barry would advise?"

"The police think they have the case solved. What about your precious grapevine? We have to keep moving."

"Orange, Kathleen," I said. "Don't forget about the orange jumpsuits Charlie will be wearing for the rest of his life if we screw up and can't clear him."

"He's my son. I can't quit." She paused. "Mom's coming tonight. She'll help."

I took a deep breath. Both physical and mental exhaustion left me nearly unable to speak. I certainly didn't want to argue. "I'm not saying 'quit.' I want to help both you and Charlie. But I've got to think about the information we have so far. What does it mean? Do some planning so we're not running off in all directions. I don't want to miss anything that could help Charlie's case."

Kathleen threw up her hands and stormed off, slamming the kitchen door behind her. I heard the garage door, and then her rental car squealing out of the driveway as she sped away.

Fine: it was time to regroup.

I spent the early part of the day catching up on my life—grocery shopping, going to the hardware store, paying bills. It encouraged me to make progress on routine chores, but my mind drifted to Charlie in odd moments. What now? I felt guilty doing nothing. And without doubt Kathleen would insist on action.

Late that morning a thunderbolt struck me. I should have realized before. KC could be on the right track. I had been looking at the case with blinders on, searching for someone who'd been seen at the murder scene. But to date, only Manolo, Lorna, and I had actually been seen near the crime scene, and we had all arrived after the gunshot. Jim admitted he'd been somewhere at Fleisher, but I didn't know where, and I'd only vague hints of a motive as yet. Josh and Mark acknowledged they'd been at the Hall, but both claimed they hadn't gone in the building, and the motives I'd discovered for them were pretty sketchy, mostly guesswork, though neither liked Felix.

Myles had the only convincing motive we'd found so far, Felix's affair with his wife. The motive police thought Charlie had dealt with Felix's effort to seduce Ana. Even KC believed in sex as a motive. And yet I hadn't investigated it.

The idea of using a different tactic encouraged me. Of course, the murderer still needed to have been at Fleisher, so where could this lead? But a different method had to turn up different results.

I thought about Felix's last words: "Tell her she was the only one . . .." I'd start with a visit to Lorna.

Kathleen returned just then. She'd been for a drive, she said. She wanted to go to Lorna's with me, apparently, thankfully, having forgiven or forgotten our row.

I hoped we'd get a new slant. But as the blocks rolled by, I rethought Kathleen's presence. Lorna knew me, but my welcome wasn't certain. I had figured it would be harder for her to turn down my request to see her if I were already there. Kathleen she didn't know at all. And Kathleen had the same last name as the supposed killer. Her company wasn't such a good idea, I reasoned.

When we pulled up in front of the house, my sister got out of the car.

"Kathleen, I think it's better that you don't come in."

"Why?"

"Because the woman in there is mourning her husband, and she's been told your son shot and killed him."

Kathleen responded hotly. "But he didn't!"

"That's not what the police believe. They've convinced Lorna Charlie is the killer.."

"That's their mistake." The pitch of her voice had risen 'til she sounded like a piccolo.

"We both know it's a mistake, but Lorna doesn't."

"That's not fair!" Kathleen crossed her arms.

"You're smarter than that. Think. Suppose Lorna knows Charlie is your son? We won't find out anything, and we'll cause Lorna unnecessary pain. We'll be lucky if Lorna hasn't already heard I'm Charlie's aunt."

That silenced her. I could see her anger dissipating. Her arms fell to her sides and her shoulders slumped. She asked in a voice I could barely hear, "Swear you'll tell me everything?"

"I swear."

Lorna lived in an enormous contemporary villa, suitable for the entertaining she and Felix had to do, with white columns and not much lawn, but a colorful and abundant garden. It bordered the park near Fleisher Hall and the college, hidden away on a dead-end street. At this time of year, the outdoor flagstone patio was deserted, its furniture removed. The gardens had been manicured for the winter, the dead foliage cleared away. Only evergreens remained visible.

I walked through wrought-iron gates which, strangely, stood open. I think I would have shut out the world under the circumstances, but to each his own. I know some people are comforted by company. The front door featured a huge heavy knocker instead of a bell. I hefted it and knocked.

Celee O'Connor, Lorna's close friend, came to the door. We had only spoken maybe three times, but I'd seen her around a lot. As usual, she looked perfect in dangly black earrings with a matching black bead necklace, forest green fitted dress, and black heels. She had pulled her thick coppery hair back in a French braid and fastened it with a glittering black barrette.

I looked down at my jeans and grey blouse. My choice of clothing embarrassed me, not that I could have bettered it much. Orchestra musicians—or the women, anyway—have lots of long black dresses, plenty of jeans, and not much in between.

Blocking the doorway protectively, Celee said, "It's Emily, isn't it? Lorna's not accepting visitors just now. Can I give her a message?"

I guessed I might not want company, either. The shock must be terrific. The open gates must be Celee's doing. "I wanted to talk to her personally. I stayed with Felix after the shot. He had a message for her. It might make her feel better to hear it, and I'd be happy to give any details I can."

At that point Lorna appeared behind Celee. Her outfit showed signs of being both immaculate and disturbed. She wore sharply creased navy slacks and a swirly-patterned sweater which picked up the color of the pants. But her long, loose blonde hair looked mussed, with a crooked part, and her feet were covered by thick, woolly socks in bright purple. She nodded at Celee. "It's okay."

To me she said, "I heard you. Come in and sit down."

I followed her through the spacious tiled entry hall and turned left to enter a modern room with burnished hardwood floors. A large sapphire sofa formed an "L." I sat on the short end while Celee and Lorna sat on the long end. Yellow, blue, and orange pillows adorned the corner, and a huge area rug in several shades of yellow nestled in the elbow of the "L." Drawing it all together, what looked like an original abstract oil painting with a nubby texture of azure, orange, and yellow took up almost an entire wall.

"I'm glad you were there for Felix at the end. No one told me. Did he . . . suffer . . . much?" Lorna bit her lip and looked down at fidgeting fingers.

I paused and tried to be as compassionate as I knew how. I didn't think an account of his groans of pain would do her any good, so I lied in good conscience, bowing my head. "I don't think so. He didn't seem to be suffering, only weak, and even that didn't last too long. I wish I could have done more."

"You did your best." She looked silently at me for a moment, and then at Celee. "You said Felix had some message for me?"

I hoped this wouldn't be too awkward. "I only understood, 'Tell her she was the only one . . .'"

Lorna exhaled slowly, as if she had been holding her breath. "That's all?"

"Like I said, that's all I picked up. I think he said more, but I couldn't make it out. I hope what I heard is some comfort."

"Yes. Yes, of course." Lorna pulled a handkerchief from the pocket of her pants and wiped her eyes. "If you'll excuse me now, I'm not seeing many people. I hope you understand." Turning to Celee she said, "You'll make sure my guest is well taken care of?" She stood, turned, and bent to give me a hug. "Thank you for coming. I'm glad Felix wasn't alone." She left the room, seeming tired and small.

I turned to Celee. "She relies on you a lot. It's a difficult situation, to say the least. Thanks for helping her."

"That's what friends are for." She paused a moment and her forehead wrinkled. "Are you sure Felix didn't say anything else?"

I thought it strange that Celee would continue questioning me after Lorna had left. "He did mumble more, but I couldn't hear."

"That's a shame. I'm sure it would console Lorna, but I guess it can't be helped."

Trying to prolong the conversation I said, "Lorna and Felix seem like they were a devoted couple." Yet it didn't quite fit when I said it.

"Very devoted." Celee stood. "Thanks for coming."

I had been dismissed.

I walked slowly back to the car, thinking as I went, then sat in the driver's seat.

"Well?" Kathleen asked.

"Weird."

"Weird, how?" Kathleen demanded.

I frowned before answering. "It just doesn't sit right. I repeated Felix's last words—which were all I heard—while Lorna and Celee were both in the room. Then Lorna left, and Celee kept questioning me. She wanted to know if Felix said anything else."

Making one of her patented intuitive leaps, Kathleen said, "Celee must have had a reason. She could have been Felix's mistress. Why else would she want to know his last words? She must be concerned about whether he let their secret out."

"That makes sense." And it fit in well with KC's theory.

"She might even have murdered him."

"What reason do you have to believe she might be the killer?"

"Her curiosity after Lorna made her exit—"

"—could have been only curiosity. We can't go around accusing people with no proof."

"But no one saw her at the time of the murder. She had left Diane and Lorna. That's opportunity, and if she and Felix were lovers . . ."

I entertained the possibility of Celee as a murderess while Kathleen continued to try to persuade me to her point of view.

TWENTY-THREE

TUESDAY, 2:00 P.M., DECEMBER 13, 2011

KATHLEEN INVITED ME TO KEEP HER COMPANY on her regular daily visit to Charlie that afternoon. After the usual sign in procedures and greetings, Kathleen updated him.

"Emily visited Lorna this morning."

"Lorna? Why?" He looked more than a little uneasy.

"She still needed to deliver Felix's last message. 'Tell her she was the only one . . .' She figured the message must have been intended for Lorna."

Charlie snorted. "That womanizer? He could have meant anybody."

I leaned forward. "Are you talking about the rumors on the grapevine?"

"The rumors on the grapevine are true. I've personally seen Felix in bars hanging all over women that weren't his wife. What a dickwit."

KC had guessed right. Kathleen's theory looked better and better, too. I should have known. "Like who?"

Charlie sat up straighter. "I didn't know any of them. The rumors were about lots of women, from orchestra members to PR people, to admirers from the audience." He chuckled. "Even volunteer ushers."

"That's a pretty broad range. If it's true, he could really have meant anybody."

"Yeah. He wasn't exactly what you would call a stand-up guy. At least, not if you were his wife."

Alice had said something similar, though not in such mild terms. If Felix had affairs, his wife would be the one most hurt.

"Emily said Celee reacted strangely to the message." Kathleen said slowly, "Do you think she could have been his mistress?"

"Possibly. Like I said, there were lots of women. Celee could have been one of them." Charlie apparently had nothing else to say about the subject. Turning to me he asked, "How's playing the *Nutcracker* without Felix?"

"Not to speak ill of the dead, but performances are a lot more fun with Doug than with Felix. His standards are right up there, but smiles for a job well done and even bows for orchestra members are an unaccustomed reward. The players do their jobs, same as always, but Doug appreciates us."

"No ego to rub up against." Charlie smiled, then exhaled noisily. "I miss playing. I miss my friends. Most of all, I miss Ana. We should be Christmas shopping together. She loves the *Nutcracker*. She could be coming to performances. Mom, we could be having family dinners."

"I know, sweetie."

An uncomfortable pause followed, during which I felt guilty for not missing Felix more.

Kathleen cleared her throat and changed the subject. "Gramma is coming in tonight for her regular Christmas visit." She gave me a sideways glance. "I know she'll help us solve the mystery of Felix's murder."

Charlie sounded excited. "Gram! She's a dynamo!" He laughed. "She'll get to the truth, and fast."

I had forgotten about Mom's visit, and worried as we left and signed out. Mom's heart was in the right place, but she wasn't tactful. The phrase *bull in a china closet* came to mind. Aloud I said,

"We don't have room for Mom. Between you and KC, all the bed-rooms are occupied."

Kathleen said, "I know. She didn't want to be any trouble, so she made reservations at a hotel."

We found the car and climbed in, as I continued to worry. Mom's accommodations weren't my real concern. She was an unstoppable force in general, and a warrior in defense of her family. Who knows what she'd do to clear Charlie?

Before I started the engine, Kathleen turned in her seat and faced me. "Mom's the answer to our prayers." She closed her eyes for a moment. "I thought about Charlie's advice to hire someone. Like I told him, I don't want to do that. I couldn't hire anyone who would care. Besides, we aren't the kind of family who airs our dirty linen to hired private eyes. Mom believes in Charlie, and she's willing to lend a hand. She'll work constantly, and she'll welcome new ideas. Remember how she helped you when your marriage went sour? She'll be another brain and another set of eyes and ears. She'll speed things up." Coaxing me she said, "I know you have a lot to do with the performances and your students and all. Don't worry about it. I'll take care of her, starting with meeting her flight tonight."

"Don't be silly. I always have time for family. But I do have a performance tonight. I appreciate the help."

TWENTY-FOUR

TUESDAY, 11:00 P.M., DECEMBER 13, 2011

After a performance, I usually came home to a quiet house. Kathleen goes to bed early, about 9:00, and KC collapses into unconsciousness around 10:00 when she returns from the restaurant, but not tonight. As I unlocked the front door and responded to Golden's welcome with the usual belly scratch, sounds of laughter echoed down the hall from the dining room.

"What did she do then?" Kathleen's voice.

What was going on?

I hurried down the hall, Golden padding after me, to find an assembly line set up at the dining room table. My sister, Mom, and KC were processing Christmas cards. KC signed for both of us, Mom put them into an envelope, and Kathleen, who worked from the email contact list on my computer server, addressed and stamped them.

I had bought the cards weeks ago, but given recent events, hadn't felt like sending them out. I'd given myself the year off. That would be one less thing to worry about. "What in the world?"

KC answered. "I found these in the closet. We had a few hours to kill after your mom arrived and before you came home, so I thought we could get these out. We're almost done. You won't have to deal with them."

I sat beside KC. She was right. The "team" had made it to the Ts. "I don't want to mess up your system. What can I do?"

Mom answered, "How about a nice cup of tea for everybody?"

"Lemon Zinger?" Kathleen's favorite.

"Of course. I stocked up when I knew you were coming."

Kathleen smiled. "I'll help. Mom can you finish the envelopes while I'm gone?"

"Sure, sweetie."

We went to the kitchen, Golden following, and divided the labor. Kathleen chose tea bags while I prepared the tea kettle and put it on to boil.

"KC is amazing!" Kathleen found mugs for everyone as she talked. "After Mom arrived, I told her about the latest develop-ments in Charlie's case, and we were pretty glum. When she got settled in her hotel room, Mom wanted to say hello to you, so we came here. When we did, KC organized us, getting the Christmas cards and making us feel we were doing something useful. We've been talking, just about light subjects like the flight, and gossip about people we know, and what we do. KC is so funny! It's the first time I've seen Mom smile since her flight arrived."

"KC is a wonder." So true. How did she know just what to do?

Kathleen rattled on, enthusing about KC, until we took the tea to the dining room on a tray, Golden trailing behind.

Kathleen resumed her original place in the "line".

"Can I join the party?" By that time they were on the Vs.

KC said, "Sure. Help me sign. You take these." She handed me five blank cards. "If you do those and I do my four, I think we'll be done."

When we were finished, Kathleen left to take Mom to her hotel, and KC and I got ready for bed and let Golden out. Even my brain felt tired. It had been a full day, with visits to Lorna and Charlie, a *Nutcracker* performance, Mom's arrival, and then staying up late finishing Christmas cards. Not waiting for Kathleen's return, I gladly let Golden in, hugged her, and let go of the day, sharing my bed with my dog's warm, devoted bulk.

TWENTY-FIVE

EARLY THE NEXT MORNING KATHLEEN FETCHED MOM from her hotel. Then they, KC, and I sat down together. The purpose of our gathering wasn't breakfast, but KC had cut up fresh fruit and made omelets and coffee cake, then served everyone, with my help. And, of course, we had tea. The house, cozy and warm, smelled of cinnamon.

When we were all seated with a full plate in front of us, I reviewed what we knew about Charlie's situation, then started the discussion of the case by saying, "I've been thinking about Celee. Both Kathleen and I agree that Celee's behavior after I talked to Lorna seemed strange."

I looked at my sister. "Celee asked more questions about Felix's last message to Lorna after she had left the room. Kathleen believes Celee was Felix's mistress, and that she may have killed him. What do you all think? Is it a possibility?"

Nobody responded immediately.

At last KC answered. "I can't see why Celee would be so curious about Felix's last words unless it's a possibility . . . a good one, you know?"

She excelled at out-of-the-box thinking, but I didn't want to make assumptions. I'd feel better if she connected the dots. "How so?"

"Well, if Felix's last words didn't refer to Lorna, his wife . . ." She shrugged.

I completed her thought. "Then the words could be about any woman. His mother, for instance." I knew she wasn't the woman KC intended, though. In her flute lesson, KC had mentioned the likelihood that Felix had a lot of romantic dalliances. Charlie had mentioned the same possibility. "Or a mistress. Charlie said he'd seen Felix with a variety of women, and they didn't behave like business contacts."

"Felix had affairs?" Mom spoke slowly.

I put all the ideas together. "If that's all true, the affair might have been with anyone. But let's assume for now that Felix and Celee were involved."

KC went to the stove and poured herself more tea. "If for some reason Celee got mad and shot Felix, she must have been dying— I guess I should find some other way to say that—she must have been 'anxious' to know how much he had said and whether it might have implicated her, you know?"

"I think we're on to something." Mom gave a thumbs-up.

The possibilities excited me. "Suppose that theory is right. She had opportunity, too. She left Lorna and Diane before the shot, and nobody saw her again 'til after Felix's body had been removed."

We all looked at each other.

Kathleen smiled. "Sounds hopeful to me."

"We know Celee wasn't with Lorna when she came to Felix's dressing room. It's quite possible Celee had just shot Felix—or not. We need to find out whether she had a gun."

"We never have enough information." Kathleen sighed.

"I think we need to get all the answers for Lieutenant Gordon so we can convince him Charlie's innocent."

Mom stepped in to encourage us. "I know we haven't solved all the details, but I think it's a pretty promising possibility. After all, every journey begins with a single leap."

I overlooked her cracked cliché and absorbed the content of her thought, hoping Kathleen would do the same.

KC sipped her tea thoughtfully. "It's only a working theory. We'll have to find out some details. What reason did Celee have to be angry at Felix? Did she have a gun? Where was she before, during, and after the murder? But it's got some serious possibilities."

She paused for a bite of omelet and washed it down with her juice. "And there are other options, too, you know?"

"Like what?" I sampled a morsel of coffee cake. *Delicious!* It tasted as good as it smelled.

KC added more sugar to her tea and stirred it. "Charlie said Felix had a reputation as a player. Well, it makes sense to me that if the guy had several affairs, those women are all possibilities. They'd be angry at being tossed aside. Not to mention any men Felix's conquests cheated on, and Lorna, who probably wasn't happy about her husband's infidelities."

"You're right, KC. Lots of possibilities." Kathleen added, "And don't forget Josh, Jim, and Mark. We know they were down at Fleisher at the right time. And Myles. Myles had such an excellent motive. "

"I haven't forgotten them. I'll check my sources and see what I can find out. And maybe Ana can find out about Celee's gun ownership."

Mom grinned. "Oh, this is thrilling. I feel just like Nancy Drew."

I smiled and turned to KC. "I know you don't have much time because of work. But if you could let us bounce ideas off you once in a while . . ."

"Sure, Em. Wish I could do more. But speaking of work, I'd better run."

She left, but I felt a whole lot better. We had some encouraging theories which were fresh and promising, and when we worked together, I knew we'd make progress.

TWENTY-SIX

WEDNESDAY, 11:00 A.M., DECEMBER 14, 2011

KATHLEEN AND MOM CONTINUED TO SIT at the breakfast table after KC's exit.

Mom turned to me. "What are your plans for the day?"

She knew I had to work. "I planned on spending the morning on the case; then I teach this afternoon and have a performance tonight."

Mom addressed Kathleen. "Since the morning's almost over, we'd better get out of Emily's way. Why don't you come to the hotel?"

Kathleen turned to me. "If I move there we'll get more done, and we won't have to worry about disturbing you."

"I donated the money I inherited from Olive to the city's kindness campaign. I don't regret that decision, but it means I can't afford to lose income. Charlie's case is important, though. I can work around my students and performances."

My sister said, "It's okay. Really. But Mom and I can do a lot more work if we know we're not bothering you."

I put aside my hurt feelings. "Okay. I understand. I'll do what I can from here. Alone." After a moment I added, "We can keep in touch with each other via text, too."

Kathleen gathered her suitcases and put on her coat. When she and Mom left, they were chattering a mile a minute.

Their departure saddened me, but I could still be helpful. I decided to call Alice Smithson, an orchestra cellist. She always knew the grapevine's latest, and she'd called Felix "a player". She would know all about his extracurricular love life, if anyone would.

"Hi, Alice. It's Emily. It's been so long since we talked, I thought I'd call and say hello." I'd actually been avoiding her. My friend Olive's murder last year had brought home to me the dangers of gossiping. But I didn't know any other way to find out about Felix, or more accurately, Felix and Celee.

"Emily! It's good to hear from you."

We spent a few minutes catching up. Alice's daughter would finish her master's this semester, and her husband would have surgery to replace his knee this coming Monday. Then we moved on to the topic of the day. She brought it up. I knew she would. She revels in digging up dirt.

"I can't believe Felix is dead, and that Charlie killed him!"

Cautiously I said, "I hope there's some other explanation. I'm Charlie's aunt."

"Yeah, I'd heard that."

Interesting. "Really? I didn't think many people knew. Who did you hear it from?"

Alice responded with gusto. "It's a funny story really. I took my dog for a walk with a friend. You know Betty Longman? The violist?"

Alice didn't wait for me to answer before she continued, "Well, we ran into a friend of hers, Shirley Finkelstein. Shirley had been to a pops concert. You know, the Cowboy Classics show?"

Hoping it wasn't important, I mumbled encouragement, wishing she'd get to the point, but I knew from experience that it behooved me to listen to the whole story. If interrupted, Alice might lose the thread altogether. It would be difficult to get her back on track.

She continued. "Well, when Betty introduced me as a member of the orchestra, we started talking about the symphony. It seems Shirley has season tickets. Anyway, that led to talking about Felix's murder. Shirley knew Leon Brown. He's her son's roommate. Leon told Shirley that you'd talked to him, and that you'd said you were Charlie's aunt."

Leon. Apparently, he hadn't kept our visit a secret.

"According to Shirley, Leon said that you were looking for some explanation other than that Charlie killed Felix. He said you accused him of the murder."

I sputtered. Of course I didn't accuse Leon, and he'd been nothing but helpful. I wondered if the inaccuracy came from him, or Shirley, or Alice.

After a short pause, during which I fumed quietly, Alice continued. "If you're looking for other explanations, Shirley had a couple of theories."

"Really? What were they?" I could use any help I could get.

"Oh, things you'd never think of. Like, if someone wanted Felix's job and shot him."

I thought about it briefly. Assistant Conductor Doug Jones took over as Felix's successor, at least temporarily. Could he have wanted Felix's job? But it seemed too ridiculous, a tiny little motive and a long shot. Nobody had mentioned seeing him until he conducted at the first concert, and I hadn't seen him, either. If he'd gotten to Fleisher early enough to kill Felix, surely someone would have recognized him and told the police about it. For now, at least, I'd assume he hadn't had the opportunity.

"Or if somebody thought it would spike an interest in the symphony, and therefore ticket sales, so they killed Felix."

A preposterous idea it didn't take any thought to reject. I rolled my eyes, glad that Alice couldn't see over the phone.

"But, I mean, someone killed Felix, and the police think Charlie did it. That's good enough for me. Everybody knows how rudely Felix treated Charlie."

I couldn't argue the point. "Yeah, including me." Eager to set the record straight I said, "I hoped to prove somebody else murdered Felix. Leon might have known something. But I don't know why he would say I accused him. As far as I know, he didn't have either motive or opportunity. But he might have known something about

Felix that would lead to a solution. That's why I talked to him." I directed the conversation back toward my main concern. "I'm having trouble finding anyone with a motive to do it."

Alice tsked. "Well, Felix didn't have many friends. I'd be more surprised if you could find someone who *didn't* have a motive. You've seen how he treated the orchestra. He dealt with most everyone that way. Except for the ladies. He could be quite charming with his female audience."

Ah! Now we were getting to it. I felt ashamed, but I couldn't see any other way. "Really? Anybody I know?"

"Oh, you've seen the sweet young things that hung around backstage. Felix's groupies."

"So, no one specific?"

"There were rumors about Celee O'Connor. But he chased skirts all the time. It's disgusting, but I guess that's common for handsome, powerful men."

"Bet Lorna wasn't happy about that."

"We can only imagine." Alice sounded quite satisfied.

I imagined, all right. But Alice didn't seem inclined to pursue Lorna's reactions. Possibly she didn't know them. I couldn't push the subject any further. If Alice knew, or even suspected, anything, she'd tell me, I'm sure. Knowing her, I wouldn't have been able to stop her.

We moved on to other topics—next year's planned schedule, salary negations with management, speculation on a new conductor—and then said our goodbyes. It appeared the grapevine had known about Felix's dalliances and had suspected Celee was one of those. Inadvertently, Alice had also reinforced suspicions of Lorna, who couldn't be happy about Felix's flirtations and affairs. I'd have to see what else I could find out.

TWENTY-SEVEN

I HADN'T BEEN ABLE TO SLEEP LAST NIGHT. Too many thoughts were in my head: sorrow at Kathleen's leaving my house and moving to the hotel, hurt feelings that my efforts were not appreciated or acknowledged, questions about Charlie's case, and concerns about Megan. I didn't get to sleep until two or three in the morning, and I overslept.

After I dressed and ate breakfast, I called Barry and asked about a gun registry.

"The state of Colorado doesn't require registration of any particular type of firearm. It's considered a violation of the rights of the private citizen."

"You'd think if it's not a violation of individual rights to register cars, guns could be registered."

"I know, Em. We're singing from the same song sheet. But the constitution doesn't mention cars." He continued. "The state does, however, require that a gun dealer register details of transactions involving guns, whether in their shop or in a gun show, in a record that is kept internally. That includes background checks. The ATF could audit the shop's records at any time. But even the police can't just go fishing. They have to have a specific reason to suspect a specific gun shop sold the gun involved, and get a warrant for the records of that shop, unless the shop owner voluntarily consents to surrender his records. As an ordinary citizen you wouldn't be able to get those records, and neither would I."

A dead end. Unless Ana could find out something. I added texting her to my to-do list.

"Also, I've been meaning to call you. I'm afraid the news isn't good. My source at the PD called. In response to warrants from the PD, the phone company submitted Charlie's phone records. They showed his phone pinged at Fleisher Hall starting at 5:28 p.m., and that he remained at the Hall 'til 5:59 the day of the murder."

"That doesn't sound good, does it, since the murder took place a few minutes before 6:00?"

"Nope. We need to talk to Charlie and find out his whereabouts and what he did."

WITH KATHLEEN'S MOVE TO MOM'S HOTEL, I shifted my teaching from the living room back to the studio, which my sister had been using as a bedroom, and where all my music, CDs, and other supplies were. I'd been giving flute lessons there since three o'clock. Megan Green was my five o'clock. I prayed her family situation had worked out since last week because, despite the best of intentions, I knew nothing about psychology. If things hadn't gotten better, I wouldn't know how to help her.

Silly me; no dice. Things had not only *not* gotten better since last week, they'd gotten worse. At least, that's what I assumed when I saw Megan's face, sad and miserable. She put together her flute without saying a word.

Since I didn't know what to say either, I resorted to a monologue on the usual. "Hi, Megan."

Uncomfortable silence.

"Let's start the warm-up with long tones on an A flat major scale."

She began the long tones, but her vibrato sounded uneven, and a big tear rolled down her cheek. At that, she put her flute into her lap. Her eyes teary, she said, "I'm sorry, Miz Wilson. I don't know if I can play."

In the past, Megan had responded well to silence. The tactic had the added advantage of ensuring that I didn't say the wrong thing. So I quietly waited for her to go on.

Megan stared out the window, then said, "Dad's been working from home, and he's been grouchy. Mom told us not to bother him." Hesitantly she continued, "Today was her day off. When I got home from school my parents were in the office, and I heard . . . I heard . . . that is . . ." She started to cry, but I managed to understand, "I heard yelling and a thump, and then crying."

Golden left the corner she occupies during lessons and sat in front of Megan.

"Oh, honey." I moved the box of tissues close by.

She took one, ignoring Golden. "I heard Dad leave. Mom ran to her bedroom, still crying. She tried to muffle the sound and stayed there 'til time to leave. Miz Wilson, I'm pretty sure he hit her."

"What makes you think so?

"Besides hearing her cry, when I saw her, she pretended everything was fine, but her eye didn't look right."

Concerned, I turned and hugged her, then held her at arm's length and said, "I know I've asked you before, but I'll ask again. Has your dad ever struck you?"

She twisted away. "No way! He's my dad. He wouldn't. Would he?"

I didn't mean to scare her. "The most important thing is that you're safe. I'm just making sure." I knew that abuse most often didn't confine itself to the parents, and I worried.

She threw herself into my arms again, crying on my shoulder.

Golden crowded closer.

I held her until her sobs became sniffles, then suggested, "Let's go have some tea."

Megan followed me to the kitchen.

Golden padded along, her eyes seeming soft and concerned.

By now Megan knew where I kept the supplies. Wordlessly she picked blackberry tea and chose orange spice for me, then got mugs from the cupboard and sat at the table.

Meanwhile, I filled the kettle and put the water on to boil, thinking what to say. "You don't know why they were arguing?"

"No. The fight started before I got home from school. I don't know how long they'd been at it. But when I saw Mom, I could tell her eye had swollen and begun to change color. She'd tried to hide it with makeup, but . . ." She hiccupped and gasped, in her efforts not to cry.

Damn. I didn't know what to do. Should I try to calm her down or encourage her to let it all out?

Leaning against Megan's legs, Golden laid her head on the girl's knee.

Megan smiled and petted the dog.

As I stood beside them, stroking Megan's hair, I said honestly, "Sweetie, I don't know what to say. It's a difficult situation."

"Miz Wilson, I feel so helpless! I try to do my best. My grades are okay, and I don't do drugs or have boyfriends or—"

I interrupted. I'd said it before, but it obviously needed to be repeated, with emphasis. My heart aching, I said, "Megan, there's nothing you can do to make it better. It's between them, and their issues are buried deep in their relationship. Even before you were born. It's not your fault."

Megan heaved one gasping sob, then pulled Golden closer.

It wasn't my fault either, but I was the adult. Supposedly, I knew what to do. I thought furiously. I needed to talk to Megan's mother, Serena Green. If I asked Megan for permission, though, she might say "no." But she shouldn't be feeling these pressures. Only a conversation with her mother would be helpful.

By the time Megan released Golden, I'd decided to speak to Mrs. Green as soon as possible. Megan might feel betrayed, but I felt more concerned about what might happen if I did nothing. "Honey, I think I should talk to your mom."

"No, please don't, Miz. Wilson. If she thinks I've told you about it, she'll be so mad. And embarrassed, too. We can't let her know I told you." She hiccupped in her distress.

I wanted to put her mind at rest, and I'd thought of a plan. "I don't think I need to bring you into it at all. We'll make sure your mother comes in tonight, and then I can say I saw the black eye."

Megan begged softly. "She won't know I told you?"

"I promise."

Megan hiccupped again.

Golden put a paw in her lap and gave a soft, inquisitive bark.

That, and maybe relief, did it. Megan giggled.

I couldn't help it. Irresistibly, I joined her laughter. The serious mood broke. When the kettle whistled, we fixed our tea and took it to the studio, where we played a duet.

After years of teaching, I have a built-in sense of how long half an hour is. That sense told me our lesson was over, even though we hadn't done much playing. I glanced at my watch and saw that, sure enough, the lesson time had ended, but there of no sign of Mrs. Green at the door. Through the window I could see her car parked at the curb.

Fine. "Megan, you need to pack up your flute now. I think your mom may not want to come in. I'll go out to the car with you."

"Thanks, Miz Wilson."

I went out to the Green's Honda and talked through the window about plans for the next recital. I asked Mrs. Green to help serve refreshments afterwards. She said she couldn't and kept turning away from me. But I'd seen her eye. Like Megan said, even with makeup I could see the shiner.

I said my goodbyes, but called later. I told Serena I wanted to talk about Megan and invited her to lunch.

She hemmed and hawed and tried to make excuses, as if she had an inkling of the real subject. She kept claiming "family responsibilities."

At any rate I pushed. "I really need to talk to you."

After a lot of negotiating, she finally said, "I'll come on my lunch hour tomorrow. Ben can't complain about that. He won't even know," and made an appointment with me for noon. I had to gather my thoughts before then so Athena's wisdom would be on the tip of my tongue.

TWENTY-EIGHT

FRIDAY, 8:30 A.M., DECEMBER 16, 2011

KATHLEEN CALLED ME FROM HER HOTEL the next morning, anxiously and needlessly making sure I hadn't forgotten Charlie. She reminded me to keep looking into Celee, Lorna, Diane, Josh, Mark, Jim, and Myles, and asked if Barry had been able to help with the gun registry. I explained what he'd told me. She took a moment to express her discouragement, and then went on to describe Charlie's experiences in jail, most of which I'd heard before, but some of which were new. Besides dismay over the dangerous company, no privacy, no music, uncomfortable bedding, and bad food, Charlie now expressed concern that the other prisoners didn't seem to like him very well, and that his cell mate, awaiting trial on armed robbery charges, didn't keep his part of the cell clean.

"So, anyway, I thought if Mom and I pick up a few things at the store we can take them to Charlie. Make him a little comfier. I wanted you to know we won't be by this morning."

Shopping. It appeared that she and Mom were channeling their concern for Charlie into a buying spree. And who knows? With a bit of luck, they would find something to make him more secure and cozy.

"Don't forget the crosswords and Sudoku he asked for."

"I brought those to him yesterday, but thanks for remembering."

My mind wandered as she described her ideas for purchases.

". . . some slippers . . ."

Nervously, I listened with half an ear. I'd scheduled my meeting with Megan's mother today, and I wanted to get everything right. I worried about my student. Charlie might not be happy, but at least he had Kathleen hovering over him frantically. I'd leave him and his problems to her, for now. Megan needed me, and she needed me today.

MEGAN'S MOM, SERENA GREEN, AND I got to the Articulate Artichoke at the same time.

"Hi, Serena."

"Emily!"

We exchanged a hug and went in together.

While we waited to be seated, I made small talk. "Megan's an excellent flute student. Do you know if she wants to pursue the instrument in college? She works so hard, and she seems to love it."

"That's good to hear. I'm not sure she's thought about it. It's early yet. She's only fifteen."

At that point the waitress seated us and took our drink orders. "It's not too early to be thinking about college. If Megan wants to, she should try for a scholarship with her flute playing."

"I'll tell her you have confidence in her. I guess it's never too early to start planning."

We studied the menu, and when the waitress returned, placed our orders. A salad for Serena. I went for the comfort of a grilled cheese sandwich. When we were alone once again, I continued the conversation, praising Megan until the waitress brought our meals. "Well, whatever she wants to do, I'm sure she'll do it well. I'm not worried." Seeing an opportunity to transition into my real purpose I said, "I have been concerned about you, though. I noticed your black eye at Megan's lesson yesterday."

Serena looked down at her plate and turned away from me. "Oh, clumsy me! I banged it into a cupboard."

I knew she lied because her makeup didn't entirely hide the shiner, and because of what Megan had told me, but I'd promised I wouldn't bring my student into it. "I used to use that explanation all the time when my husband hit me and left bruises. Are you alright?"

"Of course. It looks worse than it is." She hadn't denied that she concealed the truth. "It'll heal."

"You need to take better care of yourself. Megan and the other kids need you." I hoped to plant a seed, even though she told me a fib.

She looked up. "It's nice of you to care about Megan." She continued hesitantly. "I'm afraid I'm not a very good mother."

"That's not true." I looked into her eyes. "I've seen how devoted you are to your family."

"That's kind of you to say. I appreciate it." She picked up her fork. After several moments of silence, she cocked her head as if asking a question, then nodded, as if she'd received an answer. When she spoke again her voice was different, softer and fainter. "I haven't told anybody, but I'm so tired of feeling alone all the time. If your husband hit you, you'll understand. Please, can I be honest? Will you promise to keep a secret?"

I didn't say anything. I wasn't going to make promises I couldn't keep.

She continued, though, as if she couldn't stop now that she'd started. "I can't tell the kids. When Ben . . . when he is . . ." She looked into my eyes. "Actually, he gave it to me."

I remained silent. Was she talking about her eye? I didn't know how to draw her out and thought about it so long that she went on without prompting from me.

"Funny expression. 'Gave it to me.' Like it's a gift to be treasured." She paused a few seconds before she went on. "Ben has always had a temper." She paused and looked into her plate, pushing lettuce leaves back and forth with her fork.

"A temper?"

She bit her lip. "When things don't go well. That's what happened yesterday. Ben worked from home. I had the day off. I heard him curse, so I didn't go near the office. I kept my distance and tried not to disturb him."

She stopped, and I held my breath, waiting for her to go on. "And then?"

It seemed a long time before she continued. "He came to the door and shouted for me. Still shouting, he said he couldn't work in such a filthy environment. Usually, he likes to take care of cleaning his office so I don't disturb his papers. But he frightened me, so I came back with a rag. I started to dust, working as quietly as I could." She put down her fork. "That really sent him up the wall. He said I distracted him. I didn't know what else to do because he'd told me to clean, so I kept dusting along the shelves. They didn't need it as far as I could see, but I did it anyway. My back faced him."

Up to this point she'd sounded timid, but now she sobbed once, and her face became expressionless, her voice a monotone. "The next thing I knew he crossed the room and pulled me backward in a stranglehold. When I tried to get away, he punched my eye. He accused me of stomping around and hit me again, in the ribs this time."

Throughout the description of his violence, she remained impassive. Why? Had she lived with Ben's anger so many years, her feelings had shut down? Her lack of expression was more chilling than tears would have been.

"I'm so sorry." I held her hand and gave it a squeeze. "You didn't do anything to deserve that. You were trying to help him." His actions were the dictionary definition of abuse. "Does he hit you often?"

"No. Only when I get on his nerves. I can't seem to help annoying him." She began to tear up.

"Annoying him!" I fumed. "Have you ever thought about seeing a counselor, or even leaving Ben?"

I shouldn't have said it. She wiped her unshed tears, and defended him. "Oh, usually he's very good to me and the kids."

"Usually?"

"He makes an excellent salary. There's always enough money if I need it."

That confused me. Serena worked as an insurance adjuster. Why did she sound like she needed to come to her husband for money? Megan had told me she guessed that her parents budgeted that way. *I* guessed Ben demonstrated his power by controlling their money.

She smiled. "And sometimes he's very gentle. He's a wonderful dad. He makes a point of having a huge party for each child's birthday with lots of presents." She leaned closer. "He doesn't hit me often. Just when I've pushed him too far. And each time he's so sorry; he swears it'll never happen again." Her eyes met mine, and she seemed to be begging for understanding. "He gets on these rants. I know I can be very irritating. And the kids need a father."

I interpreted what I heard to mean that when Ben got upset he took it out on Serena, then made up for his abuse by giving her and the kids money or parties. But it sounded like she wouldn't see it that way. I guessed her sense of self-worth was lower than a string bass's low note. "Have you ever called the police?"

"Of course not! Ben doesn't mean it. And he'd be really mad." She looked down at her lap. "A wife's supposed to make her husband happy," she whispered. She managed to say, "I can't!" before she began wailing, loudly, like a three-year-old who'd lost her mom in the grocery store.

I didn't know whether she meant she couldn't make him happy or she couldn't call the cops—probably both.

People on all sides of the restaurant stared, and I saw the waitress, who had been headed our way with the check, turn away.

Handing Serena a tissue from my purse, I said, "It's not your fault."

She sobbed harder.

"Someone you love, Ben, for so many years has insisted you're to blame. It's hard to see anything else. But what he says isn't true. My husband tried to convince me our fights were all my fault and I 'made' him hit me . . ." I made air quotes, ". . . but the fact is, lots of people get annoyed with their spouses, even hate them, without hitting them."

The sobbing gradually became faint cries, and I hoped what I said had sunk in. "You have to consider your children, Serena. Will Ben ever lose his temper and hit them? Hopefully not. But no guarantees. And what if someday Megan's boyfriend hits her? Do you want her to think that's all right . . . that it's normal?"

Serena sat up straight and, between sniffles, told me sincerely, "I'd protect her. And besides, she'd have more sense than to have a boyfriend who hit her." She didn't seem to see any inconsistency between that statement and her current situation. "Anyway, the kids don't know anything about it. We never fight in front of them."

"Kids can hear. They can see. If I noticed your shiner, they must have, too."

"Why? Has Megan said anything?" Serena leaned forward.

I'd promised to leave Megan out of it, so I replied, "Anyone can see your eye."

Serena blew her nose and wiped her eyes, dabbing the injured one gently. "Well, it's nice of you to be concerned, but I think I can handle the situation."

Because you're doing such a great job, now, I thought.

She checked her mascara in a small mirror she withdrew from her purse and carefully rubbed a finger along her lower lids, wincing when she touched the injured left eye. She looked straight at me. Sounding increasingly angry she said, "You may be a very good flute teacher, but you should stick to music and stay out of things that don't concern you, like my marriage."

I didn't take offense, realizing she needed the anger to give her strength.

"You're not even a mother. Don't tell me what's good or bad for my children, or how to parent them."

Ouch. Why did she believe only mothers could understand decency and caring? I knew using another human being as a punching bag was wrong, and I didn't have to be a mother to recognize it.

"Now, if you'll excuse me, I'd better visit the restroom and make some repairs and then I need to get back to work."

I gave up. I'd done all I could do, for now. "It's okay. I have a matinee soon." I glanced at my watch and gave her an out. "I'll get the check and ask for a doggie bag. I'll be gone when you get back. But Serena, please remember there are lots of people that want to help, including me. There are resources available. Give me permission, and I'll be glad to offer support."

Without saying another word or looking back, she went to the restroom, her back ramrod straight.

I'd give Serena a chance to do something. But if she didn't take action, I'd have to report the situation. Megan's safety, and that of her brothers and sister, was at stake. I asked for a box, paid the bill, and left, having touched little of my sandwich. I'd eat it at home.

LUNCH WITH SERENA HAD UPSET ME. Fixing myself a cup of tea, then finding a plate and nibbling the leftovers slowly, I finished my sandwich while wondering how I could have done better.

There were so many things I hadn't thought to mention. I contributed to a battered women's shelter in town, the same one that had supported me. The shelter could help Serena develop a plan to leave her husband safely with the kids, and provide a place to stay. Its attorneys would take her case *pro bono* and use legal means to get money from her husband if he tried to control her by withholding it. Counselors would provide free mental health sessions for both her and the kids. The shelter could supply free career clothes in case Serena needed them, though since she already had a job, that wasn't a benefit she would use. The family could use the services even if they weren't living at the shelter. I should have told Serena all of that.

And what about my own role? Would I be willing to help? Unenthusiastically, I pictured me, KC, Megan, her mom, and three pre-teen kids in my tiny house. But people had helped me when I needed them. Now it was my turn. I knew the level of anger and violence Megan endured was unacceptable. If the family couldn't find space elsewhere, my home would offer shelter to Serena and her children. I'd let her know. The information would help with the tough decisions she faced.

She needed options, but I'd done a poor job of presenting them. I should have been more prepared when I talked to her. I hoped, at least, I had let her know she had support, if she wanted it. But to date I hadn't helped Megan, and the solution to Charlie's problems eluded me. It seemed I wasn't lending a hand to anyone in a meaningful way.

While I finished my sandwich and questioned myself, Kathleen called, hysterically angry, to tell me about her visit to Charlie. "I don't believe it!"

"See if you can calm down, Kathleen, and tell me what's wrong."

"They wouldn't allow any of them!"

"Who wouldn't allow what, Kathleen?"

"The guard! When we checked in! He wouldn't allow us to give them to Charlie!"

"I still don't understand. What wouldn't he allow?"

I heard her take a deep breath and the phone hummed with silence. After a moment she continued, a little more calmly, so I could understand. "The stuff Mom and I bought for Charlie. The guard wouldn't let us bring it in. We spent all this money. I figured Charlie's sanity made the expense worth it. But the video games, the eReader, the iPad and ear buds, the aspirin, the therapeutic pillow, the weighted blanket, the laptop, the rechargeable toothbrush, the incense, the mini-fridge . . . all of it necessary for Charlie's mental health, and all not allowed!"

Kathleen paused, and when she went on, I could hear the anger in her voice. "On top of that, the guard nearly denied me future visits. He kept insisting that I'd tried to supply Charlie with 'contraband.' I told him that I'd had no idea they had all those silly rules, and that I'd only been trying to be good to my son. I begged and pleaded as hard as I could for nearly twenty minutes before he finally said that even though my actions were against the rules, he'd ignore them this once. I could come again, but only if I'd promise not to bring any 'contraband' in the future."

I wasn't surprised she'd worn the guard down. Kathleen could be pitiful and heartbreakingly persuasive, and her son's welfare would have engaged all her emotional mother bear arguments.

"He made me put everything that wasn't allowed in a locker and take it home with me. The only thing he let me bring in were the shampoo, but not the conditioner."

"He allowed shampoo but not conditioner?"

"He said the shampoo came in a transparent bottle and was less than sixteen ounces, so it was okay, but the conditioner I'd brought came in a thirty-two-ounce opaque bottle. That made it forbidden."

She paused, and, calmer now, she continued. "He wouldn't even allow the shopping bag because it wasn't transparent, or the gourmet ham sandwich topped with poppy seeds, which apparently aren't allowed, either. And the sandwich wasn't vacuum-packed and pre-printed with the manufacturer's list of ingredients. As if any good food has ever been vacuum-packed and pre-printed with the manufacturer's list of ingredients!" Anger still in her voice she said, "I swear that before we left, he ate the sandwich."

I almost laughed. It would have been funny if it hadn't been so sad. Kathleen and Mom had been trying to make life more pleasant for Charlie. But Kathleen should have known. A mini-fridge and incense, for goodness sake! I felt forced to be a wet blanket. "The good news is you still get to see Charlie. You'll have to play by the prison rules for a while."

Sounding discouraged and squelched, she said, "I knew I could depend on you for good common sense. But he's my son. I can't stand to see him so unhappy."

I understood. She'd spent a lot of money she couldn't afford in an effort to make Charlie more comfortable. But she needed to follow the jail's rules. If flouted, those rules could result in her being forbidden to see Charlie. As I changed for the matinee, I thought again: Kathleen needed comfort in her pain, and I didn't know what to do.

TWENTY-NINE

FRIDAY 2:00 P.M., DECEMBER 16, 2011

I COULDN'T GET UP ANY ENTHUSIASM for the matinee performance. I felt tired and defeated. Megan's family was torn by violence, and Kathleen's anger had drained me. On top of that, the ballet was getting old . . . again. It wouldn't be too much longer until we ended the run, though. Today began our next to the last weekend. I reluctantly dragged myself to the performance.

I'd played the first half by reflex. At intermission I made my usual rounds then headed back to my seat. I hadn't meant to eavesdrop, but an alcove formed by the curtain hid me when someone said, "They're beautiful!"

I recognized Celee's voice when she answered. "They were a gift. From an admirer."

Now curiosity made me stop and listen, still hidden by the curtain. "They're stunning with that dress!"

I exited the alcove and walked by Celee and her friend, a cellist. I nodded to them. Celee wore an elegant little black dress with no adornment. It allowed her huge squash blossom necklace and matching earrings to take center stage—dazzling. The jewelry must be the subject of the conversation.

As the second half started, my mind wandered to the necklace and earrings. Celee had said they were a gift from an admirer. Who would give Celee an expensive gift like that? As far as I knew she didn't have a relationship. What could the occasion have been? Her birthday? An early Christmas gift?

Fortunately, I knew the music almost by heart, so my performance didn't suffer from my lack of attention.

OUR NEXT SHOW WASN'T UNTIL EIGHT O'CLOCK, so I went home to eat. Both KC's car and Kathleen's rental were outside. Golden greeted me, lying down for a tummy scratch, and enthusiastically thumping her tail against the floor. After unconditionally dispensing affection, I went in search of KC, Mom, and Kathleen. Golden followed.

I found them in the kitchen.

KC greeted me. "Hi there! I have the afternoon off from the restaurant, and Kathleen and your mom needed a break from sleuthing, so we're baking Christmas cookies."

She had organized them with the efficiency of a general. KC greased pans and mixed the batter. Kathleen rolled out the dough and used cookie cutters to shape stars, Santas, Christmas trees, and candy canes. She helped Mom arrange the prepared dough onto cookie sheets, then Mom decorated their handiwork and slipped the edible creations into the oven.

Amazed, I sat at the table. KC had, once again, gotten my mom and sister to relax. "Want to join us?"

"No thanks. I had a light lunch and now I'm starving. Have you eaten?"

Kathleen replied, "Yeah, we ate earlier."

"Okay. I'll try to stay out of your way."

Originally, KC traded housekeeping and cooking for flute lessons. Now she seldom has much time to cook. It's still true that if anything is home cooked, it's cooked by her. I mostly survive on microwave dinners and salad. Braving the kitchen's hostile territory, I managed to work around the cookie assembly line, find a saucepan, and start heating some split pea soup KC had made, listening with pleasure to the teasing and laughter of the bakers.

Noticing my clumsiness, KC left her post at the mixer, whipped out a knife and a loaf of homemade bread and made me a cucumber, avocado, and tomato sandwich with some kind of spice added. "Here. You'll starve if you depend on your culinary skills."

When the soup boiled, I filled a bowl, KC transferred the sandwich from the chopping board to a plate, and Kathleen, who had left her rolling pin, made tea. When Mom slid the cookies into the oven, she, too, joined us, and we all sat at the table.

"I'm glad you're here. I have news." I paused dramatically.

"Do tell." Mom rose, found a mug, and poured herself some tea.

"Celee came backstage at today's matinee. She wore a gorgeous squash blossom necklace and matching earrings." I took a spoonful of soup and blew on it, then swallowed it cautiously. "I overheard her tell a friend an admirer gave them to her."

"Who's the admirer?" KC asked.

"She didn't say. And the grapevine hasn't connected her to anyone, except possibly Felix."

KC and Kathleen exchanged knowing looks.

"So, looks like we were right." Kathleen flipped her long hair over her shoulder.

Mom took her seat at the table and tsked. "Felix cheated on his wife with her best friend. Disgusting!"

Kathleen went over the theory again, possibly to reassure herself. "Felix had a reputation as a player. As Lorna's best friend, Celee had excuses to be around all the time. And she exhibited a strange interest in Felix's last words. Now you find a mysterious admirer gave her expensive jewelry, and as far as anyone knows she has no boyfriend, but there are rumors about a liaison with Felix." Sounding convinced now, she said, "I'm telling you, they were lovers. Celee wanted to find out what he'd revealed. Like we said." Thoughtfully she said, "I wonder if she's the 'her' in 'Tell her she was the only one.'"

KC nodded her head.

I had finished my soup and pushed the bowl and spoon away. "It sure sounds like that's the solution. But, logical as it is, let's not be too hasty. The grapevine and guesses wouldn't be considered reliable in a court of law."

Kathleen shrugged. "I wonder if the police have checked into Celee as a suspect?"

"The police are convinced Charlie committed the murder."

Kathleen's lips pressed together and she looked like she was about to say something.

I hurriedly added, "They're not investing time in other possibilities. It's up to us to give them evidence to the contrary. Something they can't ignore. Proof." I didn't mean to discourage Kathleen, so I tried to be more positive. "But at least we've got a start now. Celee is looking better and better as a suspect. We'll get this, one way or another."

Kathleen and Mom had decided they wanted to come to the *Nutcracker* performance—Mom loved the *Nutcracker*—and prepared to leave for their hotel so they could change. I'd pick them up on the way to the performance and we'd go out for ice cream afterwards. KC geared up to leave for the restaurant's dinner rush. As I collected my flute satchel for the ballet's evening performance, I puzzled over the next step. Suspicion and a theory were fine, but we needed indisputable proof that someone other than Charlie, Celee, if our hypothesis was right, had killed Felix. How would we get it?

THIRTY

SATURDAY, 4:45 P.M., DECEMBER 17, 2011

THE NEXT DAY I PUT WORRIES about both Megan and Charlie aside and took refuge in the music, resulting in an enjoyable matinee performance of the *Nutcracker*. Afterward, I figured I'd have time before dinner and the evening performance to finish my Christmas shopping.

I stopped at a pricey department store to buy some pricier perfume as a gift for Kathleen. My sister keeps herself on a tight budget, but she deserves nice things. It made gift giving easy, though. I picked a trendy new scent, all the rage. I shouldn't spend that much, but at least I felt good about providing my sister a taste of luxury.

Now, Mom . . .

Jewelry would be nice. She liked unusual things, so I decided to forego the department store offerings and visit the jewelry store across the street. Maybe they'd have something imaginative, but not too expensive.

The store, Kokapelli's Jewelry, specialized in Native American jewelry and repairs. It had everything from reasonably priced earrings to huge antique rings and necklaces, as well as a liberal return policy, which would be helpful in my mother's case. The staff had been there ever since I could remember, and valued connections with the Native American community. The store occupied a small, square space, with room for no more than three customers. Upon entering, I immediately became aware of Celee, who stood at the counter.

"Emily?" She wore a different little black dress, low cut. It seemed bare, with only earrings for accessories, not like her at all. She loved her jewelry and could make the plainest dress seem elegant with the judicious addition of necklaces and bracelets.

"Hi, Celee. What brings you here?"

"I'm waiting for my necklace," she explained. "Friends of the Symphony wants to honor the ballerinas, and I love shopping, so I volunteered to pick up a few things for them between shows. I'll present the gifts backstage before the performance. I'm giving the welcome speech to the audience tonight, so I'll be there anyway." She rolled her eyes. "But then, while I shopped, my necklace caught on a display and broke. Luckily, the jewelry store was nearby, and their repairman works on Saturdays. He's being nice enough to fit me in and fix it right away, while I wait."

She took a breath and seemed ready to add more, when the clerk emerged from the workspace behind the side wall of the store. "This should do it. The clasp must have bent when the necklace snagged on the peg. I replaced the whole fastener."

"Thanks for helping me out. What do I owe you?"

"All our jewelry is warranted for two years. Let me look up the number on the necklace." He referred to the necklace, then turned to his computer. "Yes, Mr. Underhayes bought it less than two months ago. There'll be no charge."

Felix!

Celee looked at me sideways and flushed, seeming suddenly uncomfortable.

"Thank you." She put on the necklace and turned to go.

I blocked her path. "How beautiful! It's perfect for you. Felix had good taste."

Celee backed away from me. Her look clearly said, "*Mind your own business.*"

I persisted. This might be my only chance to find out more

about her relationship, or lack thereof, with Felix. "It's lovely. Was it a special gift?" Had Lorna bought it for her, and put it under Felix's name? But no, Celee had told her cellist friend it had been given to her by "an admirer." I gazed at it, fascinated.

"Really, I don't have time to talk." She donned her coat so I could no longer see the necklace.

I'd pushed as far as I dared. "Well, I'm glad we ran into each other. Nice seeing you."

"Nice seeing you, too." Her tone left me unconvinced.

I found some earrings for Mom while I puzzled over the meeting with Celee. It appeared that Kathleen guessed right. If an "admirer" had given Celee the necklace set, and Felix had purchased it, then she and Felix must have been having an affair. Why else would he buy her such a magnificent necklace? And why would she be uncomfortable talking about it?

BY THE TIME I GOT HOME FOR DINNER, I had to hurry. KC wasn't home, so I heated a frozen dinner in the microwave and wolfed it down. Later than I liked to be, I dragged myself in the stage door reluctantly. *Nutcracker* had become a mechanical exercise, for this series anyway, so when the orchestra tuned, I anxiously waited to get it over with.

But for some reason no one came onstage to give the welcome speech. The audience rustled impatiently. The delay got on my nerves. When Diane Gelbart, President of Friends of the Symphony, finally came out and greeted the audience, I puzzled at the change in plans. Celee had told me not two hours ago that she planned to give the speech. And what about the delay before Diane appeared? What was that about? I devoted my mind to the problem, while my fingers played by rote. Where was Celee?

THIRTY-ONE

SUNDAY, 7:30 A.M., DECEMBER 18, 2011

BETWEEN *THE NUTCRACKER* AND CHARLIE'S WOES, I hadn't had a chance to walk Golden for days. To Golden's relief I'm sure, Ana, Mom, Kathleen, KC, and I planned to meet and walk while we talked. KC had to help early with Sunday brunch at the restaurant, and I wanted her to be part of any discussion. So, we had all agreed to an early start and met on the greenbelt.

"Brrr. A midwinter Colorado morning at 7:30. Do you do this often? If so, you must be crazy." Kathleen buttoned her coat, put on her gloves, and rubbed her arms.

I shrugged.

Deserted by Golden, who took off running down the trail as soon as I let her off the lead, we walked and talked. First, I told them about my encounter with Celee yesterday in the jewelry store.

"So two days ago Celee told the cellist from the orchestra the necklace came from an admirer, and it turns out Felix bought the necklace? And Celee didn't want to talk about it?" Mom tossed her scarf around her neck, then tucked it into her coat. "That seems pretty obvious to me. I bet Lorna, her supposed best friend, doesn't know a thing about it. If she did, why would Celee be reluctant to talk about it? She and Felix snuck around behind Lorna's back, I'm thinking. It's as plain as the knee in your leg."

I ignored the mangled cliché I'd spent a lifetime failing to correct.

With shining eyes Kathleen said, "And the paperwork the store has is concrete proof that Felix bought the jewelry. Hallelujah! We're finally making progress."

"It'll encourage Charlie when I tell him we've finally found some real evidence." Ana smiled.

I agreed. "It definitely makes the theory that Celee killed Felix more believable. Gives her a possible motive."

KC got into the spirit and contributed her theory. "Celee might have killed Felix over a lover's spat." She tucked her long hair into her hood. "Or Felix might have tired of her and dumped her," she added.

"She could have caught him with another woman." Kathleen lifted her knees high as she walked, in an effort to keep warm. "With such a hound-dog, I wouldn't be surprised."

"Or he could have refused to leave his wife." Mom wrapped her scarf more tightly around her neck. "Hell hath no fury like a woman embarrassed."

Kathleen didn't bother to correct Mom's turn of phrase and continued. "If they were having an affair, there could have been any number of reasons for Celee to be furious with Felix. Whatever the reason, she killed him over it." She shrugged. "The relationship gives her motive. The Membership Committee gave her an opportunity to come early. We just have to connect her to a Glock 27 for method. Ana? Did you have any luck with that?"

"Since there's no centralized gun registry, I started with the gun shops in town. It took some doing, since it's confidential information and the means I used weren't strictly legal. There are a lot of stores, and I had to hack into the database of each one. I resigned myself to a long, nearly impossible search. Do you know how many gun shops there are in this town? I started with the shops close to Celee, then radiated outward. Thank goodness, I got lucky. I only had to go through eight of them. There's a place downtown, Gun Market, that lists a sale two years ago to Celee of a Glock 27."

"Ana, you're amazing!"

She blushed. "Well, this is important to me."

"Between Diane's statement, the jewelry store's records of the sale of the necklace, and the gun store's records, we should be able to convince Lieutenant Gordon." I paused to think a moment before I continued. "We still don't know why, specifically, Celee would do it. And we can't reveal our gun sale source. I wonder if Diane's statement and the jewelry store's records are enough to push Lieutenant Gordon to investigate Celee. I'll see what Barry thinks."

We all pursued our own thoughts silently for a moment.

"I keep thinking about Lorna." I felt for her. "She and Celee are friends. Good friends. Best friends. How could Celee kill her best friend's husband?"

Kathleen, Mom, and KC all gave me pitying looks.

"You're so *nice*, Em. Not everyone's as nice as you are."

Glancing at them, I could see that they agreed with KC. "I can see how you might have that opinion, KC. But Mom? And you, Kathleen? Since when are you so cynical?"

"I read." She sounded defensive. "And I watch television." Her tone shifted and she grinned. "Even if we don't know everything, I'm encouraged. We're making progress."

Mom, who walked next to Kathleen, put her arm around her. "That's true. Besides Celee, who's our best suspect, we have four excellent prospects in Jim, Josh, Mark, and Myles. Did you find out anything on the computer, Ana?"

"Nothing interesting came up about Jim. He has those overdue parking tickets, and that's all I found. Myles we already knew about; a recent divorce and he said, she said testimony about an affair naming Felix. Nothing else. But Josh interested me. His wife owns Regan Cosmetics. It's a small but successful local company that makes natural skincare products. Margo Regan started it two years ago as a sideline, and it's doing well; so well she's already getting offers from national companies for big bucks."

"So the Regans have income not only from his symphony job and her job at the bank, which she apparently hasn't given up, but from the cosmetic business. Would that explain their spending levels?"

"Yup. In fact, one designer dress and a nicely decorated townhouse would represent restrained spending in their situation. Other than that, nothing interesting, except a student loan that Josh recently finished paying off."

"That doesn't eliminate Josh, but it explains away money as a major part of his motive. What about Mark?"

She grinned. "I've saved the best for last. Mark threatened a neighbor last year with a gun. Apparently the guy keeps letting his dog mess on Mark's lawn. He threatened to shoot first the dog, then the neighbor. The cops were called, Mark apologized, and the neighbor didn't press charges. Since Mark had a permit, the cops couldn't do anything."

That excited me. "What kind of gun?"

"The article didn't say. Just a short item in the police blotter. No details. I'm checking gun shop records, but like I said, it's slow."

Mom said, "None of that eliminates anybody, but it sure makes Mark sound like a good possibility. And Celee sounds even better. So let's make that three excellent possibilities—Myles, Celee, and Mark—a highly suspicious possibility in Jim, and a maybe in Josh. We'll find the proof we need. It's coming. Somehow. The truth can't hide. Charlie will be home for Christmas."

"And someone who's *not* Charlie will be in jail." Kathleen added.

Their enthusiasm carried me, Ana, and KC along. I whistled for Golden. When she came running, we headed for the car, all walking a little faster, Kathleen's smile as big and bright as a floodlit theatre, and Ana's laugh high and eager.

THAT AFTERNOON MOM, KATHLEEN, AND I visited Charlie at the jail. I'd have to race from there to the *Nutcracker,* so I already wore my performance black. But I had a serious purpose I didn't feel I could entrust to Kathleen. I needed to find out where Charlie had been during and after the murder.

As soon as the guard brought Charlie in and we'd exchanged greetings, I explained. "The phone company gave the police department the report pinging the movements of your phone. Apparently it showed that you remained at Fleisher during the murder. Barry wanted me to get an explanation."

Charlie leaned his elbows on the counter and lowered his head to his hands. "This just gets worse and worse. It's true. I met with Felix at five-thirty. Our talk was tense from the beginning. He complained about my attitude and claimed my 'sloppiness and laziness' presented a problem . . ." Charlie used air quotes, ". . . and then mentioned the incident at the first rehearsal when he didn't conduct enough chimes. I tried to point out his conducting was the problem, but he interrupted me. I yelled to make myself heard. He shouted that I'd just given him another example of my 'insubordination' . . ." Again Charlie used air quotes, ". . . and put me on probation. One thing led to another. Finally, I couldn't take it anymore and threw a punch. He didn't defend himself, just backed away, got on his high horse, and ordered me out of his dressing room. I went gladly, let me tell you. That was about five fifty."

"The so-and-so!" Kathleen's nostrils flared. Mom patted her hand.

"Then what?"

"I had parked in the space right outside the stage door, next to the loading dock and under the overhang. I knew it wasn't smart to drive feeling like I did, so I sat in the car trying to calm down. I pounded the steering wheel a few times and did some deep breathing 'til I felt calm enough. It wasn't long. I left, I'd say around six."

"Can anyone else confirm that?"

"Josh Regan arrived just after I slipped into the car. He parked kitty corner across from Fleisher, in front of the junkyard. He got out and stood by his car for a while. It's unlikely he saw me. Two sides of the loading dock wall hid my car, and I had parked nose in, covered by the overhang. I have tinted windows, too. I didn't say 'hello' to him because I didn't feel like talking."

Kathleen's head jerked up and her eyes met mine.

"What? You're sure about Josh? Why didn't you tell us earlier?" I couldn't believe it.

"I didn't think of it." He sounded sheepish. "I guess that sounds crazy, but everybody asked about the murder and the dressing room. Why were my fingerprints in Felix's dressing room? Why did we argue? Why did I hit him? What was our relationship like? You're the only one that's asked what happened after I left Felix's dressing room. And anyway, I don't think Josh would have seen me."

"But he might be able to confirm your movements?"

Mom looked from me to Kathleen and back silently and smiled. Big.

"Yeah, *if* he saw me. I noticed him because he has a classic Corvette. Beautiful! I figured he had come for his appointment with Felix. Remember? Felix ordered Josh and Mark to meet with him. I remember thinking, right before I took off: *Good luck!* I got hung up at the light at the end of the block, and in the rearview mirror I saw you arrive and Josh take off right after that. He pulled up at the light behind me, but it had changed to green, and we turned in opposite directions."

"You didn't see Mark?"

"Nope."

"Did you see anything else?"

Charlie frowned and his eyes rolled up and to the left. "Not that I remember."

Besides telling me why his phone had pinged at Fleisher Hall at the time of the murder, Charlie had unknowingly corroborated Josh's story and removed him as a suspect. As for Josh's conspicuous spending, Ana had found the answer in her computer, and Charlie had provided him with an alibi. It was none of my business now.

But the big news was that Josh might have seen Charlie outside when the shot went off. It could clear Charlie. *If* Josh had seen my nephew, he could prove Charlie couldn't have killed Felix. I held my breath and released it slowly. Why hadn't Josh come forward when Charlie was arrested? Maybe he really hadn't seen Charlie, or didn't know Charlie had been in the car. "Okay. I'll let Barry know. If he has any questions, he may contact you again. Sorry I can't stay. I've got to get to the performance."

"I understand, Auntie Em. Break a leg."

I would have liked to stay and provide encouragement to both Charlie and Kathleen, but the *Nutcracker* awaited.

WHEN I GOT TO THE MATINEE, everybody milled around backstage, talking.

"Have you heard?" Alice Smithson, cellist and my grapevine connection asked. Her eyes sparkled. She loved spreading scandal, so her obvious excitement couldn't be good news for somebody. "It's Celee."

The news must be big. Had the connection between her and Felix been traced?

I moved discreetly closer to Alice. "What about her?"

Alice moved nearer so she wouldn't have to shout. "They found her body in her car after yesterday's performance."

Dead? First Felix, and now Celee? And Celee Felix's apparent mistress? Just this morning we'd convinced ourselves Celee murdered Felix. There had to be a connection.

Alice went on. "Shot dead as a *Nutcracker* mouse. They're saying the killer must have used a silencer in the closed car. Otherwise, someone would have heard."

I saw Lt. Gordon out of the corner of my eye.

"Thanks for telling me, Alice. I'm sorry to run off, but I need to warm up. Unless they're delaying the show?" I knew the powers that be would never do that.

Alice understood. "No. We'd better go, or we'll be late."

I glanced at my watch and saw I had fifteen minutes before the performance started. "Okay. See you." I did my best to lose myself in the crowd of musicians, while moving toward Lt. Gordon. I had to tell him about meeting Celee in the jewelry store.

"Lieutenant Gordon?"

"Ms. Wilson."

"I have some information that I think might be helpful with Celee's murder investigation, but right now I need to get ready to play."

"Apparently everybody here has the same problem. When can we talk?"

"I can meet you right here. As soon after the performance as I can get here."

"Okay. Don't hurry. I have several people to talk to."

"I've got to run." I hurried down the stairs to the pit, dialing KC as I went. She didn't answer, but I left a message. "Tell Steve the you-know-what is about to hit the fan. Celee was murdered last night." I arrived in the pit with only ten minutes to spare, but at least Lt. Gordon would have my information. KC's boyfriend, the symphony spin doctor, Steve, would have as much warning as I could give him, too.

THIRTY-TWO

SUNDAY, 5:30 P.M., DECEMBER 18, 2011

BETWEEN RUSHING TO THE PIT LATE and having little time to warm up, I felt off-kilter the whole performance. Fortunately, I could have played the *Nutcracker* in my sleep. When the performance ended, relieved, I put the flute away, packed it and my purse into my satchel, retrieved my coat from the green room, and ran up the stairs to meet Lt. Gordon.

He had settled in the security break room, if you could call an area surrounded by knee-high brick walls a room. It provided a view of the door, twelve feet or so away, and contained a long table, several chairs, and a vending machine. Ordinarily, the security guard could relax a bit there, and still see who came and went. But since Lt. Gordon had commandeered the break room, Bernie, the afternoon's security guard, was relegated to the security desk, closest to the stage door. Across the empty space of the lobby, the security lounge gave Lt. Gordon privacy for his interviews, as long as they were conducted at a reasonable volume.

I waited quite a while as he talked with one person, then another. Eventually the crowd around him dispersed and I slung my satchel and coat onto the table in front of him, then sat across from him.

He got right to the point in the manner of a man on a mission. "Now what's this information you have?"

I didn't delay, either. "Yesterday, I ran into Celee between shows in a jewelry store. I had gone to Kokopelli's Jewelry looking for a Christmas present for my mom. Celee was there getting a necklace repaired. We had a short conversation. She mentioned she planned on giving the welcome speech to the audience."

"That's helpful. When was this?"

I wasn't sure, and thought out loud. "I had time to make my purchases, go home, eat dinner, and make it back for the eight o'clock show. I like to arrive around seven-thirty but I was a little later than that, maybe seven-forty. So, it must have been around five-thirty when I saw Celee."

He scribbled on the pad in front of him.

"Anything else?"

I leaned forward. "I overheard the salesclerk say Felix had bought Celee's jewelry. And I'm telling you, a necklace that pricey isn't something you buy for someone who's just a friend."

My juicy information didn't even raise Lt. Gordon's eyebrows. Had he missed the point? Or did he already know?

He watched me as he thought. This was the first time I had been this close to him, and I noticed his hands were huge and the fingers long. He would have made a good pianist or bassoonist, or maybe bass player or cellist. But his scrutiny made me nervous, so I fiddled with the satchel's strap in front of me.

After a silence that seemed long, he asked, "Did you see Celee again before the show?"

"No, and I thought it strange when she didn't give the welcome speech."

"So far, Ms. Wilson, you're the last person to see her alive."

Uh, oh. "Why are you always trying to blame me?"

He arched an eyebrow. "The better question is, why are you so defensive? I'm just doing my job, trying to collect the facts."

Considering he'd put out an APB on me following my friend Olive's murder last year, and now arrested my innocent nephew, I didn't think "defensive" applied, but I considered his words. Truly, there had been strong evidence against me last year, and currently, against Charlie. I willingly believed he intended to do his job. But the lieutenant wasn't taking into consideration the nature and personality of his suspects. I supposed that was natural to an evidence-based mind. Maybe we could help each other. I thought rapidly, continuing to play with my satchel strap.

"So that puts the time of death between five-thirty and eight." He sat silently for what seemed a long time.

I tried tactfully to plant a seed in Lt. Gordon's brain. "Do you think the murders of Felix and Celee are connected?"

"Nope. We'd already arrested your nephew when Ms. O'Connor was killed."

"What if you arrested the wrong person? Felix and Celee were lovers according to the grapevine, and I confirmed that by finding Felix purchased Celee's necklace. If they were lovers, that would certainly give Lorna a motive, and maybe Celee, too, if they'd had a lover's quarrel. And Diane Gelbart says she, Celee, and Lorna split up shortly before Felix's murder, giving any of them the opportunity to kill Felix."

"Look, Ms. Wilson. I know you hope to prove your nephew's innocence, and I know you'd like to convince me somebody else is guilty of Mr. Underhayes' murder, but I have to consider the evidence. Your nephew had a contentious working relationship and quarreled with Mr. Underhayes. They were overheard. Your nephew had a pageful of conductor literature which shows his contempt on his Facebook page. Then Mr. Underhayes put your nephew on probation, and they quarreled again, ending in a fist-fight. That was also overheard. Mr. Underhayes' DNA ended up on your nephew's ring. *And* the phone company pinged your nephew's phone, and presumably your nephew, as present at Fleisher Hall at the time of the murder. Those are the facts. Wishful thinking won't alter them."

All that did sound damning. "So you won't change your mind?"

"Only if the evidence backs you up. If, for instance, the bullet in Mr. Underhayes came from the same gun as the bullet in Ms. O'Connor. That would be solid evidence. Your nephew couldn't have committed Ms. O'Connor's murder. He sat in jail, in our custody."

"What if somebody saw Charlie outside Fleisher when the shot was fired?"

"That would be hard evidence. Unfortunately, no one has come forward with that information. Unless you've heard differently?"

I considered telling him about Josh, but wasn't sure what either Barry or Josh would say. "No. But there must be somebody. Charlie says he was sitting in his car at the time of the murder." I thought a minute. "Do you have the results of tests on the bullets?"

"Nope. The coroner hasn't done Ms. O'Connor's autopsy yet."

"Do you have the murder weapon in either Felix's or Celee's murder?"

"Not yet." Lt. Gordon's voice had risen, and, to avoid offense, I decided to go in a different direction. After a decent (or indecent, depending on your point of view) interval, I changed the subject and asked about Myles. "I understand Myles Lewis was a disgruntled employee whose wife had been seduced by Felix. Good motive."

"Yeah. But again, I have to go by the facts. No one has reported seeing him near Fleisher, and signed receipts prove he bought car parts across town at the time of the murder."

News to me. Okay, scratch Myles.

"And Charlie's insistence on his innocence has no weight." It wasn't a question.

"Miz Wilson, murderers always lie."

After an uncomfortable silence, blushing, Gordon changed the subject. He looked around the lobby. It held no one except for Bernie, sitting across the room at the security desk reading a book. Even though the lieutenant was already speaking in a soft voice, he lowered his voice still further and asked, "Is your sister still visiting?"

I didn't know how things stood between him and Kathleen. She seemed to be interested in him, but she also wouldn't consider seeing him until he recognized Charlie's innocence. Would she get mad at me if I discussed her and her affairs? I wasn't sure. I responded carefully, "Yes."

"For how long?"

I didn't want to discuss her plans, but I didn't see any way to avoid his direct question. "At least until Christmas or until Charlie is released. Whichever comes last."

He nodded gravely and, to my relief, asked no further questions.

Continuing my thoughts from a moment ago, I found it difficult to believe, as the lieutenant did, that Celee had been Felix's mistress, they were both killed, but the murders were unconnected. Lorna, Felix's widow, it seemed to me, would be a logical suspect in both killings. By murdering Felix, she ended the affair, avoided the messiness of a divorce, and collected both condolences and insurance as the tearful widow. By killing Celee, she got her revenge. Sounded like a perfect plan to me if she wasn't caught. But Lt. Gordon hadn't come to the same conclusion. He didn't have the incentive of *wanting* to find Charlie innocent, or of being willing to consider that a mistake had been made. Well, I guess I really couldn't blame him for that. From his perspective, the pinging from the phone company appeared particularly damning. I had to talk to Barry and to Josh, and soon.

"Well, thanks for the info, Miz Wilson."

I remembered the way Kathleen had flirted with him. I couldn't blame her for responding to a good-looking man. It wouldn't hurt to be on better terms with him, so, for the sake of world peace and peace in my little corner of the world, I made a stab at cordiality. Putting aside my disappointment that he didn't see things my way I said, "You can call me Emily, you know. We're not really strangers anymore."

He paused and his eyes traveled from mine to the table's edge and back. "It's generally not a good idea to get too familiar with informants . . . or suspects."

My good intentions vanished. "Your choice. I just thought it would be friendlier."

"Nothing personal."

I made an excuse. "I'd better be getting back to my dog. She needs to eat. And I need to let her out."

"No problem."

We both stood.

"Thanks again, Miz Wilson." He shook my hand. "Safe travels."

THIRTY-THREE

SUNDAY, 8:30 P.M., DECEMBER 18, 2011

WHEN I FINALLY GOT HOME, Golden greeted me with wild enthusiasm, leaping and pawing and bringing me her bear. I got on the floor with her and threw it.

KC came into the entry hall. "Em, thank goodness you're here!" She had called her boyfriend Steve, the symphony's PR man, and delivered my message hours ago.

I stood and stowed my flute satchel in the studio closet. "What did Steve say about Celee's murder?"

"He said the president of the Symphony Board had already told him, but he asked me to thank you for thinking of him. He'd described Celee as a 'family friend,' and hoped no one picked up on the idea of Celee as Felix's mistress. Fat chance. People have dirty minds."

She smiled a Mona Lisa smile that made me think that wasn't all they had said to each other. "I figured you'd want Kathleen and your mom to know about Celee, too, so I called them. They came over to wait for you so they could get a full report, but then you didn't show up after the ballet." She looked a little embarrassed. "We got hungry and ate without you. I have leftovers."

"Don't worry about it. Leftovers will be fine."

Entering from the living room, Mom asked, "Where have you been?" Apparently the question came naturally to her. After all, she had raised me and survived my teenage years.

"I waited for Lieutenant Gordon. He was busy with other people, and I wanted to tell him about my encounter with Celee in the jewelry store. I thought it'd help both Lieutenant Gordon and Charlie."

Mom scowled. "Well, you might have called. We saved you food."

Kathleen, who had followed Mom in, asked, "How could you help them both?"

I sighed. "It's a long story. I'm not sure my efforts to help did anybody any good." As an afterthought I added, "Lieutenant Gordon asked about you."

Kathleen blushed. "He did?"

"He wanted to know how long you'd be in town. I told him I didn't know. At least 'til Christmas." I paused. "Mostly, though, we talked about the murders."

Mom nodded. "Let's go into the kitchen and have some tea. You can tell us all about it."

KC got the leftovers out of the fridge. Mom and Kathleen sat at the table while I put water on to boil and placed a teabag in four mugs, talking as I worked. "The police found Celee's body in her car after the performance on Saturday."

Mom said, "Your message to KC said as much."

Kathleen first thought of her son. "So that means Charlie's off the hook, right?"

Distracted from my point, I didn't follow Kathleen's reasoning. "How do you figure?" I sat down while I waited for the water to boil.

She gave me a "that's obvious" look. "He's in jail. He couldn't have killed her."

I didn't understand. "Yeah? So? How does that prove Charlie's innocence in *Felix's* murder?"

Kathleen abruptly sat down beside me and leaned over. She put her hand on my arm, and spoke patiently and slowly, as if to a small child. "First Felix is murdered, then his mistress. The same person must have killed both people, and it must have been Lorna."

I'd had the same thought, but there were loads of loose ends and unsupported conclusions. Besides, that would require Lorna to shoot Felix and come back minutes later to feign a faint. I suppose she could have done it but, most importantly, Lt. Gordon wouldn't consider the possibility. So far, Lorna might have a motive for both murders, had access to a Glock 27, and had been at Fleisher both before and after Felix's murder, so she had opportunity, if a slim, split-second one. But we knew nothing about Celee's murder.

Mom said, "Is the pope Christian?"

Mom's way of saying she and Kathleen agreed.

I smiled. "I admit it's a good possibility. Unfortunately, Lieutenant Gordon isn't convinced."

KC spoke up. "Lorna would have a good motive for killing both people. Both of them were betraying her, and in a pretty awful way."

"Divorce would have been a simpler option. What can we find in the way of evidence?"

Hearing the teapot whistle, I went to the stove. Pouring water over the teabags in all the mugs, I brought Kathleen and KC their tea, then got my own and Mom's, and sat down while KC brought over the leftovers: meatloaf and mashed potatoes—comfort food. Yum!

KC sat and stirred sugar into her mug. "What was Lorna doing last night during the murder? If she and Celee are always together, she must know something."

Slowly I said, "Before the show, when I met Celee at the jewelry store, she told me she planned on giving the welcome speech. She wasn't with Lorna then. After all, they aren't tied at the hip. Celee never showed at last night's concert. Diane, president of Friends of the Symphony, delivered the audience welcome. Celee must have already been dead at the start of the performance."

Kathleen said, "For sure."

I continued my recollections of last night. "I don't remember seeing Lorna." I paused to sip my tea. "It's possible I just didn't see her, or they weren't together. Or she could have murdered Celee and then disappeared."

Mom interrupted to ask, "Where are those cookies"

"In the cupboard above the plates."

She brought them to the table. "You left Celee at the jewelry store, around, when?"

"No later than six. Probably around five-thirty."

"Okay, between five-thirty and the time she was scheduled to give the speech, at eight, somebody killed her."

That returned me to the original topic. "Yeah, that's why I told Lieutenant Gordon I bumped into Celee and shared what I learned. I wanted to make sure he knew that Felix had bought Celee an expensive necklace, which suggests a motive for Lorna to be involved in both Celee's and Felix's murder. Lorna could have found out about the purchase from the paperwork—credit card bills, warranties, receipts—who knows? She would have been furious at Felix. And she would have seen Celee's new necklace. Then the fact that Celee was alive as late as 5:30 but didn't show for the speech helps fix her time of death. I hoped to help both Charlie and Lieutenant Gordon at the same time."

Kathleen rose and began to pace. "Despite what the lieutenant says, it's only a matter of time 'til Charlie is released. Did you tell him about Josh?"

"No. I want to talk to both Barry and Josh first."

KC put down her mug. "What's this about Josh?"

I'd forgotten KC hadn't heard Charlie's revelation. "Josh might have seen Charlie outside Fleisher during the murder. Charlie saw Josh."

"Can we call Josh right now?" Kathleen urged me.

I glanced at my watch. Nine-fifteen. I didn't want to offend him by calling too late. "It's past nine. Let's wait 'til tomorrow."

Kathleen stopped at the back of my chair and hugged me from behind. "Okay. Thanks, Emily. I feel like we're making progress now. We couldn't have done it without you."

I allowed myself to be cautiously optimistic.

"Now that Emily's home safe and sound, let's go back to the hotel. I'm exhausted." Kathleen did look tired, and I would welcome bed myself.

I saw them to their car and breathed a sigh of relief, then slowly returned to the house.

KC hugged me. "I'm glad you're okay. You've had a long day. I'll take care of Golden while you get ready for bed."

"Thanks, KC. I don't know what I'd do without you." Before I could go to bed, though, I knew I'd better call Ana and update her. Knowing Celee was dead might affect her computer searches. Besides, she had a huge stake in the investigation, and this changed everything.

THIRTY-FOUR

MONDAY, 9:00 A.M., DECEMBER 19, 2011

KATHLEEN AND MOM JOINED KC AND ME. We had all planned breakfast together. They'd just arrived when the landline rang. I answered the phone hanging on the wall of the breakfast nook.

"Emily..." Thick and unrecognizable, I couldn't identify the voice.

"Who is this?"

"It's . . . it's Lorna," she wailed.

She had never called me and must have gotten my number from the orchestra roster. "Lorna? What's wrong? I can't understand you."

"You've got to help me. I don't know what to do."

I had no clue what she had called about, so I waited for her to go on.

After a short time, less than a minute, although it seemed much longer, she said, "According to my lawyer . . . the one who did my will . . . he's the only lawyer I know . . . we're supposed to meet Lieutenant Gordon here. He's coming to question me." She took a deep breath and continued in a wobbly voice. "Emily, he wants to talk to me as a person of interest in Celee's murder . . . " a sob ". . . and I can't prove I didn't kill her."

"I'm sorry, Lorna. I know that's worrisome." Not very comforting, but what could I say?

"I thought of you. I know you proved your innocence last year . . ." She took a breath and continued in a steadier voice. "Mom has been staying with the kids since Felix's funeral so I can have some time to myself. I was home alone when Celee . . . when she . . ." She gasped and didn't finish her sentence. "I don't think even my lawyer believes me. He keeps asking how I can prove it." She continued between pauses and unclear words. "The police told him they think the murder weapon must be Felix's gun. According to the paperwork they found, he had a Glock 27, but they couldn't find the gun itself."

This was the same caliber as the gun that killed Felix; more support for our theory that Lorna killed both victims.

I heard her take a breath and hold it. When she went on, she had more control. "Felix had it to protect himself. I didn't kill anyone. I don't even know how to use a gun. Celee had her own weapon . . ."

Confirmation that Celee had a gun and knew how to use it. It made the possibility that she'd killed Felix before she was killed herself more believable. I'd use Lorna's information as proof of Celee's gun ownership. Ana's sleuthing could remain confidential.

". . . and both she and Felix told me I should learn how to shoot, but I never did. The whole idea of guns upset me . . . one person killing another . . . Felix said a public figure needed to be prepared if any audience members ever became deranged and came after him . . . I *told* him that wouldn't happen, but . . ."

I heard snuffling and Lorna blowing her nose. "How could I murder Celee? I knew about her affair with Felix. I don't understand how she could want him, but she could have him for all I cared. I fell out of love with him long ago." More snuffling, then she said in a steadier voice, "Seeing her kept him away from home, and I couldn't have been happier. Our home life embarrassed me. Insults. Demands. And in front of the kids. He treated me like his servant." Anger strengthened her further and she said, "He hit me, too. I can't remember why I ever loved him. I used to wish he'd die. And then he did." She began crying softly.

I felt like I'd dropped into another world. In just a few days, two wives had confided to me that they'd been abused by their husbands. And my ex-husband had been violent, too. Exactly how common was it? More importantly, Lorna had a different motive than I thought to murder Felix.

"Lorna, I'm not your lawyer and I'm not giving you advice, but you shouldn't say that in front of Lieutenant Gordon."

Through her tears, she went on as if she hadn't heard me. "Felix Junior is only nine, and he's already beginning to treat me like his dad did. He even threw a punch at me the other day. It's awful."

She stopped crying and her voice picked up speed and emphasis. "But I adored Celee. She laughed with me, cried with me, spent Christmas with me and the kids, listened to me vent, kept me company, shopped with me, even went to my father's funeral when Felix wouldn't go last year. I couldn't kill Celee. I don't know what I'm going to do. My kids have already lost one parent. They can't lose me, too."

What a different way of looking at things. I didn't know Lorna well. She had seemed like a grieving widow at the funeral, but she could have reacted with shock when her wishes came true and Felix died.

I had told Lt. Gordon about Felix giving Celee the jewelry set. KC, Mom, Kathleen, and I had concluded the facts made Lorna a good suspect for Felix's murder. For Celee's murder, too, we thought. Now Lorna claimed she hadn't killed Celee, but she told me she had access to a gun the same caliber as the one that killed Felix, and said that she wished he would die. It looked bad for her one way or another. But I knew how lonely and frightening being the object of suspicions, especially the cops', could be. I tried to be as sympathetic as I could.

"Are the kids okay? Do you have someone to take care of them?"

"Thank goodness they're still at Mom's, and they can stay as long as they need to."

I couldn't figure out why she had called me. "What do you think I can do, Lorna?"

"I know you did your own investigating. Can you help me, too?"

What was I? The Google search answer to "amateur murder investigators in Monroe, Colorado?" I didn't want to get involved, especially if she *was* guilty. On the other hand, despite my earlier speculations, maybe Lorna had told the truth and she hadn't killed Celee. "I'll keep my eyes and ears open, but I'm not sure I can help."

"Oh, Emily! That makes all the difference. I feel so much better. At least someone's on my side."

I didn't know that I believed her or supported her, but if it made her feel better to think so, I wouldn't argue. "Do you want the name of the attorney who represented me when Lt. Gordon suspected me of murder?"

"That might help. My lawyer works with finances and wills. He's not a . . ." Lorna's inhale quivered. She paused and I thought she might be crying. Finally she said, "He's not a criminal defense attorney."

Another client for Barry. Maybe he'd put me on the payroll. I gave her his number. By now I had it memorized.

I heard the doorbell ring on her end.

Lorna said, "That's either Lieutenant Gordon or my lawyer. With my luck, the lieutenant got here first. I've got to answer it. This is a nightmare!"

As I hung up, I realized Mom, KC, and Kathleen were all watching me intensely.

"That was Lorna."

Kathleen huffed impatiently. "We know that. What did she say?"

"She says she didn't kill Celee."

"A likely story." She tsked.

THIRTY-FIVE

MONDAY, 9:20 A.M., DECEMBER 19, 2011

I STARTED SETTING THE TABLE FOR BREAKFAST, gathering plates, silverware and teacups. "I don't know, Kathleen. She sounded pretty sincere."

"Whose side are you on?" Kathleen, who pulled muffins from the breadbox, sounded upset. "Who else has a motive to murder both Felix and Celee?" She put the rolls into a bowl with what I thought was unnecessary force.

"I don't know." If Lorna wasn't guilty we would have to start all over. No wonder Kathleen didn't like to consider the possibility. I didn't either. "But things aren't always what they seem, and I don't want to jump to conclusions the way everybody did with Charlie. And with me."

That got through to Kathleen. "Sorry. But Lorna seems to have such an obvious motive. And I'm so sure Charlie wouldn't have murdered Felix."

Mom, who had gotten eggs from the fridge and started breaking them into a bowl for scrambled eggs, stopped what she was doing, crossed the kitchen and put her arm around Kathleen. "We all are."

I tried to sound encouraging. "We'd better keep trying to find out who really killed Felix. It might have been Lorna. She could have lied to me. And if she wasn't lying, we'll find the real killer."

Mom went back to the eggs.

Kathleen said, "The important thing is to prove Charlie's innocence." She drummed her nails on the table. "How about if you talk to Josh now?"

"I'll call him right away."

Kathleen, who had put the muffin bowl on the table, started pacing.

Silently hoping Josh would talk to me when I had no good excuse for asking questions, I punched in his number. "Hi, Josh. This is Emily Wilson."

I could tell from his "Yes?" that he wasn't thrilled to hear from me.

"I'm still trying to figure out what happened the evening of Felix's murder, and I wondered if you'd thought of anything else you might have seen, since you were positioned kitty corner from the door."

"I've told you everything I saw. I've told the police everything I saw. What more do you want from me?"

"Charlie says he sat in his car diagonally across the street from you, and that he left right before the murder."

"Sorry, Emily. I occupied myself looking for Mark. I didn't know what kind of car he drove, so I wanted to be alert to any vehicle that pulled up. Not only did he not show, there was no other action on the street, other than when you arrived."

"You don't remember seeing a sedan parked across the way?"

"I vaguely remember a car—black? Or gray? Tinted windows. Nothing unusual about it. Parked front bumper against one side of the building, passenger door along another side, under the overhang, completely sheltered. I didn't see anything but the outline of a head occasionally popping out from behind the headrest. I wasn't particularly interested, and I was preoccupied. Between looking for Mark and hustling to leave, I didn't notice much. I *do* know that when I left, the other car was just ahead of me."

I felt excited. "Okay. Even that little bit is helpful. Thanks for talking to me."

"I don't mind talking to you. I just can't be of any more help."

"It's okay. See you at *Nutcracker.*"

I smiled in response to Kathleen's quizzical look. "Josh vaguely remembers a black or gray car across the street, and Charlie has a gray Nissan Sentra. Josh couldn't see the occupant of the car. but he does remember it left just before him."

"So he sort of supports Charlie's story. That's good. Right?" Kathleen stopped pacing and bit her cheek. "Right?"

I reassured her "That's very good. I'll tell Lieutenant Gordon about it. It should make a difference."

"Call him right now."

"Sure." I called his office but had to leave a message. "I have some new information I wanted to give you. Can we meet?" I called his cell phone, too, and left the same message.

"Why didn't you leave the deets for him?" Kathleen seemed dismayed.

"I want to see him in person so I can see his face and get a read on whether or not he gives Josh's statement any weight."

Kathleen scowled.

KC put the butter plate and knife on the table and said, "Seems to me we still need to find out more specific information about Celee and Lorna, and their movements the evening of Felix's murder. As alternative suspects to Charlie for Lieutenant Gordon. You know?"

"Kathleen?

Mom? Any ideas?"

Mom had finished cooking the scrambled eggs, and we sat down to eat.

"I'll have to think." Kathleen sounded hesitant. "We already know Celee, Lorna, and Diane separated before Felix's murder, thanks to Diane's account. Since Celee didn't come to the dressing room with Lorna after the shot, either Celee or Lorna would have an opportunity to shoot Felix. But now Celee's dead. So, unless Celee shot Felix, and then Lorna shot Celee, Lorna must have committed both murders, in spite of her denials." She sounded frustrated and blew her bangs away from her eyes, then slouched deeper into her chair. "But the lieutenant won't accept that. There must be other possibilities."

At the risk of discouraging her further, I said, "I also told Lieutenant Gordon about Myles and his certainty that Felix ended his marriage. He said Myles's alibi checks out."

Kathleen huffed. "All I know is Charlie didn't do it. What about Mark and Jim? They've both admitted they were at Fleisher."

"That's true. That gives them opportunity. I heard Felix embarrass Mark in front of the orchestra, too, so that could be a motive, although it seems pretty weak to me. *And* Mark has a gun, which we know thanks to Ana's computer work. Assuming the motive's strong enough, it could have been Mark, but Lieutenant Gordon doesn't buy it. He's fixed on Charlie. Charlie alibied Josh, but we know nothing about Jim's movements." I pushed back from the table, frustrated, too.

Mom stepped in to buck up our spirits. "What's important is that, even if Myles's alibi checked out, whatever Lieutenant Gordon says, Felix's affairs are a credible motive for the first murder, whether with Celee or with somebody from the grapevine's rumor mill." She paused. "But why should anyone have a reason to kill Celee unless they found out about the affair and exploded with rage? Maybe the two murders were coincidence and entirely unconnected, but I find that hard to believe."

We all looked at each other. I think I spoke for everybody. "You're right. There's got to be a connection."

KC buttered her muffin.. "Lorna is the most obvious link I can think of. There might be others, though. A cuckolded boyfriend or husband, a jilted girlfriend. Anyway, I think the connection piece is important. We're on the right track, you know?"

Kathleen sat up straighter.

For her sake, and Charlie's, I hoped KC was right. I worried.

THIRTY-SIX

TUESDAY, 8:00 A.M., DECEMBER 20, 2011

Lt. Gordon had checked Myles's alibi and eliminated him as a suspect. Although Charlie had vouched for Josh and I would give the lieutenant that information at the meeting we'd arranged on Friday, Josh didn't have a firm confirmation of Charlie's story. Mark didn't seem to have much motive, unless you were willing to believe he would kill over a disagreement about bowings, in which case Josh had better watch his back. Wouldn't it make more sense for Mark to kill him, rather than Felix? Only Mark and Celee had so far been confirmed to have guns, and, although the caliber of Mark's was a mystery, Celee's was the right caliber. But Celee had been killed. Lorna, as the betrayed and abused wife who had access to a gun of the right caliber, appeared to me to be a good suspect. But Lt. Gordon didn't believe she'd killed Felix and she claimed she hadn't killed either Felix or Celee. Jim was so hostile he wouldn't talk to us, and Ana hadn't found any information about him on the computer. As a result, I didn't know much about him. Unless Josh's tentative confirmation of Charlie's presence outside Fleisher during the murder proved his innocence for Lt. Gordon, Jim appeared to be our last hope, so I fretted about how I could get more facts.

Brainstorming, it occurred to me that my friend, Cal Nelson, as manager of Fleisher Hall and Jim's boss, might know something.

I texted him requesting a meeting. I knew normally there were no gaps in his schedule, but he responded, "Cancellation today. Lunch? Sandwich Smorgasbord, one." I didn't have a student until three, so I confirmed and arrived at the same time he did.

Cal's wife, Melanie, was my insurance agent. I had met Cal when I dropped some papers off for Melanie after hours at their condo. Since then, Cal and I had seen each other often at various symphony functions and he'd always greeted me heartily.

"Emily! Long time, no see. What you been up to?" Cal was a blond, blue-eyed giant who displayed the same enthusiasm for everybody. A friendly puppy, if the puppy was a Great Dane.

"Hey, Cal. Let's get our sandwiches and I'll tell you about it."

He pushed open the door.

Sandwich Smorgasbord was sunny at that time of day, with a long counter on the right, behind which various employees added ingredients you chose as you moved down the line, ending with the cashier, who totaled your purchase. The seating area was on the left, with tables lining the windows and wall, and a few tables in the middle. The lunch rush almost over, a small white table in a corner by the window opened up. I claimed it.

"How's Melanie?" I hadn't seen her for a while.

"Busy. The mayor appointed her to the Task Force on Financial Security for Single Women and Children, and that takes up a lot of her time. It's only for a year, though, so I'm looking forward to seeing her in July. It's on my calendar."

We laughed.

"What about you? Your text sounded urgent."

"It is. Thanks for making time for me." I hesitated only briefly before I decided how to proceed. "You've heard Charlie McRae's been arrested for Felix Underhayes' murder?"

"Sure. It's been all over the news."

"Well, Charlie's my nephew, and I don't think he killed Felix."

"Hoo, boy." He twirled his pretend mustache and tapped his pretend cigar. "That's a fine kettle of fish."

I wouldn't have thought it possible to be amused about the subject, but I laughed. "The police have all kinds of circumstantial evidence, which doesn't look good, but they haven't found the gun, yet. Charlie doesn't know or like guns. The police won't be able to connect him with any kind of firearm, let alone the murder weapon."

"Okay, so how can I help?"

"I've been looking into things. One of the names that keeps coming up is Jim Plank. By his own admission he was at Fleisher, but he seems to have disappeared shortly before the shooting. He might have a motive, because he didn't seem to like Felix, but I haven't been able to find out anything."

"Did anybody like Felix?"

"Not unless you count the people at the funeral." Cal had been there and heard the kind eulogies.

He chuckled. "Yeah. I don't know where they came from."

I waited but he didn't say anything else.

"Anyway, I wondered if you could shed any light on Jim's whereabouts at the time of the murder. I know you were around that day, because I saw you talking to Lt. Gordon after the murder and you let us use your office when I gave my statement."

Cal's large ears turned red. "You have to promise not to pass this around."

"As long as it doesn't affect Charlie's innocence or somebody else's guilt, I promise."

"Okay. You have to understand; all the employees at the Hall have jobs that are cyclical. In the ticket booth there's a rush before performances, but otherwise the phone and the walk-ins are pretty quiet. A lot of people make purchases on-line these days. I give tours to people who want to rent the hall or city dignitaries who want details on the facilities, and I also handle hiring and any employment problems that might come up, but there are times I'm free. The stagehands, too, are needed when they're needed, but there's a lot of down time."

Rubbing the back of his neck, Cal continued. "So, we have a poker game when we can. Low stakes. Just to pass the time. Felix found out about it. Came into the office blustering about 'employee gambling' and threatening to talk to the Board. It's not illegal and not even disapproved, as long as we do our jobs, and do them well, and don't get anybody into financial trouble. But Felix had to be his usual insufferable self."

"What about the evening of the shooting?"

"Jim had unlocked the door for Charlie and Felix, and he and I were playing poker with two people from the box office when we heard the shot."

There went my last, best suspect. Jim hadn't fired the shot, but it was no wonder he had been evasive about his whereabouts during the murder.

"Everybody knew a shot had been fired. I ran toward the sound. Jim ran the other way, I assume outside. I didn't see him again that day."

"So you were with him up until the shot."

"Yeah, but I don't want to advertise the poker game or the participants. I'll tell the cops if they ask."

"Well, I guess that leaves Jim in the clear, then."

We discussed this season's *Nutcracker* challenges, speculated on a new conductor, and talked about next season, which had already been planned.

"Good to see you, Emily. I'm sorry to eat and run, but I have a two o'clock, and I have to get back."

"Good to see you, too. Say 'hi' to Melanie for me. And thanks for working me into your schedule." I tried to sound upbeat, but he had blown a hole in all my hopes. I needed to name Felix's murderer to convince Lt. Gordon to release Charlie. I considered. The killer wasn't Jim. Probably wasn't Mark, either, since he had no reason to want to kill Celee, as far as I could tell. Lt. Gordon had checked out Myles's alibi, and cleared him. The lieutenant refused to consider Lorna as the perpetrator of Felix's murder. Who else was there? So far, our only accomplishment had been to discover who *didn't* commit the crime.

I WAS TEACHING WHEN KATHLEEN AND MOM arrived late in the afternoon after their daily visit to Charlie. They started dinner and by the time I'd finished, a scrumptious vegan soup and pasta salad awaited. We hadn't even sat down to dinner before Kathleen asked when Lt. Gordon and I would meet about Josh's evidence.

I told her we'd set up a meeting for Friday.

"You're kidding." She looked as if she might cry. "That's a long time to wait."

Two and a half days. I understood that she wanted Charlie released immediately, if not sooner. But, "That's the soonest he had a break in his schedule. It'll be worth the wait. You'll see."

"I don't see why you couldn't talk to him over the phone."

"I told you, Kathleen, I want to see his face. Josh's evidence is so vague, I want know if Lieutenant Gordon takes the information seriously."

She huffed her response.

To distract her, I described my meeting with Cal. "So Jim and Josh are in the clear, and only Mark is left. What do you think?"

Kathleen crossed her arms and leaned on the table. "I think if he's all that's left, he must have done it."

"Okay. I'll keep working on finding a motive." I tried to sound hopeful, but inwardly I thought the prospects looked dim. "How is Charlie doing?"

Mom and Kathleen exchanged a glance.

Kathleen answered, "It's awful! He tries to keep up appearances, but I can tell. There are dark circles under his eyes, he's losing weight, and he looks pale. He's trying so hard to be cheerful for me and Mom, so I don't feel like I can let down, either. But I just want to take him in my arms and rock him."

Mom sat beside her and put her arm around Kathleen's shoulders. "Don't worry. When Lieutenant Gordon finds out about Josh's evidence, it'll all be over. The truth will come out."

"In two and a half days." I didn't know if Kathleen was comforting herself or accusing me.

THIRTY-SEVEN

WEDNESDAY, 11:30 A.M., DECEMBER 21, 2011

The police continued questioning Lorna as a "person of interest" in the murder of Celee.

It being Wednesday, KC didn't have to go to the restaurant until dinnertime, and I didn't have students until afternoon. Mom and Kathleen, still insisting that Lorna must have killed both Felix and Celee, were hopeful Lt. Gordon would discover that. Optimistic that Charlie would be released any moment, they had joined us to await a call from the cops. KC and I were doubtful, but then, we had first-hand knowledge of how the police worked. Ana kept us company in spirit, and called twice for updates.

KC had been in contact with her boyfriend Steve, the Symphony's PR man. He consistently got details on Celee's murder before I could. When the police hadn't called by eleven-thirty in the morning, I decided to visit him before my first student arrived at two. KC texted him I was on my way, but didn't come with me, since she didn't want to bother him at work. Instead, she stayed home to get in some practice time on her flute.

I parked in the underground parking garage for Steve's downtown building, then took the elevator to the fourteenth floor, which his business shared with an accounting partnership and a firm of financial advisors. I followed the signs to Media Masters and entered.

I found chaos.

In the foyer with a cell phone pressed against one ear, Steve ordered the receptionist, "Tell him not to say anything until I call."

He lifted his chin in greeting to me, then returned to the phone.

I tried not to eavesdrop, but closed in the same room with Steve I couldn't help but hear. He turned and headed out the door and down the hall while saying into the phone, "They want to dig up dirt. Don't give them anything to work with." Several "uh-huh"s and "yeah"s followed. Sitting close to a large-leafed potted plant, I took off my coat and buried my nose in my latest book. I always carried one with me for occasions like this. Steve would get to me when he could.

Two chapters later he came into the lobby and shook my hand. "KC told me you were on your way. Come on back to the office." He walked as he spoke, and I trailed along behind.

Steve had a large corner workplace, with windows in two outside walls, one facing west toward the mountains, the other south, with a view of the city and, beyond that, along the Front Range. On the east wall, the dark wood of a large desk was almost invisible, covered by untidy stacks of files and papers. I sat in the blue armchair that faced the desk.

He got right to the point. "Pardon my French. I'm up to my ass in alligators here, so I'll skip the niceties. I appreciate the heads up about Celee's murder. Now, how can I help you?"

I didn't have time to waste, either, so I said, "I guess it'd be best if you could tell me the facts you know. Do you think Celee could have murdered Felix before she was killed herself? Or could Lorna have committed both murders?"

"I don't know anything about who did what to whom. I only know that I've had to hush up Felix's affairs before. Now he's gotten himself killed, and the symphony muckety-mucks tell me to handle his murder and make him seem socially acceptable and a great loss to the community. I succeeded in doing just that, but now his mistress, who, oh yes, happened to be his wife's best friend, has been killed. According to my information, the police say Felix's wife put a bullet into his mistress. The police are still questioning the wife, trying everything but cattle prods to find where she hid the murder weapon. My instructions are to silence it all. How am I supposed to do that? I keep referring to Celee as 'a family friend,' but why would Lorna want to kill a family friend? It's all going to come out. I'm trying to limit the damage. Distance the symphony. That's the best I can do."

Better him than me. "How?"

His look told me I'd asked an unwelcome question. "I don't know. But I'm working on it. I'll come up with something." Sounded like he knew it would be a difficult job, and he planned to punt.

"Well, I don't want to keep you. I'm trying to fit all the pieces together."

"Sure, Emily." He stood to show me out. "I'll help however I can, but that's all I know for now." He escorted me down his office hall, crossed the foyer, and opened the main door for me. "Sorry to rush you off."

I found myself standing in the building corridor, struggling into my coat. Well, I understood. I'd interrupted Steve's day, and he'd been understanding with me. He'd corroborated the grapevine by confirming Felix's past affairs, and supported Lorna by telling me that, even after a day and a half spent questioning her, the police still hadn't found the murder weapon. Beyond that, I guess I'd have to be patient. More facts had to come out later.

THIRTY-EIGHT

WEDNESDAY, 1:45 P.M., DECEMBER 21, 2011

I SPED HOME AND ARRIVED JUST BEFORE my first student. Hurriedly I told KC, Kathleen, and Mom what Steve had said, and asked Kathleen to call Ana. Later, during spare minutes, I checked with Kathleen. By five o'clock we hadn't heard. Charlie had not been released, nor the murder charge dropped. I concluded Lieutenant Gordon wasn't yet willing to consider the theory that both murders were committed by one person, or that he had that person, Lorna, in custody. Hoping Barry had different information, I called him.

"Em. My favorite former client."

I'd called on the landline and knew the whole household could hear my end of the conversation, so I only said, "Hi, Barry," but I could feel my face heating at his enthusiasm.

"I hope you called to ask me to dinner, 'cause I'm just leaving the office, I've had a hard day, I'm *starving*, and your companionship would help ease the pain."

I wanted a vacation from the tension of the day more than anything. The symphony didn't have *Nutcracker* tonight, so I turned my back on my audience, the better to ignore them, and lowered my voice, hoping they wouldn't hear. "How about the Chili Pepper? I'll meet you there in half an hour."

"At last. You're not busy. You don't have to ask me twice. I'll be there."

We hung up, and I explained to the others that I would find out what Barry knew about Charlie's status and tell him about Josh's information.

Kathleen asked, "Why isn't he talking to me? I'm Charlie's mother." She smiled. "I bet he wants a private tête-à-tête with you. That's okay with me, but I don't want to pay for it."

"I'll make sure there's no charge. Don't worry."

THE CHILI PEPPER INHABITED A DOWNTOWN NEIGHBORHOOD that had thus far escaped urban renewal. You would have expected a dive, but its chile rellenos and guacamole tostadas were to die for. It had a fireplace, and the restaurant's walls picked up the colors of brightly colored wooden chairs carved with birds. The vibrant colors warmed the spirit and pleased the senses. At 5:30 p.m., with the city already cold and dark outside, the restaurant welcomed me.

Barry had arrived first and sat at a corner table by the fireplace. He waved and pulled my chair out as I threaded my way amongst diners to join him. "You have no idea what a welcome surprise this is."

"A surprise to me, too, Barry. I have some new evidence I want to talk to you about. And Kathleen, Mom, Ana, and I have been waiting all day on pins and needles. We knew Lorna was being questioned about Celee's murder, and Kathleen, Mom, and Ana were thinking that Charlie would be released. But there's been no word. We hoped you'd have more info."

"Let's talk after we order."

We studied the menu. Everything sounded good, but I couldn't pass on the chile rellenos. Barry ordered chicken enchiladas and a couple Mexican hot chocolates with tequila for both of us.

I relaxed into my chair and sighed contentedly. At that moment, there was nowhere I'd rather be.

When we were settled, Barry brought up Charlie's case again. "By the way, thanks for recommending that Lorna see me. I referred her to another attorney. I have my hands full with Charlie and a few other things. Then too, I didn't want there to be a conflict of interest. I wouldn't want to be trying to prove Charlie's innocence by pinning Felix's murder on Lorna, if she depended on my defense. I wouldn't want to face you, either, if I couldn't talk about Charlie's case because of confidentiality issues with Lorna."

"I hadn't thought of that."

The hot chocolates arrived, and Barry took a sip of his. "What's this new information you have?"

I described Charlie's explanation of the phone's pinging and why it had shown him at Fleisher during the murder, including Josh's presence.

Barry raised his eyebrows. "Even if Josh is vague, it's a piece of evidence that can't be ignored. Creates a little bit of doubt." He crunched one of the chips the waiter had left and washed it down with water. "Now, explain to me why anyone would think Lorna's arrest for *Celee's* murder would get Charlie off the hook for *Felix's* murder."

"I know it's not indisputable proof, or really proof at all, but I've discovered that Celee was Felix's mistress. It wasn't a very well-kept secret. Lorna claims she wasn't in love with Felix and didn't care, but she also claims he was abusing her. That points to a logical motive for his murder. She also, conceivably, had opportunity to kill him, although she would have had to have considerable acting skills. The police think Lorna had access to Felix's Glock 27, and killed Celee with it. But it's also the caliber gun that killed Felix. We hoped the police would see the connections and investigate them, and that uncovering all those possibilities would free Charlie."

Barry chuckled. "The police have a lot of pieces to put together. It's a good bet they haven't even completed Lorna's interrogation or the search for the murder weapon yet."

Steve *had* told me they hadn't found the gun. I nodded.

Barry continued. "When they find the gun, they have to do ballistics tests. It's perfectly possible that Lorna only committed Celee's murder, if that." Barry kept looking at me while he paused to sip more of his chocolate. "And it's hardly surprising that they haven't reinvestigated Felix's murder. They consider that already solved."

I ducked my head and gulped my water. I didn't like looking foolish in front of Barry.

"I'm not saying Lorna didn't murder Felix, but it's a little unrealistic to expect the police to connect the dots this soon. According to my friend at the MPD, Lieutenant Gordon thinks Lorna discovered Celee and Felix were lovers after his murder, then killed Celee. He didn't say anything about whether Lorna did or didn't love Felix. The way I see it, nothing's changed. "

Our dinners arrived then. Barry tried his enchilada. "Hot!" He chugged down his water, then wiped his mouth with a napkin and took a breath to recover before he continued. "On the other hand, I thought the information about Myles's divorce had possibilities. He has a good motive."

"Lieutenant Gordon told me that Myles has an alibi for the time of the murder that checked out."

"Oh. Too bad. For us I mean."

"It frustrates me that there's no gun registry. How do the police *ever* make an arrest?"

"When they zero in on a suspect and a source for the gun, they can get a warrant. It's awkward. Write your congressman." Barry shrugged. "Lots of pieces to the puzzle, Em, and some are still missing."

I felt more at peace than I had all day. The alcohol in my chocolate and the easing of my hunger pangs relaxed me. I offered Barry a taste of my chile rellenos and sampled his chicken enchiladas. They couldn't beat my rellenos. "So, tell me about your awful, terrible, very bad, no-good day."

Barry huffed. "Even if I wanted to talk about it, which I don't since I'd rather forget, I can't, because of confidentiality issues. Since you've already told me about your day, and the state of the world doesn't bear thinking about, how about we discuss cute little puppies or kittens."

I laughed. "Sounds good to me."

As we ate dinner we caught up on less legal, more friendly topics.

Barry's kids were both in college now, and his daughter made noises about having a serious boyfriend. Barry planned to volunteer next summer on the Hopi reservation and looked forward to it; he told me about his hopes and preparations.

I didn't contribute much to the conversation. I could only tell him I dealt with family dynamics, played in orchestra, and tried to remain sane while my suspects proved innocent one by one. That wouldn't cheer Barry up.

We took a break to order sopapillas, then moved on to other topics. Barry was well-read and interested in everything, so we talked companionably. The sopapillas came, we ate, and still we talked, until we realized the staff wanted to close the restaurant.

"I'll get the tab." He took out a credit card and put down several bills for a tip.

I felt so relaxed, I didn't even defend my strong, self-sufficient womanhood by insisting on paying my share.

Barry walked me to my car through the cold of the evening. "Em, it's been amazing having you to myself for the evening. Let me know if you have free time again. I'm always available, for you, at least."

I looked down at my gloved fingers. "I'll be sure and let you know, Barry. Bye for now."

Expecting to open my own car door, it surprised me when Barry reached past me and pulled the door open.

I turned to thank him, and he tenderly and slowly kissed me goodbye.

He lifted my chin with his finger and smiled. "See you soon, I hope."

I sank into the car seat behind me. Barry had kissed me before, but . . . this time I wanted more, and it wasn't the spiked chocolate making the decisions. I kept my new feelings to myself, though. Who knew?

DESPITE THE LATENESS OF THE HOUR, Mom and Kathleen hadn't gone back to their hotel. Kathleen "read" the paper (upside down), while Mom played solitaire on the computer. KC had worked the dinner rush, then returned from the restaurant, and she practiced flute in her bedroom. The sound of a popular song I couldn't quite place filled the air.

Kathleen jumped up, tossing the paper aside. "Where have you been? You've been gone for hours! What did Barry say? You can't have been talking about Charlie's case all this time."

Barry and I hadn't talked more than a few minutes about Charlie's case, but I wouldn't confirm Kathleen's suspicions. She only needed to know about the police investigation. Paying no attention to the rest of her questions, I said, "Let's get everybody together so I don't have to say this more than once."

Kathleen said knowingly, "I bet you've been canoodling with Barry."

I ignored her and called up the stairs to KC. Mom abandoned her card game.

KC ran down the stairs. She hugged me, then said, "You're back! Give!" She scooted into an easy chair, legs dangling over the arm, waiting for my account.

I had to smile at her enthusiasm.

"I couldn't get any information on Lorna's status. Barry referred her to another lawyer. He doesn't want to appear to have a conflict of interest or neglect Charlie's case. Even if he had taken the case, he wouldn't have been able to give me any information, because of confidentiality."

"That makes sense," Kathleen affirmed. "What did Barry say about Charlie? Did you tell him about Josh?"

"I did tell him about Josh, and he thought Josh's account could be important."

Her reaction swift and total, Kathleen clapped her hands and bounced in the chair.

"It's not all good news, though." Sorry to be the bearer of bad tidings, I continued. "Barry talked to his friend in the PD, who confirmed what we already knew; Lieutenant Gordon thinks Lorna murdered Celee. He's convinced that Felix's murder is entirely separate, and that Charlie killed Felix."

KC and my family didn't have to know the other things Barry had said. The sweet things. They had nothing to do with the investigation. I felt the heat rise to my face and hoped no one noticed.

With a gleam in her eye, Kathleen said, "The lieutenant will change his mind when he hears Josh's story." She smiled. "Then I'll tell him 'I told you so.'" From the light and bubbly tone of her voice, that's not all she'd tell him.

I said, "For now, I think it's best to keep following the leads we have, like we agreed. Josh's evidence may not convince Lieutenant Gordon."

Kathleen said, "Although we've eliminated Myles, Jim, and Josh because they have alibis, we do have another possibility. Mark was at Fleisher, Felix embarrassed him in public, and he has a gun. But we'd concluded the two murders were connected. And Mark has no reason to kill Celee, as far as we know. He's all we have, though, if we don't consider Lorna." The air vibrated with the strength of her feelings. "Josh's statement has to make a difference. It has to. It will, won't it?"

"Barry thinks it might, and that's enough reason for me to hope." I just wished Josh's story was more certain and emphatic.

I paused a minute to think. "Charlie didn't kill Felix. The police will get information that clears him soon. Until then, we"ll just have to keep searching for the real killer."

Kathleen looked up and pulled at her lip. "I wish I could think of another way to help, but I can't." She stared down at her hands and sagged further into the chair.

"Sleep on it. The cops, and Charlie, need all the help they can get."

The room quieted suddenly.

KC said what we were all thinking. "In spite of my fears, I hoped they'd let Charlie go. With both Felix and Celee dead, it's so logical that Lorna killed them both."

I thought of my earlier conversation with Lorna. "I don't know, KC. I guess it's too simple. Lorna said Felix's infidelity wasn't a motive since she didn't love him anymore. And Celee was a good friend, despite her love life."

"You believed her?" KC scoffed. "Of course, Lorna wouldn't admit it if she committed the murders. Trust me. It's true that 'hell hath no fury like a woman scorned.' And a wife whose husband is unfaithful is a woman scorned, you know? Besides, he beat her. How awful for him to beat her, while being charming to his mistress. It must have been infuriating."

I had to admit, "True."

We all looked at each other.

KC stood. "Well, I'm sorry to go, but I promised Steve I'd meet him for a late dessert after I practiced. He's been working overtime trying to keep Felix and Celee's connection out of the media, or at least distance the symphony, in spite of Lorna's involvement. We both thought we could use a break." She hesitated, then bent to give Kathleen a one-armed hug. "I'm so sorry. I thought everything would be easy from here on out."

Kathleen returned the gesture. "It's okay. We'll find the truth. We're making progress." Her words were hopeful, but she sounded discouraged.

I knew why she felt discouraged, but I couldn't bring myself to join in her dejection. Instead, I hugged my evening with Barry to my heart. Kathleen and Mom went back to their hotel. Golden kept me company, snuggling close. For me, it would have been a perfect day, if only there had been a break in Charlie's case.

THIRTY-NINE

THURSDAY, 8:30 A.M., DECEMBER 22, 2011

KATHLEEN AND MOM HAD COME OVER and were having break-fast with KC and me, as had become our habit. I wished Ana could join us, but she had to work weekdays.

We were interrupted by the ringing of Kathleen's phone. She answered it and after a moment responded, "You're certain, Barry?" A pause while she listened. "I'll be right there."

Kathleen ran for the coat closet followed by Mom. My sister pulled out her own coat and purse, then shoved Mom's at her. "I've got to get to the jail right away. Charlie needs me. No time to explain." And just like that, she disappeared.

I assumed Barry had good news. With police attention on Lorna for Celee's murder, all of us had spent yesterday waiting and hoping for the news that she had killed Felix, too, and Charlie had been released. The call came later than we expected, but it must mean the police had discovered that Lorna, not Charlie, had murdered Felix.

KC left for work. I smiled to myself, convinced that Charlie had been freed. I put it out of my mind as I taught a full day of students.

As usual, I'd scheduled Megan's five o'clock lesson as the last of the day. This time she didn't wait. As soon as the previous student had gone Megan burst into tears.

"Miz Wilson, Dad hit me. He hit me!"

Golden, who had been offering her usual welcome, stopped short. She looked from Megan to me, ears down, worry in her expressive brown eyes.

I wrapped my arms around Megan while she sobbed for what seemed hours to me, but couldn't have been more than a minute. Using the time to deal with my own shock, I tried to think what to do and say. When Megan's tears slowed and she took a breath I asked, "Are you okay?"

Hiccupping and trying to catch her breath she said, "I guess so. He didn't really hurt me. My ribs are a little sore, is all, but it's not bad."

Megan hadn't earned anything but loving affection and parental pride. Of course, her father had hit her ribs, where it wouldn't show.

Rage clouded my vision. "It *is* bad. You didn't deserve it. "

"Really. It's okay," she said, as I led the way to my studio where I taught, now that Kathleen had moved to Mom's hotel.

Her bravery pulled at my heartstrings. "Whatever problems your dad has, this is not the way to handle them."

"But I forgot to clean the kitchen. Mom left, and he asked me to do it. I had a book report due the next day that I hadn't finished, and I didn't . . . do it . . . and I told him . . ." She hiccupped all the way through this before she collapsed into the student chair behind the music stand.

Golden sat at her feet and whined.

How dare he? Angrily, I told her, "People forget things all the time. Kids even mouth off to their parents. He just needed to remind you. Or scold you. He didn't have to hit you."

She slumped to the floor and slid her arms around Golden, weeping again, her face buried in the dog's velvety fur.

Golden leaned back and licked Megan's ear.

Still crying, she hugged Golden closer.

"Listen to me, Megan. I'll say it again. Your dad's behavior is not your fault, no matter what you've done or not done." I moved to the chair she had vacated and sat down, putting my hand on her back.

After a time, her crying began to soften, and huge gasps of air broke up the tears, though her face stayed buried in Golden's fur.

I asked, "Did you tell your mom?"

She looked up, sniffled, and said, "Mom has her own problems. I don't want to make them worse. And I should have cleaned the kitchen." Gulping breaths, she rubbed Golden's ears.

My dog responded by licking Megan's cheek.

She giggled, wiped her face, then took a deep breath. Hiccupping and sniffling, she looked at me pleadingly, hair hanging in her face. "Ms. Wilson, I'm scared. I have my father's genes. What if I hit people, too, when I grow up?"

Damn! I wasn't trained to say the right thing, and I prayed I wouldn't say the wrong thing. "Honey, of course you won't. Abusing is not hereditary. You know how it feels, and you would never hurt anyone else that way." Was it a lie? I didn't know, but it sounded good and calmed Megan a little.

Between Golden on the floor and me on the chair, we sandwiched the unhappy girl between us and surrounded her with love the best we knew how. As I tried to radiate caring to Megan, I reflected that her dad could ruin his daughter's life. I had to take action.

I waited until she'd quit crying, and then suggested we have a lesson, since I figured music would help soothe her emotional pain. As she got out her flute, I reflected that talking to Megan's mom hadn't done any good. This time I would call Social Services. The law didn't consider me a mandatory reporter since I taught privately and wasn't a health professional, public school teacher, or Child Protective Services worker, but ethically I considered myself involved. Megan's dad wreaked damage in people's lives, people I cared about. I couldn't let him get away with it.

After her lesson, without saying anything to Megan, I called Social Services. I gave them her name, address, and phone. They assured me the report would be confidential, and I would remain anonymous. I felt sick.

THAT NIGHT MUSCLE MEMORY AND LONG HOURS in the practice room kicked in, and I played the *Nutcracker* instinctively. Serena

Green, Megan's mom, had to be told what I'd done and, more importantly, what her daughter had been through. I didn't want to betray Megan's confidences, but I needed to prioritize. Most importantly, Serena had to know the whole family, including Megan, suffered from her husband Ben's cruelties.

When I got home after the performance, KC had gone to bed. Kathleen and Mom hadn't left a message about the situation at the jail. Kathleen must have been so carried away by the good news that she forgot me. I felt hurt, but they say no news is good news.

Only Golden was available to discuss Megan's situation.

"Think I made a good decision?"

Golden cocked her head and whined. I took that for approval, and went to bed, convinced I had done the right, the only, thing.

FORTY

FRIDAY, 8:30 A.M., DECEMBER 23, 2011

Kathleen and Mom would arrive soon for our usual breakfast meeting so, assuming this would be a celebration, I wanted to do something special. KC made her coffee cake. Meanwhile, I managed to slice fruit without cutting myself.

Mom and Kathleen entered the house in silence—unusual for them.

I felt bright and cheery. "Where's Charlie? I thought you'd bring him to breakfast."

They exchanged looks. Kathleen responded, "Charlie hasn't been released."

"But . . . when you left in such a hurry yesterday for the prison, I assumed—"

"Well, you assumed wrong." Her eyes red as if she'd been crying, she continued. "Yesterday's call from Barry confirmed Charlie won't be released. You've heard it before. The cops believe Lorna found out about her husband's affair with Celee after Felix's murder, when she saw the credit card bill including the charge for Celee's necklace, and that led her to kill Celee. They haven't found it yet, but they've found the paperwork for Felix's gun, a Glock 27, which they believe Lorna used to kill Celee. They haven't done the autopsy yet and don't have the bullet, but the casing they found belongs to a Glock 27."

Kathleen dropped into a kitchen chair. "I'm so frustrated! The two homicides are being handled completely separately. Lorna isn't suspected of killing Felix, even though his gun is the same caliber as the one that killed him, and they think she used it to kill Celee. Glock 27s are a common weapon, apparently, and the evidence against Charlie is strong." She choked off a sob and looked accusingly at me. "And you still haven't met with Lieutenant Gordon."

"Our meeting is this afternoon."

Kathleen continued as if she hadn't heard me. "I rushed off because I wanted to comfort Charlie the moment I found out. I had a regularly scheduled visit to the jail in the afternoon, so I thought if I got there earlier . . . but the prison personnel made me wait 'til our regular visit time, even though I begged and promised banana bread."

KC and I both leaned over and hugged her. "I'm so sorry."

Kathleen hugged us back as a torrent of tears cascaded down her cheeks. "I had to wait until after lunch to comfort Charlie, and he's so discouraged! Every little bit of hope has been snatched out from under him. I told him about your meeting with Lieutenant Gordon to discuss Josh's evidence, and that cheered him a little, but I'm so worried!"

By now, Kathleen had run out of words, so Mom, seating herself, continued the explanation. "After the visit with Charlie we went to dinner and tried to figure out what to do next. We called Ana and she met with us. She used the laptop to comb through past editions of the newspaper and find members of Friends of the Symphony—the big donors—the ones that were well known in the community for their philanthropy, the ones that Felix would have known personally. They might know details about the Underhayes' marriage that would show Lorna's motive for killing Felix. What she told you the other day about the abuse she suffered would certainly be motivation. We figured somebody might provide corroboration. Or there might be somebody that arrived at Fleisher early the day of the murder, either for the tour or as a donor or both, someone who might be Felix's killer."

Mom took a breath and patted Kathleen's hand, then continued. "Kathleen and I will call them later today with the excuse of soliciting donations for the symphony. Hopefully we'll draw one of them out and connect Lorna or someone else to Felix's murder."

I couldn't believe what I heard. "What? Do you know how much trouble you could get in if you get caught? Impersonating a symphony employee to extort money won't be taken lightly."

Kathleen raised pleading blue eyes to mine. "We're running out of time. Charlie has been in that jail cell over two weeks now. I've got to get him out!"

KC, who had been working at the counter, turned and, standing behind Kathleen and Mom, raised her eyebrows at me. She mouthed, "This is crazy. Do something."

But I couldn't do anything else. I had warned them. Kathleen ignored me. It seemed a hopeless and desperate idea to me, if not downright dangerous. At best they were wasting their time. At worst . . . who knew? They could even cause problems for Charlie.

LEAVING KATHLEEN, KC, AND MOM TO CLEAN UP the breakfast dishes, and keeping the conversation quiet and private, I called Serena Green from the studio and asked her to tea at my house.

She argued. "Last time I saw you we had an awkward talk that was *way* too personal. You stepped over the line."

And this would be no different, though I didn't say so. "I'm concerned about Megan."

Serena demanded, "What are you worried about?"

"I don't want to discuss it over the phone. Can you come today?" I'd learned from our last meeting. We could keep our conversation confidential at my house. Since she didn't know what her husband had done to Megan, I had to give Serena the information as soon as possible. I confess I also wanted to get it over with right away.

"Today? I have to work."

"Can you come during a break in your schedule? Believe me, it's urgent."

Now she sounded concerned. "I suppose I could come at lunch. But Megan's such a good kid, I don't know how anything 'urgent' could come up."

I didn't enlighten her. "I'll explain when we meet. Thanks for arranging your schedule."

By the time I got off the phone, KC had left for the restaurant and Mom and Kathleen had dashed off again. I assumed they were going to make their phone calls. Their desperation and lack of perspective made me squirm, but at least Serena and I would have the house to ourselves.

Now, what would I say? That would be the hard part, and I didn't have long to think about it.

"THANKS FOR COMING ON SUCH SHORT NOTICE." I reached out to give Serena a hug, but she backed away.

"My kids are my first priority. If you're concerned about Megan, we need to talk."

"Thanks for understanding. Come on in." I led her down the hall and through the living room to the kitchen. I had put out two cups and saucers. "Have a seat."

She sat down and waited for me to join her.

I stalled. "Is tea okay, or would you like coffee?"

"Nothing for me." Serena pushed away her cup. "Let's get this over with."

Though I guessed that wasn't her intention, I felt, if possible, even more uncomfortable. "I told you I needed to see you urgently."

She gazed steadily at me. "So? Explain."

I hesitated. Only one way of dealing with nerves had ever worked for me: to ignore them and go ahead anyway. I do it whenever I have a big solo—no reason to delay. "I've, uh, reported the abuse in your house to Social Services."

"Abuse!" She slid back her chair, and her eyes filled with tears. "How could you? What do you mean, abuse?"

I couldn't believe I had to explain this. "You have a black eye."

"So? Ben loses his temper now and then. I thought you and I were friends."

"We are friends, and friends help each other. I'm worried about your whole family. Megan can't know I've told you, but her father hit her, too. She told me, and she's heard you two fighting. I can only guess how that would affect the little ones. I'm sure they at least hear you."

"Wait! Ben hit Megan? That can't be!" The shock sobered her and dried her eyes.

"That's what Megan said. She wouldn't lie to me. She'd have no reason."

"But . . ." Serena seemed at a loss for words.

I reached to pat her back, but she shrugged away and turned to face me. Still dry-eyed, anger vibrated in her words. "Hitting my kids is not okay."

"I know it's not okay. That's why I called Social Services."

She squinted her eyes. "Nobody hurts my kids. Not even Ben."

"Just hearing the fights could be hurting your kids. They're not stupid. They know what's going on. You don't want them to think people in love behave that way."

She hesitated. "I want them to know people in love have their disagreements."

I couldn't believe what I heard. "This is more than a disagreement. It's violence! You don't deserve it, and your kids don't deserve it, either."

"Well, my kids don't deserve it, anyway." Momentary silence. "It's almost impossible to imagine, but you're right. I've never known Megan to lie."

I waited as she silently processed the information.

"I guess I owe you, Emily." She blew her nose. "I'll have to think about it. My first thought is to leave, but how can I leave home . . ."—she sobbed once—" . . . with four kids?"

"There are lots of options." I told her about the battered women's shelter, emphasizing legal help, and available counseling for the kids. "You and the kids can stay together and be safe. Or you can stay with me, too." I gave her a card with the shelter's contact information and the name of someone to talk to.

She looked at the card carefully and tucked it in her purse. "Thanks, Emily. I know you're concerned about Megan, but I'm going to have to think about this." She stood. "Can I use your rest room?"

I pointed her in the right direction and watched her stumble down the hall. I had upset her, upset her badly, but Megan and her siblings needed help.

I turned off the burner under the tea kettle and emptied the coffee pot. The drinks had been useless, and my meeting with Serena, I suspected, was over.

MID-AFTERNOON KATHLEEN AND MOM APPEARED through the connecting door from the garage to the kitchen. I only had time to greet them before the bell rang at the front entrance. Lt. Gordon had arrived for our scheduled meeting.

Golden barked until I answered.

"Thank you for coming."

The lieutenant followed me and Golden down the hall to the living room.

Relying on Mom's training I said, "Have a seat."

He took off his hat, tucking it under his arm, and chose the straight-backed cane chair that I had begun to think of as "Lt. Gordon's chair" because he'd chosen it every time he sat in my living room.

Kathleen and Mom materialized in the living room as soon as they heard his voice.

"Miz McRae. " The lieutenant nodded and rose, giving no clue that they'd met before, other than his acknowledgement of my sister's name.

I introduced my mother.

She glared at him. "So you're the idiot who—"

"Mom!" Kathleen and I shouted together.

The lieutenant looked Mom up and down, but just nodded. "Ma'am."

The two of them sat on the sofa while Lt. Gordon reseated himself.

I dragged Golden and settled her on the floor next to my recliner, prepared to give Josh's information.

But the lieutenant cleared his throat and seemed uncomfortable, shifting in his chair. "About half an hour ago I received a call from Mrs. Franklin Grundquist."

I knew Mrs. Grundquist. She belonged to Friends of the Symphony, was on the Board, and was a huge contributor. Ordinarily I wouldn't know the donors or Board members, but Mrs. Grundquist particularly loved the flute. She had played in high school, maybe sixty years ago, and had a keen ear. She never failed to congratulate me after a concert if the second flute had been prominent, as it had earlier in the season when we played Dvorak's *New World Symphony*, and last year in Ravel's *Daphnis and Chloe*. Her husband was a senator. A call from her would have been top priority.

"Apparently she received a call supposedly soliciting donations for the symphony." He cleared his throat. "She told me it puzzled her, since she had already made a large donation and didn't usually receive solicitation calls."

A sense of dread filled the pit of my stomach.

"Mrs. Grundquist became more and more convinced the call was fraudulent when the female caller began pressing for details of whether Mrs. Grundquist knew Felix and Lorna Underhayes, and if she knew anything about their family life."

Kathleen seemed to shrink in the sofa and reached for Mom's hand.

"Mrs. Grundquist's alarm became urgent when she hung up and realized the caller ID had registered the call as being from Kathleen McRae. She recognized the last name as the same last name as Felix's alleged killer. Now she thinks she's being 'stalked' by the killer's family."

Silence.

I shattered the guilty quiet. "Kathleen?"

"I didn't think . . . we didn't think . . . that is . . . we didn't know . . . we just wanted information that would help Charlie."

Lt. Gordon gave me a sideways glance. "Harassment requires more than one incident to prosecute. But there's also the problem of fraud. Since it's a crime against the public, the police department could look into it on its own; however, Mrs. Grundquist didn't want to be a part of an investigation. She and her husband want to avoid a scandal." He glanced quickly at Kathleen, then away. "Luckily for you, you're off the hook, so far. I like you, in spite of your rash actions. I assume you're a concerned mother, so I'll just give you a warning and review the possibilities. It will not help Mr. McRae if his mother and grandmother are jailed for fraud. The Board, including Mrs. Grundquist, might conclude that all of you, Charlie and Ms. Wilson included, are responsible. If this happens again, I won't be able to overlook it. I'd hate to put you in handcuffs. But protecting the public is my job. So make sure you stay out of trouble." He didn't crack a smile.

"I'm sure Kathleen—"

"I've said all I have to say on that subject. Tell me your new information." He raised his eyebrows at me.

I explained that Charlie had sat in his car outside Fleisher at the time of the murder and seen Josh.

"Did anyone else see them?"

"I've told you everything I know."

"Okay. Thanks. I'll talk to Mr. Regan. We'll get to the bottom of this."

Finally, a reason to hope. His help made me more optimistic.

Kathleen rose from the sofa at the same time I started to stand.

She raised her eyebrows at me, and I understood she wanted to show the lieutenant out.

He rose from his chair, nodded to both me and my mother, and plodded down the hall to the front door with Kathleen.

I heard her say, "I am *so* sorry . . ." before they went out the door, closing it behind them. Mom and I ran to the door's side window and watched as Kathleen and the lieutenant, standing close together, talked in the front yard for several minutes, despite the December cold.

When Kathleen turned and headed inside, we ran back to the living room.

As far as she could guess, we hadn't moved.

"You were lucky Lieutenant Gordon gave you a warning." I didn't want to say, *I told you so,* but I had warned them. "How did making a few innocent phone calls turn into terrifying old ladies and breaking the law?"

Kathleen sniffled and blew into the tissue she produced from her pocket. "That's not fair! I didn't intend to scare Mrs. Grundquist, and I'm sorry I did. I told Lieutenant Gordon so. I didn't think a few phone calls would be against the law. My name being on her caller ID never crossed my mind. I asked questions that would help us find information that might help Charlie."

Unwilling to argue and mentally tired, I shrugged and changed the subject. "Are either of you hungry?"

"No thanks." Speaking for them both, Kathleen turned her back on me and said, "I just want to be alone." She headed for the back door. "C'mon Mom. Let's go back to the hotel."

Mom seemed torn between her two daughters, but rose to go, looking back at me. She caught up with Kathleen, talking and rubbing her back as they went out to the car.

FORTY-ONE

SATURDAY, 8:30 A.M., DECEMBER 24, 2011

I EXPECTED MOM AND KATHLEEN FOR BREAKFAST today. My sister had called and apologized for leaving so abruptly yesterday. She admitted her short-sightedness and poor planning in calling Mrs. Grundquist, and hoped it wouldn't rebound on Charlie and me. She barely mentioned Lt. Gordon's scolding, but instead focused on his responsiveness to Charlie's alibi. I wanted to be able to encourage and support her if I could, but also wanted to discourage any more crazy plans, of which both she and Mom had proved themselves capable.

KC wasn't home. Either things were going well with Steve and she hadn't returned from yesterday's date, or she had gone into the restaurant early. I didn't know which.

Feeling frustrated and out of the loop, I cracked eggs for me, Kathleen, and Mom into a bowl. After fishing out the eggshell that fell in, I whisked the eggs, but didn't season or cook them, unsure what seasonings to use or in what amounts. I located the remnants of the coffee cake KC had made yesterday and sliced it along with some fruit, then sat at the table drumming my fingers. I focused on the fact that circumstances were more hopeful than they'd ever been for Charlie. But if Josh didn't come through, I didn't have any more bright ideas.

About ten minutes later, Mom and Kathleen poked their heads in the door. Both were silent.

"You're both awfully quiet. What's going on?"

Mom answered. "I hoped to make some more progress on Charlie's case today, but Kathleen convinced me not to do anything until we'd heard from Lieutenant Gordon."

"What progress were you hoping to make? It seems to me that we've done all we can."

Mom glanced sideways at Kathleen, then returned her gaze to me. "I thought maybe we could go to Lorna's house and look for proof she killed Felix."

This confused me. "She wouldn't let you in to do that. Besides, the police might still be questioning her."

"If she's there we wouldn't try anything. But I have lots of talents, one of which is not needing a key for everything."

In other words, she was planning to break in.

"I told you. Lieutenant Gordon is going to talk to Josh. That has to vindicate Charlie." Kathleen's raised her voice and her face reddened.

"Okay. Okay. But I still don't think we should fill one basket with eggs like that." Her voice was soothing.

"Mom!" Kathleen angrily ignored her contorted cliché and responded, "There's no reason to flout Lieutenant Gordon's warning when Charlie is all but cleared."

"I agreed not to do anything. Now let's not mention it again."

An uncomfortable silence followed, during which Kathleen glared at Mom.

To break the tension, I changed the subject. "I got everything ready for breakfast. The eggs just need to be cooked."

"I'll do it." Kathleen mumbled something and took over the cooking, beating the eggs, though I'd already beaten them, and beating them, and beating them. Finally, her frustration relieved, I assumed, she spiced them with salt and pepper.

While she heated olive oil and poured the eggs into the pan, I arranged the sliced fruit on a platter. That seemed most likely to help, and keep me out of the way of Kathleen's obvious frustration. "What are your plans for the day?"

Kathleen spoke to the scrambled eggs. "We're just going to finish up some Christmas shopping and wait for the lieutenant's call. He has my number, and he said he'd let me know how the interview with Josh went. How about you?"

Several students had cancelled because they had plans today, Christmas Eve day. Unfortunately, the cancelled lessons weren't consecutive, so there wasn't enough time between them for productive activities before I left for the symphony's last *Nutcracker* performance.

"I'll just be teaching. Probably wrapping presents in between students."

At that point KC flung open the door from the garage dressed in evening wear. She blushed when she saw us all in the kitchen. "Sorry. Can't talk. Late for work. Gotta run." She hurried up to her bedroom.

Looked like I had been right. Things were heating up with Steve.

THIS EVENING'S PERFORMANCE WAS THE FINAL *Nutcracker*, and I hadn't watched the show since the run-through. It's rewarding to see the finished product. Boredom with my part had set in too, so, with my fingers following well-known patterns, I pressed the flute's keys and watched the show whenever I could.

Seeing the ballet jogged my memory. When I ran into Celee shopping between shows right before her murder, she'd told me she'd come to buy gifts for the ballerinas. Had she seen them before she died? If so, they might have information about Celee's murder. I'd promised Lorna I'd keep my eyes and ears open for clues.

But who were the ballerinas Celee referred to? Surely, she didn't intend to buy gifts for the entire *corps de ballet*. She must have been referring to the *prima* ballerina and the girl who plays Clara, the twelve-year old who has the dream that sets up the whole ballet.

I considered Clara. The *Nutcracker* is usually the first starring role for talented female dancers and deserving of celebration, so it would call for a gift. I couldn't bring myself to question a child, though. Wasn't there supposed to be a special technique used for kids so the questioner didn't prejudice the answers? It would be easiest to leave her for the end. If I couldn't get information any other way, she'd be a last resort.

That left the *prima* ballerina. Lily Hawthorne, the review said. Had she seen Celee before the murder? This might be the last chance to find out.

Oops! Missed a minor entrance. In a loud spot, fortunately; the second flute wouldn't be missed. But I scolded myself. Professional discipline required that I keep my mind on the performance. So, with practice honed from long experience, I brought my mind back to my part. I had one last *Nutcracker* to play, ending the run for the season. I'd concentrate on the music now and leave speculation until later.

FORTY-TWO

SATURDAY, 10:30 P.M., DECEMBER 24, 2011

AFTER THE PERFORMANCE I FOUND pure chaos backstage. It was packed so tightly with people that I had to weave, sometimes sideways, often stopping, to get from here to there. The uproar made ordinary talking impossible, and I had to shout to make myself heard. Costumed and garishly made-up dancers were exuberantly spinning, kissing, and accepting flowers from admiring audience members who had made their way backstage. Orchestra members met family and friends and arranged to get together for drinks. Small children, mice in the show, scampered around their parents and grandparents, posing for pictures. Doug, in his tuxedo, accepted congratulations from orchestra and audience members. Fighting my way to him and yelling to make myself heard, I congratulated him, too. He'd done a fantastic job of stepping in to lead the orchestra with no rehearsal, making sure everything went smoothly in difficult— no, unprecedented—circumstances.

I knew that talking to the *prima* ballerina in these conditions would be difficult if not out of the question, so I determined to wait. It would be a long time, but if I didn't talk to her now, I wouldn't get the chance. Ballet stagehands were already starting to pack their trucks with scenery and props to be used at the ballet's next stop.

Creeping into a corner, I found a chair and applied myself to reading the program. Donna Donnelly danced the role of Clara—a typical young dancer's resume. The *prima* ballerina was Lily Hawthorne. From her bio it sounded like she had the experience to be about thirty, old for a ballerina, but then she had to be old enough to build the necessary skill.

About half an hour later the area started to clear. There were still plenty of people around, though, a lot of them lined up outside Lily's dressing room.

I did everything I could to occupy myself—drank from the water fountain, chatted with waiting symphony members, got another drink, went to the bathroom, slurped yet again at the fountain, went back and read the program cover to cover including advertisements—and finally looked up to see the area was now deserted except for me, the occasional scurrying stagehand, and Lily's closed dressing room door.

She might have been the last to see Celee alive. Her information had to be important. I wanted a witness to our conversation, but there was nobody. Kathleen's presence would have been helpful. But instead, I turned my cell phone to record, put on my parka, and shoved the phone into its right pocket. Then I knocked on Lily's door.

"In a minute, Gil! I'll be there in a minute."

Who was Gil? I didn't see anybody else around. "It's not Gil. I'm Emily Wilson, from the orchestra. I'm a fan."

Lily opened the door dressed in jeans and a tight tee shirt, one eye devoid of paint, the other still made up. "Oh, my apologies!" She reached for her bare eye. "I thought you were someone else." She blocked the door. "I'm getting ready to go. Can I help you?"

Knowing the best way to a show person's heart I said, "I wanted to congratulate you on a great performance."

"Thank you." I apparently hadn't engaged her. She started to close the door, so I enthused. "I know you must hear that all the time, but I took the opportunity to watch from the orchestra pit today, and found myself entranced by your dancing. You're so elegant, so graceful."

She still didn't look interested and hadn't moved from the door.

I fibbed desperately. "I sometimes write articles for the orchestra newsletter." What orchestra newsletter? "If you have a minute, I'd like to get some quotes."

She opened the door wider, motioned me in, waved me to a seat, and sat in the small room's only other chair, facing me. On the floor between us sat a small stool. On top of the stool I recognized Lily's pink costume from the Dance of the Sugar Plum Fairy; to her right and slightly in front of her was an open suitcase; behind her were shelves, empty now, except for her purse.

"I am glad you enjoyed the show." She didn't actually have an accent, but she sounded a little foreign. Was it her o's? Her speech seemed a little stilted, too.

"You're so lovely. A treat to watch."

"Thank you." She smiled, but the smile didn't crinkle her eyes. "Practice. Lots of it."

"I know about practice." I paused. "Sorry you caught us at a bad time. Felix's murder was, well, a unique situation. Did you know him?"

She turned her face away from me and her voice sounded . . . different. "Just from working on the tempos of the Sugar Plum Fairy dance."

I waited, but she didn't go on. "Well, I hope the murder didn't upset you too much."

She turned back to face me. "Oh, no. Douglas did a fine job."

Interesting that she thought I referred to the music she danced to. "And then to have a second murder!"

She gave me a cold look. "A second murder?"

"Celee O'Connor? The lady from Friends of the Symphony?"

"Oh. Her." She looked away and down. "I thought Felix's wife was being questioned in the woman's murder."

"She is." I tried to catch Lily's eye, but couldn't. "Celee intended to present you with a gift from Friends of the Symphony."

"Really?" Lily sounded surprised. "I don't expect presents."

"Did she ever connect with you?"

Lily continued to avoid my eyes. "No. Why? Did you want to give me something in her stead?" Was she trying to understand my presence, or playing dumb?

"No. I'm trying to figure out what happened. Celee was kind of a friend of mine." Lily wouldn't know that I fibbed again.

"Well, I'm sorry I can't help you. I never saw her." Lily turned her head and looked straight at me, sounding increasingly suspicious. "How will you fit this into a newsletter? I'm really in quite a rush."

I stubbornly stayed put.

"I'm in an odd position because Lorna, Felix's wife, is also a friend of mine, but she's suspected of my friend Celee's murder."

"That *is* awkward." I heard no genuine sympathy in her voice. Her fingers drummed on the side of the chair.

"Especially since Lorna swears she didn't commit the murder."

"Would you expect her to confess? Don't guilty people always claim they're innocent?"

She had a point, but my intuition and Lily's body language—she'd crossed her arms and begun tapping her foot—were telling me she knew more than she admitted. She impatiently waited for me to finish. I had no evidence to back up my suspicions, other than Celee's comment that she intended to see the ballerinas before the performance. If Lily insisted she had no knowledge of Celee's murder and hadn't seen her, I couldn't prove differently. Was she telling the truth? Or not?

Hoping to wrest the facts from her, I tried another gambit. "Felix had a reputation as a player." True as far as I knew. The grapevine and Steve said so. "Rumor had it that he and Celee were lovers." My theory and the police's, as well as gossip from the grapevine. "Actually, he had a reputation as a ladies' man." Charlie's info. "There were always women around. He'd use one for a while, then cast her aside for another." A logical conclusion. "And then, of course, there was Lorna, his wife." *Fact.*

"Really. What on earth does all this have to do with me and my dancing?" Lily had moved to the edge of her seat.

Desperately, I ignored her and babbled on.

"There were even rumors the two of you were having an affair."
An out and out lie, but I sensed Lily hid something behind her half
made up face and tapping toe. Besides, I never had to see her again.
I didn't need to make a good impression.

In a conversational tone I continued, "You have to wonder
about the women. To believe his lies!" I made use of his last words.
"'You're the only one I've ever loved.' Give me a break. A woman
would have to be a fool to fall for his cheap flattery."

"It wasn't cheap flattery!" Her face reddened, and her voice rose.
"I am not ashamed. Lies were for the others. Felix *did* love only me.
I could tell by the look in his eyes. He had a special love for me. He
said so." She flushed, and her voice had risen.

"And you believed him?"

"Enough! Why are you telling me this?" She stood and turned
away from me, facing the shelf and fumbling in her purse.

"Just repeating the gossip."

"One mustn't listen to gossip." When she turned back, she held
a gun.

Apparently, I had hit a nerve.

Pointing the weapon at me she said, "I, myself, am far too intelligent to listen to the tittle-tattle of small minds. Felix and I had
something special, no matter what you, or anyone, says. Unlike
anyone he ever knew. He said so."

Her face clouded. "Still, like all men, apparently he lied when it
suited him. Not to me, but to the others. He had to be taught the
limits of my patience."

I told myself to keep my head. Fear wouldn't help me. I pressed
for more information. "Taught?"

"Even though we had been together the night before, he
seduced Celee at the run-through. He could have had me forever.
But he spoiled it."

Hoping the cell phone recorded without a problem I reached in
my pocket and touched it lightly with a trembling hand. "So you
killed him?"

"I didn't plan to, but I carried the gun in my pocket. Celee, too,
needed to be taught. She tried to steal a man who belonged to me."

Clasping the gun with both hands, she continued. "They forced me. I had to show both of them. At first, I only thought to wound Felix, to educate him. He enraged me. Who knew he would die of his wounds? But I am not a fool. I will not settle. He could not have me and other women, too."

A small smile crossed her lips and broadened.

But then her brow furrowed. "It seems that only you have suspicions. Eliminating you eliminates all questions. You are the only one who will ever know the truth, and you will be dead."

Uh-oh.

While I wanted to get details for the cell phone, which I again hoped documented the conversation without a problem, more importantly, I needed to buy myself time. "You'd kill me in your own dressing room? The police will know you murdered me. They'll figure it out. What will you do with my body?"

"I've already gotten away with murder twice. What makes you think your death will be any different?"

"But why would you put yourself at risk?"

She shook the gun at me. "I'm confused. Are you asking why I need to kill you, or why I risked Felix's murder? Because either way, the answer is the same."

"Explain so I get the picture . . ." I looked into her eyes. ". . . please."

She laughed and sat down in the chair again. "Very well. I suppose you have a right to understand it all." She still held the gun in both hands. Now she pointed it at my stomach, though.

The thrillers I read said gut shots were a horrible way to die, extremely painful, so it relieved me when she started to talk again.

Holding the gun steady, she said, "The night the ballet arrived, I went to a late dinner, then came to the auditorium to get a feel for the stage. The orchestra had gone for the most part, and the last of them left as I arrived, but Felix remained. He charmed me. We talked of the tempo of the Sugar Plum Fairy dance. We laughed. We walked through the number. He complemented me and said he wanted to support such grace to perfection." She hesitated and then smiled.

I encouraged her by nodding and mirroring her smile.

Never lowering the gun, she continued. "I cannot be a ballerina forever you know, but I do not meet many people on tour. Charming men with money, an intimate knowledge of the music of the dance, who are attracted to women, are rare. Talent connected to talent, and one thing led to another. Felix walked me to my hotel. We drank wine and laughed, shared soft words and passionate glances. His eyes were only for me. We went to my room and, well..." she paused a moment, searching for words. "...we showed our appreciation for one another." She glanced down, for the first time, modestly. "He wouldn't spend the night and explained that he had a wife and children. He apologized and said that he would free himself from his marriage."

Again, I nodded, trusting that she would take the nod for support.

But the smile disappeared replaced by an angry scowl, and she waved the gun. "The very next night, the night of the run-through, I walked into Felix's dressing room eager to give him best wishes for the coming rehearsal. But there he embraced Celee, and she gazed lovingly at him. I left quickly, without saying anything. Felix's back faced me, but Celee's eyes found mine."

Lily trained an intense stare on me. "Can you understand? He infuriated me! He had told me he loved only me, but he held another woman, a woman not his wife, not twenty-four hours later. I wanted him only for me, embracing only me. But he thought he could have Celee, too." Her eyes flashed at the memory.

I murmured sympathetically. "I *do* understand. *Of course* you were livid. What did you do?"

Her eyes blazed. "I planned to talk to him, so I gave no hint of what I had seen. After the run-through he, the *primeur danseur*, and I worked on the *Pas de Deux*. I still hadn't planned what to say, and I avoided Felix's company. The *danseur* and I left quickly. But I was more and more angry. So before the dress rehearsal I went to Felix's dressing room. A man stomped out, and I knew Felix would be alone." She shifted in her chair.

"We talked. He made it clear that he would not leave his children until they were grown. In the meantime, Celee, his wife's friend, occupied his time, an amusement."

The bastard! I leaned forward, hands on knees. I had been waiting to hear this. "And . . ."

"I grew angrier and angrier. I could not wait ten years for his children to grow up! And his dalliance with Celee was unacceptable."

I'll say!

"I always carry my gun for protection. I withdrew it from my jacket pocket and shot him. He deserved it."

Charlie's proof! Again, I silently prayed the phone had recorded the information.

She glowered. "To go from my arms . . . mine . . . to her!" She paused. "He deserved to die."

Smiling, she continued. "One of my talents is cleverness. Quickly, I ran down the hall. Where it forms a 'T' with a second hall, rather than go downstairs I exited to the street. I returned to my hotel and hid the gun in my room, safe from the police. Later, in the midst of the chaos, I reentered by the stage door and acted as if I knew nothing of the happenings." Her eyes locked on mine. "Felix will never pleasure me again, but he will never again be unfaithful, either!"

Kathleen would be ecstatic. If she ever heard the story. I thought furiously. During Lily's long recitation I had been feverishly searching for available weapons. There were none. I could only reach the stool holding the Sugar Plum Fairy costume.

Lily paused as if she were expecting applause. While she focused on her cunning, I took the opportunity to slide forward in the chair. "Smart." I remembered her working on the sets with Jim Plank so calmly. She must have been certain she got away with it. "But weren't you worried that the gun would be traced?"

Lily responded calmly. "No. A 'friend' gave it to me. I requested that it be untraceable. I wanted to be anonymous if I ever had to use it."

I cast about for facts I knew. "You may not have been aware of it, but Diane Gelbart, President of Friends of the Symphony, knew Celee planned to see you before the performance to give you a gift."

Lily's eyes didn't seem to focus. "It is true that Celee came to see me before the evening performance last Saturday. She wanted to talk in her car though the weather was very cold, so we wouldn't be seen or overheard. Curiosity made me go. But I feared being alone with her and, as always, carried the gun in my jacket pocket, so I would be safe. I didn't intend to kill her. But Celee wore a necklace. She talked about Felix and how he had given it to her. She had the nerve to say it symbolized Felix's 'love' for her." Lily half turned, glanced in the mirror and touched her neck. "That necklace should have been mine! Felix hadn't left his wife for Celee, had he? He said she was nothing but a plaything."

Furious as she remembered, Lily jerked the gun.

My heart sped, the beat as fast as sixty-fourth notes played *molto vivace.*

"Celee said she wanted to talk with me because I had 'witnessed their love.' She knew that I had seen their embrace and wanted it to stay between us, now that Felix had died. No one else knew, she said. She asked me to be silent. She didn't want to soil Felix's memory. How stupid she was! The more she talked, the angrier I got."

Her face scarlet by now, the gun shook as she continued. "Finally, I couldn't take any more of her lies. They enraged me. I did not hesitate longer. I took the gun from my jacket pocket and shot her. Thankfully, I had inserted the silencer as usual, and we were far from the crowds and closed in her car, so no one heard."

Desperation planted an idea. I kept her talking. "But people must have seen you. Wasn't there blood on your clothes?"

"My coat was stained with it. But one of my many talents is quick thinking." Her lips curled in a smirk. "The performance would not begin for another hour and a half, and most people had not arrived yet. I took the coat off and entered the building, then stuffed the garment into my luggage in the dressing room. I knew the coat would be safe there until I arrived at home. Then I would burn it. I freshened up and changed into my costume, then went on as if nothing had happened."

Continuing to divert Lily by keeping her talking, pulse pounding, I slowly inched further forward in my chair, trying to keep my eyes off the stool. "How could you perform so beautifully, knowing what you had done?"

Sounding offended she said, "I am a professional. I do what I must, no matter what."

She stood again. "Now, to protect myself, I will have to kill you. You understand? I don't want to. But I must. Get up. We're going to take a walk now." She gestured with the gun.

At that moment her phone rang, distracting her. Still holding the gun with one hand, she pulled her cell phone from her jeans pocket with the other and turned away slightly. "Gil, I have already left. I will meet you there."

Simultaneously, I stood, grabbed the stool, and threw it at her with all my strength.

The stool hit Lily's chest. The Sugar Plum Fairy costume atop it flew into her face. She lost her balance and stumbled over the suitcase. The gun fired and she dropped both it and the phone.

I threw open the door, slammed it behind me, and dove out, crouching low, moving toward the connecting hall. One side of the "T" went outside, but I knew beyond the door there was nowhere to hide. The building, the sidewalk, the street, and the parking garage across the way presented blank uninterrupted concrete. The other side of the "T" went downstairs, into a maze of rooms and pipes. I chose the safety of familiarity. I leapt down the steps as fast as I could go, not knowing how much time I had.

By the time I reached the bottom, one floor down, I could hear Lily's footsteps.

I passed up the electrical room and scurried into familiar territory, the orchestra pit. The setup hadn't been torn down yet, and there, crouching between the timpani and the gong, I texted Lieutenant Gordon's cell phone.

Killer looking 4 me. Fleisher orch pit. Hurry.

I could hear Lily checking the janitor's closet.

I hoped the lieutenant wouldn't be too late.

FORTY-THREE

SUNDAY, 12:30 A.M., DECEMBER 25, 2011

LILY SEARCHED METHODICALLY. I could hear her look first in the janitor's closet, then the supply cabinet. The plumbing and electrical room followed. She must have searched all the way to the back because I heard thuds, bumps, and curses among the pipes.

Meanwhile, I searched frantically for a weapon. A plan began to form. The percussion table held a prop gun used in the first act of *Nutcracker*. It lay with the miscellaneous percussion and seemed to be the heaviest, hardest thing there. I took it. There were all kinds of mallets, made for hitting drums, cymbals, gongs, etc. Their heads had a little give to them, and the handles didn't look too sturdy, but I took the largest of them.

By then Lily had reached the darkened orchestra pit. Where were the stagehands? Having a late dinner? Gone for the day? Not around at any rate.

Lily paused at the entrance, sweeping her gun from one side to the other. "I know you're here. You may as well come out. There's nowhere to go."

I had the advantage of knowing the orchestra pit well. I don't live my life there for nothing. Lily had entered through the door nearest the audience side. I crouched in the percussion section, at the back of the orchestra on the stage side. Close to me a well-camouflaged double door used for easily moving large equipment into the pit gave access to the hallway beyond, which ran under the stage. Probably the timpani, the celesta, and the gong had all come in that way. I crawled slowly toward the door, on my hands and knees.

Silently I crept past the timpanist's chair. *So far, so good.* I leapt to my feet and purposely made noise flinging open the door, letting the light from the hall momentarily escape as I ran out of the pit. Then I slammed the door shut and hid behind it, hoping Lily would fall for my trap.

She had stood on the opposite side of the orchestra pit in the dark, and would be feeling her way to the door at the rear of the pit. I could hear her tripping and muttering profanities as she pushed chairs and music stands out of her way. When she exited, I sprang from behind the door and, using all the strength that fear and will and need could give me, struck down at her head with the butt of the stage gun.

Lily stood a head shorter than me, and she wasn't expecting the blow. Her grace deserted her, and she crumpled like a discarded doll, face first. Her gun skidded across the floor.

Quickly I grabbed the weapon and ran up nearby stairs. I didn't want to be around when she regained consciousness.

The cold darkness outside the building shocked me. Despite my parka, my pudgy body shivered with exertion and the bitter wintry wind. I blinked as my eyes adjusted to the dark.

Lt. Gordon screeched up as I pulled out my phone to text him again. He drove an unmarked car, leading a police cruiser with two uniformed policemen inside.

I quickly explained what had happened and gave him the gun, which he took with gloved hands, and directed him to Lily.

"Wait here."

As if my knees, which had buckled beneath me, gave me any choice. Abruptly I sat atop the outside stairs, chilled despite my parka, wanting only to go home to Golden. I noticed blood oozing slowly from my thigh. Lily's bullet must have nicked me after all.

The lieutenant and the two cops hurried inside, guns drawn.

Lt. Gordon returned without the other officers, talking on his cell phone. "That's right. Fleisher Hall."

He hung up and sat beside me. "Lily's downstairs, like you said. She's beginning to stir, so the uniforms are watching her. I've called an ambulance. You really knocked her a good one."

Now I could do nothing but wait. Relief and the cold enveloped me. I huddled into my parka.

Two EMTs arrived moments later. They disappeared up a ramp and into Fleisher with an empty stretcher. When they emerged, they carried Lily on it, a uniformed police officer following behind. As they rolled her by, one of her eyes, still encircled with smeared and blotchy makeup, glowered at me. I shuddered at her scowling face, oozing with hatred.

One cop went with her in the ambulance. His partner followed in the squad car. Lt. Gordon stayed with me. "First, you should go to the hospital. You look a little the worse for wear. Then I'll need to get a statement from you with all the details."

"I'll be glad to give a statement." I remembered my cell phone and gave it to him. "If everything worked, it should all be on there. I carried it in my pocket, so the recording might be a little muffled and scratchy. Your lab guys might have to amplify it, clean it up a bit. And I just have a scratch. I don't need to go to the hospital."

He tsked and took the phone from me with gloved hands. "My receipt book is in the car. Walk with me."

We went to his car together and he wrote a receipt for my cell phone. "I'll still need a statement from you. Are you sure you don't need to go to the hospital? There's blood on your leg."

"No. I'll be fine. I'll meet you at the station."

"Are you okay to drive?"

I assured him of my wellbeing, but he walked me to my car anyway. As I got in, I realized the delayed effects of stress had caught up with me. I fell into the seat, weaker than I'd thought.

I quieted my pride. "Uh, maybe I could use a ride after all." I added, "and a doctor."

The lieutenant glanced at my thigh, then held my elbow and carefully helped me out of my car and to his. "I think we'll go to the hospital. Don't fight me on this."

I let the last of my pride die. "Okay."

THE HOSPITAL LAY ON A QUIET RESIDENTIAL STREET halfway across town. Lt. Gordon drove to the emergency room entrance.

"Hey, lieutenant! Couldn't stay away on Christmas, eh?" a receptionist greeted him.

I felt like I accompanied a celebrity.

Lt. Gordon returned the greeting with a two-fingered salute. "Wouldn't want you to miss me too much." He nodded at me. "Can you get somebody to sew up Ms. Wilson here? I've gotta get her statement, and I hoped she'd get home before Santa comes."

"Sure thing."

Lt. Gordon sat in the waiting room and picked up a magazine.

The nurse took me into a curtained cubicle where the doctor looked at my thigh. "Shouldn't have to keep you too long. We'll deaden the pain, clean it out, sew it up, and send you on your way."

He left and sent in a nurse with flaming red hair. She opened a package, took out a gigantic syringe, way too big for my taste, then drew anesthesia from a vial and tapped the syringe.

I'd completely run out of bravery, and needles were among my least favorite objects. "But I don't want . . ."

"You don't want us to sew you up without a painkiller."

"Yes, but—"

Before I could protest, she had already emptied the syringe into my thigh. "We'll wait a few minutes." She left me in shock, with no way to control my thoughts.

A few minutes later another nurse came in. I couldn't say what she looked like because I had spent the intervening time imagining scenarios of pain and injury, sure she would have another needle. I had eyes only for her hands. By that time, I babbled with fear. "Don't! You can't!"

She poked me with a sterile pin.

Despite the dread gripping me, I didn't feel a thing.

"Now's the easy part," she said, cheery and upbeat.

Maybe for her.

She cleaned the wound with some clear solution. Sewing like she readied a stuffed turkey for roasting, she said, "Almost done." Despite my readiness to squeal again, I felt tugging, but no pain. Then she coated the injury with more liquid, reinforced her stitching with a couple of butterfly bandages, and gave me a tetanus shot, even as I tried to squirm away. "There now. Isn't that better?"

Better, except for the pain, anxiety, and mental anguish I had suffered.

"Have your doctor check it out in five days. He'll need to decide when to remove the stitches."

Great! Something to look forward to. Inwardly I groaned.

She left without wishing me a Merry Christmas or giving me a sucker, and my band-aids didn't even have a cartoon character on them.

LT. GORDON TOOK ME BACK TO THE STATION. "I need your statement, and then we can both go home."

I did the best I could to include everything exactly as it happened, while the lieutenant served me cups of water, telling me to drink.

When I finished at last, I pushed the signed statement across the desk to him. The lieutenant said, "From one perspective I could thank you . . ."

Could Lt. Gordon be admitting a mistake? I didn't expect it, and fortunately didn't say anything.

". . . but I don't like it when you get into these scrapes. I hope this is the last time I'll have to rescue you. Makes my job harder having a loose cannon out there."

Loose cannon? Considering that he'd wrongly accused me last year, almost arrested an innocent Lorna, and erroneously jailed Charlie, I couldn't see myself as a "loose cannon." But in the interest of peace, I ignored the term and responded, "It would be nice if you'd pay attention to my ideas. Then we could work together."

Lt. Gordon turned red in the face. "Touché. I'll try and listen better."

"I—"

The lieutenant's cell phone rang. He glanced at the number and said, "I have to get this." Turning his back, he said, "Gordon here." Pause. "Yeah." Grunt. "It's okay. Tell them she's with me and she's a bit banged up, but she's fine." Turning to face me he said, "Seems your mom and sister are worried about you. They're out front asking for both of us."

"Then we'd better put their minds at rest."

FORTY-FOUR

SUNDAY, 3:30 A.M., DECEMBER 25, 2011

KATHLEEN HAD ALWAYS BEEN THERE when I needed her. I owed her a lot. She was my big sister, my role model in my early years, and my support now. And Mom? Mom had given me life, as I'd heard many times. They were both concerned.

Lt. Gordon and I met them in the lobby.

Mom fastened her gaze on my torn and bloody pants. "What happened? Are you alright?"

"It's a long story. Lieutenant Gordon knows all about it. He doesn't want to hear it again, and I'm exhausted. I'll tell you later, but it's enough to say that . . ." I looked at Lt. Gordon, ". . . we've found Felix's killer."

"Oh, thank goodness!" Kathleen clasped both hands at her heart. "What about Charlie?"

"He'll be released as soon as we can find a judge to dot all the i's and cross the t's." Lt. Gordon smiled at Kathleen.

"Now, Ms. Wilson. I'll have a squad car take you to your vehicle." He firmly grasped my elbow and fixed Mom in a stare. "If you could go with her and drive. She may have some painkillers in her system. Be safer that way."

Mom, who wasn't used to following orders, sputtered, but agreed to his plan.

He guided me and Mom to the front of the building and outside, summoning a squad car on his cell phone, Kathleen following behind.

After a short wait, a pair of patrolmen arrived with their car.

Addressing them, the Lieutenant said, "Miz Wilson's had a hard night. Take her and her mom back to her car at Fleisher Hall." He turned to go, but called back as an afterthought, "And follow them home. Make sure they're okay."

He turned to Kathleen. They were standing close together and talking as we left.

WHEN WE GOT HOME, MOM MADE TEA and we waited for Kathleen, who didn't reappear for a good half hour. I told them the whole story then, and, after a healing rest, woke Christmas afternoon.

Nutcracker performances were over for the year and students were celebrating Christmas with their families. My nephew would have to wait his turn for release, but, thanks to me, he *would* be released.

I stretched like a cat in the sun (sorry, Golden!) and drowsed.

The afternoon was quiet and peaceful. I bundled up, and Kathleen, Mom, and I took Golden for a walk in the late afternoon sun, wishing the few people we saw "Merry Christmas." Mom and Kathleen and I discussed it, and decided Christmas would just have to wait. We wanted the family to be together.

Thinking about Felix's last words, I wondered again about the "her" in "Tell her she was the only one . . .." Surely, he wouldn't lie with his last words. But just as surely, he wouldn't beat the one to whom he directed those words and treat her with contempt. They weren't for Lorna, then. Even though he had used those words to seduce Lily, I found it hard to believe he could mean them after only one night. So, of the women I knew about, that left Celee, with her squash blossom necklace and her perfect grooming. Or maybe he *did* lie with his last words. I realized I'd never know for sure.

When the four of us got home, Mom and Kathleen prepared a Christmas meatloaf. The real celebration would wait for Charlie—and maybe KC and Ana and Barry?

Drowsy again, my tummy full, I realized I had nowhere to be, and nothing to do. I padded back to bed, snuggled with Golden, and dreamt of *Nutcracker* soldiers.

FORTY-FIVE

SUNDAY, 7:00 P.M., DECEMBER 25, 2011

T HE UNIVERSE HAD DETERMINED turnabout was fair play, and a
call from Barry awakened me.

I struggled to reach a coherent state. "Barry?"

"I just wanted to wish you a Merry Christmas. I've been dealing
with red tape. Charlie will be released as soon as possible. Ana's
going to pick him up and take him to her place."

So. The family would soon be reunited, and the real Christmas
gift would be Charlie's release. Ana would be a welcome addition.
She had earned her place in the family, along with KC. Finally,
Christmas spirit filled my being, and I looked forward to sharing
the holiday with my family at some later date.

Now fully awake, I expressed my gratitude. "Thanks, Barry,
you're a wonder!"

"To show your appreciation, and because tomorrow will be
the day after Christmas and I recall you said you'd be free after
Christmas, how about going to the theatre with me? Tomorrow?"

He didn't lose any time, did he? Remembering that kiss outside the Mexican restaurant, and all the help Barry'd been, I said,
"I'd like that, and there's nothing on my calendar 'til after the New

Year. I'll look forward to it." I smiled, already anticipating tomorrow. "What about Lorna? Is she okay?"

"I shouldn't talk to you about it, but since your sleuthing found the truth, I'll tell you that my colleague said the police have released Lorna from questioning with apologies. She's home safe, and happy to be there."

"That's wonderful! At least now her life's no more difficult than it needs to be."

With a feeling that the world had righted itself, I made arrangements with Barry about our date, and rang off. Mentally addressing myself to Lorna I thought, *"The truth will set you free."*

EPILOGUE

SATURDAY, 12:00 P.M., DECEMBER 31, 2011

WE HAD DECIDED DECEMBER 31ST WOULD BE a multipurpose celebration. For me, the main cause for festivity was Charlie's release from jail. Charlie's place of business had chosen to view his absence as his "Christmas vacation." They closed between Christmas and New Year's, so both Charlie and Ana were free for the party, and didn't have to be back at work until Monday.

But this afternoon was also our delayed Christmas celebration, and tonight we would spend New Year's Eve together. The guest list I had made in my head had come to life, with some additions— KC, Steve, me, Kathleen, Barry, Charlie, Mom, her long-distance cruise love Ira, Ana, and of course, Golden. About an hour after the guests arrived, Lt. Gordon made a surprise appearance at the door. The poinsettia he brought, ostensibly for me, he handed to Kathleen, who answered the door, with best wishes. His presence brought a radiant smile to her face, and we invited him in. At first, he was reluctant to intrude on the gathering, but when Kathleen assured him he was welcome, he joined the party.

"If I had known, I would have brought a helmet." Lt. Gordon smiled.

"Don't worry. I'm more careful with wine than hot coffee,"

Not wanting to create an awkward situation for anyone, I had asked that no one bring presents, and had presented Kathleen's perfume and Mom's earrings privately. In return I received a craft fair sweater from Mom, and a hand-crocheted hat, scarf, and mitten set, "for those early morning dog walks", as Kathleen said.

"Merry Christmas! Happy New Year!" It had turned out to be a party of couples. Steve and KC had eyes only for each other, and made a point of kissing under the mistletoe—several times. Kathleen and Lt. Gordon, starting nervously, managed to sit next to one another at every opportunity and laugh quietly together. Charlie and Ana held hands and, to my knowledge, didn't lose contact during the entire afternoon and evening they were at my house. Though no one knew him, when Mom had requested an invitation for Ira I couldn't refuse, and now he had Mom in stitches, smiling more than I'd seen in recent years.

As the oldest guest, Ira carved the ham, and we ate ourselves into a stupor. Even Golden ate like a queen. Although the ham would have endangered her, she got extra Santa-shaped dog cookies, as well as liver treats. After dinner, Barry, Lt. Gordon, Charlie, Kathleen, Ana, and I cleaned up.

After naps for all parties, tonight we would celebrate New Year's Eve.

This put an awful lot of pressure on Barry and me, since, besides Golden, we were the only two unattached persons at the party. One by one, couples had drifted off for their naps, Charlie and Ana to the guest room, Lt. Gordon and Kathleen to places in front of the TV, supposedly watching the game, but really nodding off on the sofa, heads leaned against each other. Steve's townhouse wasn't far away, and he and KC were spending the afternoon there. They said they would be back for tonight's celebration. I imagined their afternoon, and smiled.

Barry and I were drying the dessert dishes, beautiful crystal inherited from my grandmother, as the dishwasher whirred beside us and Golden paid hopeful attention to the goings on.

"I had a wonderful time during our date."

We had gone to an afternoon movie, which we discussed over dinner. Barry's comments were insightful, sensitive, and humorous. He sought my ideas, and listened thoughtfully to the answers. "Me, too."

"I was thinking we could go to dinner and dancing at the Starlight Room."

Located in the luxury hotel nearby, going to The Starlight Room would be a big step up. It was like a declaration of interest.

"I . . ." I hesitated. Barry was nothing like my ex. He was interesting, sensitive, present, listened without judgement, and increasingly, to me, he was handsome. His laugh thrilled me. But agreeing to a date at the Starlight Room? "I . . ." What the heck. I wouldn't let my ex affect the rest of my life and relationships. "I'd love to."

He smiled, and, with his hands in the soapy water, leaned over and kissed me tenderly. "That's excellent."

I could feel my face heat, but responded with enthusiasm to his caress, dropping my dish towel and putting my arms around his helpless form, his hands still submerged in dishwater.

Finishing our dish duties, we took a walk with Golden in the warm afternoon sun, which was busily melting yesterday's snow, holding hands and laughing together companionably. I would have lots to celebrate at midnight tonight. It was the beginning of a whole new life.

SIX MONTHS LATER, BARRY AND I had dinner at Le Fondue to celebrate Lily's convictions.

Barry said, "You can't blame Lieutenant Gordon for suspecting Charlie and Lorna. The evidence looked damning against both of them for a while. We're lucky Lily confessed before Gordon arrested the wrong person in Celee's murder."

"Lucky? I had a little bit to do with it."

Barry laughed. "Yes, you did." We clinked our teacups.

"Thank goodness I didn't have to testify at Lily's trials." Fortunately for me, the police lab had deciphered the recording from the cell phone that I carried in my pocket. Unable to fight a confession in her own words, Lily plea bargained; there were no trials, and I breathed at the reprieve.

"Lily didn't have a prayer."

The waitress interrupted, bringing our salads, and Barry didn't continue until she left.

Then he said, "My colleague told me the cops found Felix's gun in his dressing room. Even though it was the same caliber as Lily's, ballistics tests proved that it didn't kill either Felix or Celee. Lily's gun matched, though, in both murders. And her prints and yours were the only ones on it. The manager, Gil Sanchez, heard the gun go off over the phone. And then of course, like she said on the recording, the cops found Lily's bloody coat in her luggage. Lab tests confirmed the blood was Celee's."

I considered. "Since Lily received the maximum sentence, twenty-four years for each murder, served consecutively, I figure she won't get out 'til she's seventy-eight. Do you think the maximum sentences had anything to do with Felix's prominence?"

"Doubtless. And the strength of the case."

"Poor Steve! He tried so hard to keep the media from reporting that Celee had been Felix's mistress." I'd heard all about it from KC. "But I think he fought a losing battle. After all, Lily's motive for both Felix's and Celee's murder couldn't be explained away."

"True."

"It didn't seem to hurt the symphony, though, when all the facts came out. Ticket sales even picked up for a while. I guess it's true that bad publicity is better than no publicity." Steve had been relieved, KC reported.

I changed the subject. "Charlie went to Ana's and he's been staying there ever since. I'm happy for them. I think Kathleen wishes she saw them more often, though. After all, she moved here to be closer to her family."

Barry shrugged. "What can you do? They're young people in love."

The waitress brought our meals—cassoulet for him, poulet de Provencal for me.

Barry sipped his tea before he changed the subject. "I wonder how Lorna's getting on."

"I happen to know the answer. I saw Lorna in the grocery store parking lot not long ago, right after Lily's first sentencing. I didn't recognize her at first. It hadn't been that long since I'd last seen her, but she'd aged at least ten years." I took a sip of tea before I continued. "Instead of the perfectly groomed trophy wife I expected, she seemed frayed, a middle-aged woman with no makeup and dark circles under her eyes. And she had all three boys with her. They were racing around her and bickering while she ignored them and loaded groceries into her car. I only recognized her when she said, 'Emily, how good to see you.'"

I leaned closer to Barry. "The greeting surprised me. Lorna and I were never close. I could see she'd gone through a lot in the last few months, so I asked, 'How are you doing?' The wrong question, I guess."

"I don't know how you could have asked anything else. What'd she say?"

"I got an earful. She told me she didn't miss Felix much, except for the practical things like income and insurance, and that she felt relieved not to have to deal with his insults, his affairs, and his contempt. But when she talked about Celee, Lorna teared up and told me that she couldn't express how much she missed Celee. She'd been such a big part of Lorna's life and a great help with the boys. She said Celee had been a comfort. Lorna tried not to cry, but her chin trembled and I felt for her, so I asked if I could do anything."

I felt my throat drying out, so I took another sip of tea, then continued. "She smiled this enormous smile and said I'd already done a lot, finding the true murderer. But she told me that things were still rough here. People ask nosy questions and whisper behind her back. And then she went on a cynical rant about the police. Instead of protecting her, she said they'd interrogated her, accused her of lying, and then questioned everything about the situation including her temper, her marriage, her shooting skills, and even Felix's state of mind. You should have heard her." I gave my angry Lorna impression. "'As if that musical monster ever thought about his actions long enough to be depressed!' She'd raised her voice and begun to attract stares from across the parking lot."

I dabbed at my mouth with a napkin. "I told her that the articles I'd read in the press painted her as a tragic widow valiantly forgiving the police for hounding her."

"I thought that was the truth." Barry's eyebrows rose.

"She agreed that, yes, the symphony's PR department had done a great job making her look good, but then she rolled her eyes. Who can blame her if she's bitter? It'll take her a long time to get over it all."

"I guess I'd feel the same." Barry poured more tea for himself and offered me some.

I shook my head.

"Steve did such a fantastic job of keeping her feelings out of the news. I hadn't a clue she felt ill used." Barry sipped his tea. "Feeling that way, that's no kind of life."

I settled into my chair. "Lorna told me she thought it better that she moves away. Felix's life insurance paid out, and Friends of the Symphony took up donations for her boys. Apparently, she has enough to move to Arizona and plans on leaving next month. I told her I'd miss her, and the symphony would miss her, but I completely understood that she needed a fresh start. I almost cried when she said, 'I'm glad. I didn't want you to doubt how grateful I am to you.' I wished her well. I sincerely hope she'll find an ideal place in Arizona to start again and forget it all."

In another change of subject Barry asked, "How are things with Steve and KC?"

"They're still seeing each other, but she's a little freaked."

"Freaked? How so?"

"Apparently he wants to get married."

Barry chuckled. "I could see the light in Steve's eye. What's her answer?"

"She's *really* unenthusiastic and doesn't know why. She says he's kind, patient, generous, loving. She can't make sense of it, but it makes sense to me. Look at her history. As an escort, she routinely dealt with men who were bored, or annoyed, or angry with their wives. She's afraid if Steve becomes her husband he'll turn out to be like all the married men she knew, and he'll soon be looking for an escort. Anybody but her. At least, that's my amateur psychologist opinion. It's worth what you paid for it."

"And what did you advise?"

I sighed. "I'm not any expert in relationships, either. So, I told her to listen to her feelings, and see a professional counselor to figure out exactly what those feelings are, if necessary. Marriage is always a risk, though I didn't tell her that."

Finished with my meal, I felt uncomfortably full. French desserts are the best, though. I hoped the waitress would come back, but not too soon.

Barry asked, "And how did Steve take that?"

"He must be a great guy. KC told him marriage scared her. He said he wouldn't push her. I think he's hoping his trustworthiness and dependability will reassure her. I begged her to stay at my place as long as she wants, so I still have help with cooking, cleaning, and dog sitting. It's a win-win-woof for us."

I savored Barry's deep booming laugh, one of the things I liked best about him.

The waitress came then and took our dessert orders. When they arrived, we ate and drank slowly, enjoying each other's company and reveling in the opportunity to be together.

Finished, we went to Barry's place. Not being a girl who kisses and tells, I'll only say we made a night of it.

"KATHLEEN! OVER HERE!"

At my words Kathleen waved and hurried to my table. "Emily." We hugged. "Has KC seen you yet?"

"I don't think so. She's busy in the kitchen."

"Good. We want her to be surprised." Kathleen put a wrapped package on the table.

"It looks beautiful! What did you get?"

"It's a silly little thing. An apron, embroidered with the words 'World's Best Chef.' "

We were meeting at the Articulate Artichoke for a late dinner, planning on surprising KC. She had been promoted to head chef, and we thought it deserved a celebration. We planned to wait for her to get off work, then go party. She could sleep late on her day off, tomorrow.

I hardly recognized the restaurant. It bustled with customers. The vegan dishes were developing a national reputation and the restaurant had added an all-vegan pastry counter—KC's idea.

"How perfect!" Leave it to Kathleen. The apron wasn't extravagant enough to embarrass KC, but it served as an ideal marker of the occasion.

"Here. Sign the card." Kathleen took it from her purse and handed it to me.

"How are things going with Lieutenant Gordon—I mean Paul?" Paul and Kathleen had been seeing each other steadily since my Christmas/New Year's/Charlie's freedom party and she had moved to Monroe from Indiana a couple months ago. "This is where the people who really care about me live," she had told me. I suspected Lt. Gordon played a large part in her decision to move. She'd told me he was "funny and tender." As for me, I looked at the situation with the perspective I'd gained, and realized he had always had a good basis for his suspicions, even if they had later been proved wrong. He had taken good care of me the night of Lily's arrest, too. Most of all, though, I hadn't seen my sister so happy since her husband died.

"I'm afraid to say anything. It seems too good to be true. I didn't think anyone could fill Bob's shoes, but I love Paul's consideration, his desire to be of service to the community, and his integrity."

Between Charlie and Lt. Gordon—I mean Paul—Kathleen hadn't had much sister time, but Mom and I had discussed the developing relationship between Kathleen and Paul. True to form, Mom unconditionally supported her daughter. "If it ends well, all's well." She didn't care about anything but Kathleen's happiness. And I had to agree.

Kathleen and I studied the menu. "There are so many new dishes. What are you having?" I was thrilled to recognize two new vegan dishes KC had tried out on me and I recommended them to Kathleen. When the waitress came to take our orders, Kathleen chose the veggie platter and I ordered a lentil-mushroom burger with salad.

"So, tell me all about Paul."

She talked happily.

Lieutenant Gordon had relaxed Kathleen's mother bear anxieties a little. She'd clung awfully tightly to Charlie at first, but over the months as she got to know Ana better and became closer to Paul, she gradually calmed. Charlie had been kind to his mother, but took every opportunity to be alone with Ana, undisturbed. At our occasional family dinners, where he pampered Ana and she responded in kind, I could see he welcomed his mom's new distance.

Kathleen sipped her tea, then changed the subject. "I know you were worried about your student. How is she?"

"I'm so proud of her. She could go to school anywhere, but she wants to stay here in Monroe. Since both her academics and flute are strong, I think there's a good chance the university will give her a full ride scholarship. The school will be lucky to have her. It'll be good for her, too. She wants to major in music therapy. MU has an excellent department, and she'll be able to live at home."

I didn't want to betray confidences or take advantage of my position as Megan's flute teacher and confidante, so I didn't tell Kathleen about Megan's plans to help the family if she could. They were having a rough time. Her mom had left her dad and worked extra shifts to make ends meet. The court had convicted her dad of domestic violence, and he could only see his kids in a supervised setting until he finished counseling, anger management, and fathering classes. Megan wanted to stay close to home so she could see him. And the whole family was in counseling. She liked her therapist, too, and didn't want to start over with someone else.

The waitress brought us coffee and desserts and made sure we didn't need anything else. Kathleen waited until the server left, then asked, "What about you?"

"It seems I'm completely surrounded by domestic abuse— Megan's family, Lorna and her kids, my own experiences—so I took it as a sign. People helped me; now I need to start lending a hand. So two weeks ago I started volunteering for the Supervised Visitation Center."

"What do you do, exactly?" Kathleen delicately picked at her veggie platter.

"When the courts convict anyone of drug or alcohol abuse, or domestic violence, like Megan's dad, it orders supervised visits. That's where the Center comes in. We supervise visits between kids and their non-custodial parents. I make sure procedures are followed so they can see each other safely."

"It sounds like a wonderful program."

"It's very satisfying. Plus, Golden has finished her certification as a therapy dog, so she helps out when we need her. She seems to have a natural sense of who needs the comfort of her dogness, and when."

"Do your student and her brothers and sister use the same visitation center where you volunteer?"

"Yeah, but I don't want to embarrass her or violate confidentiality. So if Megan and her family see their dad at the Center while I'm there, I pretend I don't know them, and another volunteer works with them. "

"And how are things with you and Barry?"

I hesitated.

"What? I can tell something's up."

"Barry and I, it's hard to describe. You already know we like and respect one another, so we're seeing more of each other, and that's a dimension to my life that keeps expanding." I poured dressing on my salad. Kathleen was my sister, but I didn't want to tell her things I wasn't sure of myself. "Even though our conflicting schedules make it complicated, he's always there for me, and not just as my lawyer. That kind of commitment is rare. He seems interested in working it out, despite all our baggage. Hopefully it's worth it. So, we get together when we can. Movies, lunches, dinners, plays. And stuff." I could feel the warmth color my face. "We'll see where it goes."

Kathleen said, "Stuff? My sister radar tells me there's more."

How did she know? Was I that transparent? I took a moment to organize my thoughts. "I like my independence. Barry understands, or says he does, so he'll be spending August with the Hopi, as usual." I silently hoped that would end the conversation.

"And? What do you think of that?" Kathleen could be as relentless as our mom until she satisfied her concerns.

I hesitated. This was very private territory. But she was my sister, after all, and I had no secrets from her. "It's his life. That's what he's always done. I can't expect him to respect my independence if I don't respect his." I hesitated. "But we enjoy seeing each other. So halfway through August, while the symphony is on hiatus, I'll join him for a week. Just to see how it goes. We might stay at the Hopi reservation, or we might tour the area. The Grand Canyon's nearby, you know."

"That sounds pretty serious." She folded her arms, leaned on the table, and gave me the meddling and concerned look of a big sister.

"Kathleen, don't. You're scaring me. I'm taking one step at a time. I don't want to get in too deep too soon."

She tilted her head thoughtfully. "Well, at least you know what you don't want, and you've shared it with Barry. He's still interested. That sounds promising."

By bringing the check, the waitress interrupted a conversation that had gotten increasingly uncomfortable. Kathleen insisted on paying, and I escaped answering because just then KC exited the kitchen.

"Em! Kathleen! I didn't know you were here."

"SURPRISE!"

The celebration began then and, to get Mom's cliché right, all's well that ends well. I have to admit that I smiled at the thought of the future. I hope things work out with Barry. I like the idea of having a lawyer permanently on my side. It could come in handy, especially when you have a family like mine.

B.J. Bowen is a musician and free-lance writer whose love of music was awakened by her mother, who played the flute. After discovering her lips were the wrong shape and failing miserably as a flute player, at the age of eleven Ms. Bowen began studying oboe, and has since performed and recorded on both oboe and English horn with professional symphonies and chamber groups throughout Mexico and Colorado. Other experience includes working with various children's organizations, teaching music to children and adults, editing newsletters, and writing grants for non-profits. Her inspirational articles have appeared in *Unity Magazine* and *Daily Word*, and she was a finalist who won Honorable Mention in the 2018 Focus: Eddy Awards for her article, "Letting Go with Grace," published in *Unity Magazine*. Drawing on her quirky fellow musicians and orchestral experiences, she created the mystery series, "Musical Murders." She lives in Colorado Springs, Colorado, with two canine friends, and has a stock of musical puns, as well as a song for any occasion.